James Kenward

For Cambria

Themes in Verse and Prose

James Kenward

For Cambria
Themes in Verse and Prose

ISBN/EAN: 9783337366964

Printed in Europe, USA, Canada, Australia, Japan

Cover: Foto ©Andreas Hilbeck / pixelio.de

More available books at **www.hansebooks.com**

FOR CAMBRIA:

THEMES IN VERSE AND PROSE,

A.D. 1854–1868.

WITH OTHER PIECES.

BY JAMES KENWARD

(ELVYNYDD).

'NEC ALIA, UT ARBITROR, GENS QUAM HÆC CAMBRICA, ALIAVE LINGUA, IN DIE DISTRICTI EXAMINIS CORAM JUDICE SUPREMO, QUICQUID DE AMPLIORI CONTINGAT, PRO HOC TERRARUM ANGULO RESPONDEBIT.' (A.D. 1165.) — Ex Giraldo Cambrensi: (Cambriæ Descriptio, lib. ii. cap. x.)

LONDON:

LONGMANS, GREEN, AND CO.

1868.

TO THE

VICOMTE THÉODORE HERSART DE LA VILLEMARQUÉ,

MEMBER OF THE INSTITUTE OF FRANCE,

A MASTER IN CELTIC LITERATURE,

A GENEROUS VINDICATOR OF CELTIC NATIONALITY,

I Dedicate these Writings,

WITH TRUE ADMIRATION AND RESPECT.

PREFACE.

———◆———

IF the object of a preface is to apologise or to explain, I may well leave this little book to be its own justification, and to tell its own tale.

The opinions on Welsh Nationality, which an experience of fifteen years has led me to form, will be opposed, as such opinions have ever been, by a large proportion of the few readers who may care to examine them in their present setting. But this consideration by no means relieves me from the duty of asserting what I hold to be just and true. *Liberavi animam meam.*

On the other hand, I feel sure of the sympathy and approval of a small but happily increasing number of Celtic scholars and patriots, who, looking at the earnest purpose, will perhaps pardon the imperfect work.

Yet to those of both classes who do not know me, it seems right to say that I am not Welsh by birth, residence, or connexions. My name, formed of etymons which are at once Gothic and Celtic, appears equally in the Rotulæ Walliæ and in the Anglo-Saxon Chronicles. I have approached these

a

subjects simply as a student and as a traveller, without
personal interest, and without national prepossession.

Several of the poems have already been published
in Wales and in Brittany. They are now submitted
to an English audience. In annexing the prose pieces
I have tried to avoid deviating into the history,
archæology, literature, and bardism, connected with
many allusions in the text, and of which my inclination, and the materials at my disposal, would naturally
tempt me to treat. The present work is designed for
the general reader and the traveller. The notices,
therefore, refer for the most part to social and scenic
matters.

I have endeavoured to do justice to the themes of
my choice. I feel that the result is unsatisfactory,
but I cannot help it. If the living masters of English
Song would realize and expand the noble suggestions
of Milton, Spenser, Drayton, or Gray, the Cymric
Cause might be enshrined in numbers that would
surely charm the ear, and perhaps move the heart, of
our united Britain.

As to the poems in this collection that do not bear
on the main topics, they may be added, without special
remark, to the innumerable miscellanies of Fugitive
Verse.

                                        J. K.

SMETHWICK, NEAR BIRMINGHAM
      June 25, 1868.

CONTENTS.

VERSE.

PROSE.

STANZAS READ AT THE NATIONAL EISTEDDFOD
OF LLANGOLLEN, 1858.

Dygorvu Cymry trwy gyvergyr.
Yn zywair, gydair, gydson, gydfybl:
Dygorei Cymry !—GOLYDDAN (Seventh Century).

CYMRU ![1] first Mother of our love and pride,
Who bearest yet a bright and queenly brow
Though crowuless and contemned, for at thy side
Wait Truth and Hope to cheer thee and endow
With victory and with joy, when Hate shall bow,
And Falsehood blush, and Obloquy be dumb
Before thee; ancient Mother, favour now
Thine earnest children, who to greet thee come
From many alien paths to one dear kindred home!

Accept again our Gorsedd; favouring look
From old Eryri's head where Genii guard
Thy liberty and name, the eternal book
The Muses open to the patriot Bard,
The urn whose waters time shall not retard
Quick rushing, and the birthplace wild and free
Of all the winds; and let this high reward,
Thine *Awen* flow like wind and wave on me,
And fill my heart and song, unworthy though I !

---

[1] *Cyn-bru.*

B

Not mid the City's pillared fanes of Trade,
Where men entwine their heartstrings, and grow old
In method ; not where Pleasure's nets are laid
For idle Passion ; Art enslaved and sold,
And Science priestess of the idol Gold ;
Not in the narrow schools with form imbued ;
May Cambria's history be conceived or told
Aright, nor what she *was* and *is*, reviewed
With large and liberal mind, and weighed, and under-
        stood.

But stand beside the rock-engirdled sea
When Night looks on it with her ardent eyes ;
Or where the Carnedd watcheth solemnly
The mountain waste ; the broken pillar lies
Noteless mid nameless graves ; the owlet flies
Slow through the ruined oriel : there receive
The true impressions that within thee rise,
For elemental Spirits will reweave
The Past's rent robe o'er all, if thou their power believe.

Or seek the Cymric future when the day
Flashes from ocean to the mountain crest ;
When rolls the tide rejoicing in the bay ;
When Life leaps eager from the vale's green rest,
And all the country's fair and peaceful breast
Glows with the light and energy of morn :
Oh then, when nerve and pulse obey thee best,
Come with clear intellect and heart unworn,
And hail the Nation's day, the era newly born !

So margined, so interpreted, then range
With calm discerning eye the historic page,
And what is there obscure or weak or strange
In the mixed colours of a vanished age
Shall brighten so; as lonely haunt of sage,
Or mouldering keep of warrior, marks his clime
And life, and as where spreading seas did rage
Above the mountains of primeval time,
Eternal traces bear significance sublime.

The Briton held the Isle; avails it not
To know the story of that earliest sway;
The stream which flows through subterranean grot
Can bear no burden and reflect no ray;
But still it winneth its resistless way,
And soon emergeth to a course of pride,
And beauty and fertility array
Its banks, the heavens mingle with its tide,
Art there selects her seat, and Power and Fame abide.

Enough that in the Nation's parent fount
The force which launched the issuing stream inheres;
That on this stream the spirit may remount,
And follow Truth beyond recorded years;
And though, alas! its later path appears
Narrowed and rock-opposed, and bent aside,
Yet more its depth or purity endears,
And more triumphantly its waters glide,
While storied lakes are lost, and mightier rivers dried.

Enough for us that o'er that ancient day
Which Folly shuns, and Ignorance maligns,
A power is spread not transient all as they,
A light unquenchable as Heaven shines ;
For Mochnud fills the place his worth assigns—
Great parent of his people, wise and just !—
And for the land of green hills, isle of pines,
Rose Plennydd's song—though harp and hand are dust,
The soul survives, and well Tradition keeps her trust.

And Science then had half unveiled her face
First to the circling stars of God upturned ;
And Art accorded to a simple race
What simple needs demand ; and Labour earned
Free blessings from the soil ; and purely burned
The lamp of Virtue kindled in the fane
Of Druid worship, whose clear eye discerned
Truth darkly subject yet to Error's reign,
And led the captive forth, but could not break her chain.

The Roman came, and saw, but conquered not
Till Fraud and Discord had oppressed the land,
And Luxury unfortified the spot
Where brave Caswallon took his earliest stand,
Or reared a city where Cynvelyn planned
A camp, but sternly on that city fell
Victoria's [1] curse and red avenging hand,—
Vain the doomed Legion this last shock to quell,
Colonia Victrix sank,[2] dirged by the conquerors' yell !

[1] Boadicea (*Buddug*).   [2] Camalodunum.

Thence rose, alas! the tide of blood and turned
Back on the hapless Princess; utter woe
Consumed her, but the heroic heart that spurned
Forlorn and crownless life, and Roman show,
Lived yet again and laid the Armada low,
Spurning for Tudor England threats and chains;—
Lives quenchless yet, and may it ever glow
In her, our new Victoria, while she reigns
Invincible and free o'er ancient hills and plains!

But woe was bitter then : hear the dark Isle
Bewail her flaming groves and ruined halls;—
Sad Mona! Autumn gave its golden smile,
Spring decked thy fields, and now fierce ravage falls
On thee, and sternly purple Power enthrals
Thy rock-bound shores and blue-encircling sea;
And lone Despair thy white-robed Druids calls
In vain—too well they cheered and counselled thee,—
And such must perish first ere perish Liberty.

Paulinus flung the Briton's earliest creed
Out to the wind-swept Orcades to die;
And Edward, emulous of that fair deed,
On her own altar murdered Poesy ;—
Vain leader! vainer king! the mystic tie
Of each was proof against thy sharpest sword:
This lives renewed more holy, pure, and high,
Throned on thy seven hills, and *that*, proud lord,
Sings loftier scorn of thee, and Cambria's name restored!

Where sits conspicuous over Deva's wave
The old blind Pharos on its mount alone;
Where the green hills hold many a burdening grave,
And wood and dingle tell of tear and moan;
Achwynvan stands deep-based—dark Weeping-stone!
Saddest of all memorials of our shame,
When sank the Ordovices, overthrown
By wise and strong Agricola, whose name,
Though conqueror's it be, we honour with acclaim.

Dark Stone of Lamentation! whose the hand
That raised thee, whose the princely dust below,
What import lurk in sculptured scroll and band,
Were idle all to ask and vain to know;—
Thou silent, moveless Sentinel of woe!
The hours glide round thee, circling seasons meet,
Thy grey head wears a coronal of snow,
Brown wheat-ears deck thy sides, spring flowers thy feet,
Impassible and cold! while Time's quick pulses beat.

But we invest thee with our own emotion,
Ghost of the Past! and claim a voice to tell
How round thee, as a rock in heaving ocean,
Thou saw'st the Roman tide of conquest swell;
Heard impious Ethelfrid's and Offa's yell;
Rejoiced when Owain bowed the Norman's pride:—
Enough! Peace folds her wings o'er thee, the bell
Of Sabbath morn falls sweet, and at thy side
Rise safe and loyal homes, wave plenteous harvests wide.

In Powys, where a thousand mountain camps
Their crested heads eternally uprear
O'er crumbling fort and palace, history stamps
Three hills with name and fame to Britons dear;
For the long fiery struggle ended here,
That shook the legions, where secluded Teme
Before the mailed invaders shrank in fear,
And Freedom's shield was rent, and Victory's beam
Was quenched in Redlake's swoln and crimson stream.

Caradoc's spirit hallows yet his hill—
That triple camp; and let us look from thence
Toward his loved Siluria, victress still
When he, pre-eminent in eloquence
As war, stood uttering his high defence
To Time; for her not cruelty could tame—
Not clemency; she wrung a recompense
For all—herself alone—and put to shame
In many a struggle fierce the great Imperial name.[1]

Nor closed her ample page of glory yet,
But golden letters point the Saxon time;
For though a mark of blackest hue be set
'Gainst the arch-traitor Vortigern, his crime
Is as the river's sun-corrupted slime,
While like to ocean waves in grandeur free,
The deeds of Uthyr and Ambrosius climb
Heavenward to Fame; but Death rides on the sea,
And Hate prepared their tomb, too soon for Liberty.

[1] Tacitus, *Annal.* xii.

Yet brighter then in ancient Caerlleon rose
A name than legion or than fort more strong
To guard the land, and overawe its foes,
And Caerwent echoed to a loftier song;—
Immortal Arthur! fain would linger long
The enamoured Muse o'er all we deem of thee,
For round her, vivid shapes of glory throng—
The unsullied sword--the plume of Chivalry—
The battle-harp of Bard—the torque of Chieftain free.

Vain are the voices raised against thy state,
Birth, lineage, power, nay existence too:
Dull minds within themselves the doubt create
That overclouds them, and a picture view
Of grandest import, lovely, large, and true,
Captious of aught that envious Time have stole
Of clear and bright away--of faded hue,
Of newer colours ill applied--O soul,
Conceiving *part* so well—impervious to the whole!--

Be just; from Truth's fair amaranthine stem
Pluck intertwining Fable if you can;
But not both tree and parasite condemn,
Nor praise the picture yet deny the man;
Valour that ever led the battle-van—
Genius that guided--love that lit the fire
Laid on the Country's altars—wit to scan
Prophet's and Muse's face, and wake the lyre--
Sweetness and grace to charm—devotion to aspire;

These, these are truth, and true to truth, and we,
Shall we not credit, cherish, and esteem !
These sank not 'neath a Medrawd's treachery—
Passed not, the lifeless pageant of a dream—
Died not at Camlan :—glory's latest gleam
That bathed his shattered helm and plumeless crest,
Expanded into broader light shall beam
Immutably above our hero's rest—
Transfuse the land he loved, and fill each patriot breast !

Did'st thou, Caradoc, on thy silent hill
Discern this distant recompense ?—thy name,
Kindred with Arthur's, is united still
To his in immortality of fame ;—
Nor his alone; thy beauteous Gwent may claim
Lucius, bright bringer of the light divine ;
Mwynvawr the mild, with whom fair Courtesy came ;
Tewdric who well sustained and blessed thy line,
Armed with the sword and cross of potent Constantine :—

Of Constantine, in whom o'erruling Heaven
Restored thy empire, and confirmed thy creed ;
And though no permanence to *that* was given,
But soon the sceptre passed into the reed ;
Yet *this*, expanding still with human need,
Grew with the slow decay of Latin power,
As, noteless first, there grows till all men heed,
Above a storm-rent and time-wasted tower,
The seed, the plant, the tree, the overshadowing bower,

Where all found rest and shelter.   Oh how sweet
To blunt the curses of malignant War
By the mild blessings of the Paraclete—
To scorn the thundering of his battle car,
And list the angelic accents from afar
That tell of unity and peace on high!
And when the hapless valley-meadows are
Polluted all with blood, and Tyranny
With Treason shares the land, and Love kneels weeping
    by :—

Oh then how pure and sweet the mountain air
Fresh from eternal Heaven! and the fane
Where Passion bows his burning front in prayer,
And Resignation breaks the weary chain
Of pale Subjection, and the voice of Pain
Is hushed by Mercy, and the lurid eyes
Of Cruelty abashed, the aspiring strain
Of Genius swells mid holy symphonies,
And Liberty waits calm her lingering star's uprise!

In Arvon Clynnog holds her worship yet ;
Stern Eifl guards her, and the choral sea
Hymns in her aisles, and Beauty's signs are set
Within, without, o'er all ; a joy to me
It is to wander there with footsteps free,
Mindful how royally Anarawd crowned
Valour with Faith, and oft to bow the knee
Where Beuno gazed on Wisdom's face, and found
Devotion's heart beat warm on Nature's glorious ground.

Llancarvan, Clynnog, Enlli, Llandaff, kept
Securest refuge for the darkening hour,
Of Cymru's princes, when the war-flames swept
Around Aberffraw, Eilian, Dinevawr ;—
O'er many a palace proud and rockfast tower ;
And when the fight 'gainst destiny grew vain,
When sank anew the star of patriot power,
They guarded sleep which Treachery and Pain
Haunt not—for the crossed hands shall meet in prayer
    again !

Yet still from marble grey, and formless mound,
Where the wild winds, from out their ancient caves,
Sweep many-voiced—the mystic life of sound—
Viewless and fetterless among the graves,
As is the spirit's self, the Poet waves
His laurel wreath above the illustrious dead,
And each immortal memory clears and saves,
And crowns with worthy song each honoured head
On the broad battlefield eight centuries have spread ;—

Eight centuries, down from when the Saxon keel
Defiled fair Thanet's shining sands, to when
Demetian treachery, and Norman steel
Delivered to the insatiate tiger's den
The gallant remnant of our trueborn men,
With their last lion-hearted princes :—Shame
Lie heavy on that act, and may the pen
Of honest History yet degrade *his* name
Who, brave, spared not the brave, recked not a nation's
    claim !

Strike then the harp for high Cunedda's line,
For Arthur and a hundred epic years,
For Maelgwn, Island Dragon, valour's sign,
Who rushed exulting o'er the broken spears,
For Rhodri whom his triple sway endears;—
Would that the valiant still were wise as brave!—
For Hywel, name Humanity reveres,
Who sought, and brighter to his Country gave,
The lamp of law and truth which burned in Dyvnwal's
    grave.

And he the Heaven-favoured, Sitsyllt's son,
Llywelyn great and good, whose warlike hand
And peaceful heart for suffering Cymru won
Secure and liberal blessings:—wretched Land
That paid him death for life! he joins the band,
The glorious few who lived before their time,
Whose recompense is evermore to stand
And look from Heaven's crystal towers sublime
On hopes and deeds fulfilled in happier age or clime.

Enough! though circling on the vision crowd
Princes and Bards and Saints, a noble train,
Ere Power grew tyrannous and Insult loud
O'er Cambria's vanished royalty; and fain
The Muse would vivify the scenes again
Where Dyvrig, Dewi, Teilo taught and prayed;
Where Llywarch's, Gwalchmai's, bright Taliesin's strain,
And Cynan's, Gruffydd's, Owain's falchion made
Hope, triumph, genius, joy, from sea to sea pervade.

Alas! of episodes so bright and pure,
Enough, for Clio rises cold and stern
With other records and a night obscure,
Though yet may stars of keenest lustre burn;
See the storm-maddened billows swift return
And sweep the golden sands where sunset lay
In magic slumber, and ye might discern
Beauty in myriad types!—Oh haste away
From hideous shapes of ill that swarm to meet their prey!—

Their prey e'en Cambria, poisoning the heart
Of her own sons each against each and her:
Ambition with his suicidal dart;
Pale Jealousy; slow Hate the murderer;
Loud-tongued Dissension, like a clinging burr
On Patriotism's robe; blind Ignorance,
And sanguine-eyed Ferocity, concur
To hold their Country in distraction's trance,
While o'er her prostrate form glad enemies advance.

Yet selfishness and error, sloth and crime,
Are clouds and tempests of the human day,
Not *all* Humanity; the heavens sublime
Blend varied colours in each vivid ray,
And hold forever their unswerving way
Through all vicissitudes of time and tide;
And thus, through Cambria's many-featured sway—
Through light and gloom, decadence, power, and pride,
One cause, one soul, one love, one purpose, did abide:—

And *that* was Freedom :—O thou recusant
Of loftiest truth and beauty ! see wild Wales
With all her mighty heart for freedom pant
In Destiny's fell grip ; the foe assails—
Race after race succeeds—she faints and fails,
Down-trodden—then convulsive wakes and flings
Oppression off, and triumphs ; not avails
Such strength or ardour long, for closer clings
The giant iron-mailed, and locks the deadly rings.

Infinite wiles and weapons 'gainst her breast,
One her simplicity—her purpose one ;
Now Britain's voice supreme and arm confest—
Now beaten backward with the setting sun—
Backward to wave and mountain yet unwon—
Insulted by her own and linked with blame—
Aspersed, derided, ever did she run,
With changeless brow, with spirit still the same,
Her radiant course adown the starbright track of fame !

Nations like phantasms have haunted her,
And passed as vapours from the rising day ;
Creed, custom, speech, opinion, that confer
On them a character, have died away
To newer forms of upgrowth and decay ;
But she has kept alive her ancient fire
Through Roman, Saxon, Norman, English sway :—
Oh cherish it, and it shall not expire
Until her mountains feed Earth's last great funeral pyre !

Her mountains, Nature's own dividing line
Between the enduring and the transient set ;
They saw the Lloegrian plains unvanquished shine,
Saw Anarchy and Despotism met
In Freedom's temple there, and Change beget
His Proteus brood o'er vale and wood and shore ;
But all inviolate their rock-realm yet
They held, and nursed the seed whose sacred store
Shall ineradicably spring for evermore.

Joy then for Cymru ! though disposing Heaven
Have now her empire old and name denied,
Yet is not recompense divinely given ?
May she not lift her voice—assume with pride
Her place among the nations, close allied
With England, sharer in her triple might ?
Oh let not factious tongues that sway divide
Which shines before the world so clearly bright,
Firm on its rock-fast base, inalienable right !

One Throne is o'er the kingdom—Liberty
And Law have reared it ; not the Despot's sword,
But Love, sustains it—here may Cambria see
Her history honoured and her realm restored :
One God of peace and mercy is adored ;
Knowledge sheds on the land one common light ;
One blood for hearth and altar's freely poured ;—
Witness each field of Britain's well-proved might,
From Bosworth's royal plain to Alma's deadly height !

Long live such union fair! yet Cambria hath
Her own bright heritage apart from all;
Her genius still protects and guides her path;
The flowers faded from her coronal
Were not Truth's amaranth; the mountain wall
That still divides her from the Saxon plain,
Divides her too from many a vicious thrall,
From many a clinging care, and bitter pain—
Shadows which ever haunt Civilisation's train.

Not in the cherished dream of old dominion
Her surest hope, her fairest freedom, lies:—
See, with the Past's dull night, on broken pinion,
Irrevocably now that Error flies!
And see a clearer, happier day arise,
When safe from tyranny, misrule, and wrong,
She looks rejoicingly in Nature's eyes,
And seeks, what years shall deepen and prolong,
Truth, virtue, purity; art, science, song!

And so, while England's fevered pulses beat
For power, pleasure, territory, gold;
While change and novelty involve her feet,
And mar her speech, and leave her altars cold;
Cambria shall cherish in her mountain fold
A small, perchance, but uncorrupted band,
Whose loyal lives shall public faith uphold;
Whose tongue shall last unperishing as grand;
Whose piety shall warm, whose valour guard, the land!

Thus rising still, refined, regenerate,
Developing her greatness from within,
All the best blessings of a Christian State
Linked with enduring power, she shall win :
Even now the bardic prophecies begin
To wake the voice of vindicating Time,
Not as they *seem*, to Error's brood akin,
But as they *are*, with inmost truth sublime,
Appealing still for *one* to *every* age and clime.

O England ! thou who art so great and free,
As oft thy children vaunt, and foes confess ;
Think that thy might was not conceded thee
To scorn thine elder Sister and oppress :
No ! 'twas to aid, acknowledge her and bless,
For God hath fixed her dwelling-place apart,
And given her gifts which thou dost not possess ;
Hurt not her shieldless form with envious dart,
But bear her by thy side with nobly generous heart !

And ye her own ! a solemn task is yours
To keep her fame unsullied to mankind ;
For as the mountain-mist the sun obscures,
Though still his keen effulgence lives behind,
Yet to the lower world the day is blind ;
And ye by actions dark may thickly veil
Your Country's face, and cloud her genius kind,
While Slander tells the old malignant tale,
And Pedantry's dull taunt, and Folly's sneer assail.

Live simple lives, and worthy of the land ;
Bow not to Fashion ; heed not the voice of Gain ;
Draw near to Nature—see her stretch her hand
From rugged mountain or from fruitful plain ;
Let mild and peaceful Agriculture reign
O'er skill and industry ; let every art
Be fostered which the clime and soil sustain ;
But shun the Mammon spirit of the Mart,
Which dims the vivid eye, which mocks the swelling
    heart.

Cherish each worthy memory of the Past,
Of Saint and Warrior, Teacher, Bard, and Sage ;
Hold Christian Faith immutable and fast,
Drawn from clear fountains of an early Age,
Not from to-day's vexed stream ; pursue the page
Of human history well, and urge the car
Of conquering Science ; but whate'er engage,
Think 'tis not what ye *know*, but what ye *are*
And *do*, that hallows Earth, and sets in Heaven your star.

And O ye bearers of a princely name !
Whose birth-roll tells of Cymru's proudest sway ;
Who hold her soil, and take from her your fame ;
Whose sires stood foremost in the battle-fray ;
Lead ye the nation still, but in the way
Of truest peace and progress ; give it light
And strength, and ye shall have our praise to-day,
And in their ancestral halls your sons shall write,
Proud on the glowing shields, your name thus doubly
    bright !

And ye whom fortune or mistaken choice
Draws from your Country to an alien soil,
Still for her name and language lift your voice,
Nor let rude tongues her dignities despoil;
But still 'mid poverty, and pain, and toil,
Remember her, and she shall comfort you;
And oh! when pleasures tempt, and riches coil
Around your heart, return, and so renew
Your life with blessings pure—your path with purpose true.

One farewell word!   O friends, there is a stain
Upon your bardic robes, and it was so
With counsellor and chief since Rhodri's reign;—
Dissension! see what crimes and miseries flow
From that polluted source: behold a foe
Deadlier than all beside:—Arise, arise!—
Ye are our hope and refuge—lay him low—
The giant who has stalked with sneering eyes
Among you, and diffused the poison of his lies!

Peace, Concord, Truth, let these prevail to-day—
Prevail for ever Cambria's sons among;
Be this Eisteddfod in its bright array,
Where Genius, Learning, Birth, and Beauty throng,
A great regenerating Voice which long
Shall echo in the land from Wye to Dee,
Like that of Marchwiail—may those chiefs of Song—
Those glorious brethren,[1] our high pattern be,
While Trevor's fame shall live in Powys fair and free!

[1] Ednyfed, Madog, Llywelyn, at the Eisteddfod of Marchwiail, *temp.*
Edward III.

Awake, Deheubarth! join our patriot union—
Calon wrth galon, heart to heart, defies
The world; and Gwynedd, keep thy close communion
With beauty, lineage, and all that lies
Most ancient in thee! and Morganwg, rise—
Thou Queen of Countries[1]—Freedom's earliest stay—
Mother of warriors stern, and teachers wise!
And Powys! victim erst of many a fray,
But bright with conquering peace, and strong in love
    to-day.

Advance the Dragon Standard; raise the song
Unbennaeth Prydain; let us firmly swear
By Wood and Field and Mountain,[2] to prolong
Our bloodless contest for the great and fair:
Hark, how Dee's rushing waters fill the air!
Through night and day, and storm and calm they pour;—
One voice, one strength, one tendency, is there;—
Be wiser, truer, bolder than before,
And God shall bless our Cause, and prosper evermore!

[1] 'Arglwyddes pob Gwlad.'
[2] 'Coed, Maes, a Mynydd.'

LLANGOLLEN. (ALBAN ELVED,[1] 1858.)

LLANGOLLEN! round whose loveliest brow fondly doth wizard
    Dee
Bind his last charms ere duller plains invite him to the sea;
Fair vestibule which Nature rears to Cymru's mountain shrine,
Which Light and Beauty penetrate with all their gifts divine;
Where Grandeur sits upon the rocks that saw the primal wave
Their bastion-front like ocean-fort with slow persistence lave;
Where wood and stream gain voice and soul by old Tradition's
    might,
And arch and pillar, wall and tomb own History's clearer
    light;
Where Peace broods over human homes, and Freedom fills
    the air,
And Health exults, and Piety outbreathes her purest prayer;—
O Valley! ever dear to me, beneficent and sweet,
How oft I've wandered through thee with full heart and
    careless feet!—
Lingered with languid summer moons on Geraint's flowery
    crest—
Lain 'neath the kindling star of Love on Craig-y-Vorwyn's
    breast—
Heard the storm-echoes sigh within Myvanwy's ruined hall,
And watched the sun's most golden rays on Llan Egwestl fall;
And by the green-embosomed bank of the immortal stream,
Shaped many a lofty enterprise, nursed many a wayward
    dream;

[1] Autumnal Equinox.

And in thy hospitable homes which kindly spirits grace,
Have seen what Art could borrow from, and lend to, Nature's
    face.
But never yet did majesty so well thy brow adorn,
So proudly o'er thee roll the Night, so jocund move the Morn;
But never yet so eloquent did wood and wave and hill
Assume a voice—so glad a heart thy sweet recesses fill;
As when the azure bardic flag played in the mountain wind,
As when the ancient music swelled to heaven unconfined,
As when from far-divided homes the patriot Cymry came
On Cambria's fairest ground to bless and vindicate her name—
To rear in peace their Gorsedd-stone on basis firm and strong,
And in their great Eisteddfod to honour Art and Song!

They come from Mona's[1] sunny isle which rocks eternal guard,
Where lives the might of many a prince, the voice of many a
    bard;
They come from where the mountain-queen of gentle Clwyd's
    domain
Looks on grey tower, leafy dell, white cottage, golden grain;
From where the Eifl's crags enwrap, cold, desolate, and
    stern,
The vale that nursed the fiery snakes for traitor Vortigern;
Where Nevyn saw the pageant pass of Edward's blood-stained
    sway—
How scorns and triumphs over it our peaceful one to-day!
From where the lake of Beauty lies, and Aran's summits
    blend
Their giant cones with Eve's gold shafts that in its breast
    descend;

---

[1] No longer *Ynys Dywell*, the Dark Isle, from its groves.

Where yet round hoary Snowdon beats the quenchless heart
of Wales—
And *shall*, till stedfast rock dissolves, till rushing river fails !
Where Vyrnwy sparkles 'mid the groves and meadows rich
with kine,
And spreading uplands white with sheep and quiet home-
steads shine;
Where Past and Present meet and mix in Caerdiff's storied
town ;
Where fair Glyn Neath from Brecon's ridge her streams leads
dancing down ;
Where Towy glides through level meads and gardens of
delight,
And Merlin's spirit animates wood, waterfall, and height :
Where Usk and Wye confirm to Gwent the beauty of her
name,
And Learning holds his heritage, and Royalty his fame :
Where Merthyr's fires and circling smoke deform the air, yet
give
A recompense in art and wealth, and peace by which they live :
Where round Saint David's stormy Head the deep-voiced
breakers pour,
And howl the sea-winds through the aisles where Worship is
no more :—
They come from hall and cot remote—from factory, mine, and
farm,
Linked by one common brotherhood, led by one sacred
charm ;
And e'en from England's airless towns where Trade has
blocked the street,
For Patriotism keeps their heart though Fortune guides their
feet ;

They come with hope and purpose high, and voices tuned to glee,
To stand as stood their forefathers beside the holy Dee;
To rear in peace their Gorsedd-stone on basis sure and strong,
And in their great Eisteddfod to honour Art and Song!

Now in the beaming face of day and in the eye of light,
Beneath the freedom of the sky, full in the country's sight,[1]
See on the level greensward the zodiac stones arise
That emblem out the sun's career, the circle of the skies!
For as the eternal heavens bend o'er human chance and change,
As Nature swerves not from her course through all Creation's range,
As holiness and truth and peace immortally endure
Before God's throne, though clouds of Earth their purity obscure;
So is the bardic circle raised, the bardic colours worn,
The ancient mother-tongue invoked, the ancient symbols borne,
The gauds of pleasure cast aside, the nets of habit burst,
The mind led up to principles that shall be last as first;
And, one by one, while evil thoughts and passions disentwine,
The heart is warmed by human love, and blessed by love divine;
And spirit-filled is the temple great which time nor strength can bow,
Hallowed by faith and eloquence three thousand years ago.

---

[1] These expressions denote the conditions under which the Gorsedd must be held.

Firm on the central Covenant-stone stands the presiding Bard ;
The banners close around him there, and thronging votaries
    guard ;
Before him in his azure robe the hateful sword is sheathed,
While peace within the hearts of all on the lips of all is
    breathed :
Fair to his noble forehead the gold tiara clings—
More fair in what it typifies than vainer crown of kings ;
The mountain winds endearingly play o'er him and rejoice ;
The river sends its softest tones to mingle with his voice ;
He stands with calm eyes turned toward the ever-radiant
    East,
Proud as Christ's loyal minister, and Nature's poet-priest :
So stood Taliesin for his prince, with shining brow, and sang
Of honour, fame, and chivalry, while the battle-music rang ;
So Lucius stood—true saint and king—on many a British
    height,
Taught the pure faith, and perfected the triad rays of light !

Thus to the listening Gorsedd now the Hierophant declares
Of Cymru's Druid altars, of Cymru's Bardic Chairs ;
Of them who first in Heaven's name the sacred circle drew ;
Of ceaseless right and privilege—of ceaseless duty too ;
Of faith that found in Britain's isle a safe abiding ark,
When turned from her Creator's face, the Earth was lost and
    dark ;
Of peace that filled the bardic breast as Heaven's own hue
    serene ;
Of growth in knowledge and in good, plain in the Ovate's
    green ;
Of purity and holiness linked in the Druid white ;
Of truth that trieth, crowneth all in the Omniscient sight—

Of truth that beams like a polar star o'er every age and
    clime,
Would Man but clear his troubled eyes and view its light
    sublime!

Before the honour-giving Stone the glad expectants stand;
With reverent mien and earnest gaze they grasp the Bard's
    right hand;
The elder grave, the student mild, the maiden young and fair,
The Saxon, Celt, and Norman join in love for Cambria there:
And solemnly and fervently in the calm mountain air,
Descends to Earth that blessing, ascends to Heaven that
    prayer—
God's light be ever before thine eyes! God's truth upon thy
    lips!
God's word within thy conscience![1]   May silence or eclipse
Fall never on that utterance now burning in their heart,
When from the Gorsedd's ancient ring to the world they
    shall depart!
Illusions load the wings of Time, and feelings fade or sleep,
But may this hour's influence be durable as deep!
O Druid, Bard, and Ovate! know your duty and your joy;
Let virtue, peace, and worthy praise[2] your energies employ;
Shun sloth, contention, folly;[2] win a high but honest name.
For Honesty is sentinel at the loftiest gate of Fame;
To human thought and human work go forth, and join the
    crowd,
But be your honour still unstained, your spirit still unbowed;

---

[1] The formula addressed to the candidates for ordination in the bardic
degrees.
[2] As enjoined in the Triads of bardic duties.

Though Custom wave her leaden wand, though Pleasure's lips
    entice.
Assert your free and manly name 'gainst slavery and vice:
Around you Falsehood colours all, all gravitates to Gold,
And Passion moves in varnished masks, and Life is bought
    and sold;
But clasp your bardic lamp of truth, your bardic faith retain,
Be pure and single-minded, be primitive and plain;
For few and narrow are the needs of Man's ignobler part,
But vast the field of Intellect, and deep the mine of Heart!
And oh! forget not Cambria now, her history, soil, and
    speech;
For *her* let Genius raise his song—for *her* let Wisdom teach;
Let Beauty keep her heart for him whom *patriot* love first
    warms—
Devote the mother's watchful eye, the maiden's modest
    charms;
Let Eloquence pour winged words—Art doubly nerve his
    hand,
For her, for her, the old—the true—the beautiful—the grand:
And she shall well repay the love by many a golden hour
Of health, of clear intelligence, of privilege and power:—
Shall lead ye up from rushing time to the eternal dome
Where Peace and Virtue, Faith and Truth, sit in their primal
    home;—
Shall cool Life's fevered pulses with her fragrant mountain
    breath;
And stand Consoler, Hope, and Joy, beside the bed of death!

TO GWENYNEN GWENT.

Love ever cherishes thy name,
  Love doubly hails it now,
When, sharer of thy husband's fame,
And crowned desert and honoured claim,
  New jewels grace thy brow,
And royal favour and respect
Anew thine ancient House erect.

What noble nature e'er requires
  Titles to set it forth ?
The clear discerning soul aspires
To her own heaven, and but desires
  The dignity of worth ;
Rank little aids thy heart or hand
To win—sustain—protect—command.

Yet as some rock-fast guardian light
  Set o'er a stormy sea,
Shows more beneficently bright
To curving zones, when added height
  Lifts it above the lee ;
Llanover thus may beam sublime
To distant shores and distant time.

For thou with pure unselfish bent
  Hast loved our Cymric land,
And by that patriot love hast lent
New beauty to thy beauteous Gwent,
  And deepened all of grand,
Or fair, or sweet, in hills and dales
Which shrine the burning heart of Wales.

Of Wales—each mountain, cave, and rock,
  That guarded first the free,
And broke the untiring battle-shock,
And saw the morn (let dulness mock !)
  Of faith and liberty,
Which circling wide o'er British ground,
Have shed so fair a noon around :

Of Wales—her laws of simplest mould,
  Of wisest sense withal,
Her ancient knowledge half untold,
Her ancient virtues manifold,
  That flourished ere her fall,
And left a heritage behind—
Rich usufruct for heart and mind :

Of Wales—her song that ever poured
  In love-soft linnet's trill,
Or like to mountain eagle soared
For chieftain praised or God adored,
  Through ages good and ill—
Deep and imperishable might,
The soul of law, the source of right !

Of Wales—her speech ennobled long
 By wise and fervent lips,
And hallowed by the sacred throng
Who raised the psalm sublimely strong
 When faith's most cold eclipse
But brightened *their* lone altar-fires,
And silence swelled *their* deep-voiced quires :

Of Wales—her zone of living air
 Which Health's sweet spirit knits,
Her bower of mildest beauty where
Young Spring selects her emerald chair,
 And calm-browed Summer sits ;
Her rock-walled storm-swept palace lone
Where Winter rears his lofty throne :

Of Wales—of Wales—her present cause
 Built on her past renown—
Oh may it flourish 'mid applause,
Plainly and proudly as it draws
 Near to the future crown !
Oh let the Cymry round her cling
With close yet still enlarging ring !

Oh let the Cymry calmly rise,
 And know aright their part.—
Look on their work with chastened eyes,
Strive hand in hand till discord dies
 Encountered heart to heart ;
Then rest on loyal love to plead,
And claim for Wales her fullest meed !—

Unfettered freedom for her tongue
   In Church and Court and School;
Respect for hopes her bards have sung,
Respect for instincts that have sprung
   From unforgotten rule;
Prelates of native heart and voice,
Of people's love and sovereign's choice.

O Lady of my lowly verse!
   'Tis thy surpassing praise,
That 'mid the cares which rank immerse,
'Mid bosoms cold and eyes averse
   In Cambria's evil days,
Thou hast for her dear service still
Intrepid heart, unshaken will.

Glorious it was in ancient time
   When came a princess forth
With stately step and brow sublime,
The height of womanhood to climb
   By deed of arms and worth,
Cheered by her subjects' deep applause
To guard their altars, homes, and laws!

More glorious now when sneers abash,
   And grasping passions hold,
And jealous aliens Cambria lash,
And of her sons the warm are rash,
   The wise, alas! are cold,
And Trade and Habit bind the chains
Which Power gladly locks and strains!

More glorious, honoured Lady, now
   Is thine exalted part ;
Not Fashion's frown can make thee bow,
Nor sneering Pity disavow
   The impulse of thy heart :
Bright is thy place, but brighter yet
We own thy spirit's coronet.

'Tis thine on Virtue's mountain crest,
   'Neath Truth's cerulean dome,
To weigh the world and scan it best,
And dwarf the men of selfish breast,
   And feet that life-long roam—
Puny of eye and heart and hand—
Through vales of flowers or wastes of sand.

Oh honour to the radiant throng
   Who half redeem our Age !
Hail Art, Philanthropy, and Song,
That wax in woman fair and strong,
   To light Time's latest page !
Hail constellation great and pure,
Lind, Browning, Nightingale, Bonheur !

Another rising star shall shine
   Long in the crystal Wye,
For with our names of princely line
And princely worth, we welcome thine
   Of bardic melody—
Of strength and sweetness redolent,
Revered and loved Gwenynen Gwent.

A SONG FOR WALES.

RISE, brothers, Deheubarth with Gwynedd,[1] and render
   True praise to our Mother loved dearly and long!
Come Manhood intrepid, and Womanhood tender—
   Come graces of Music and glories of Song! .
United, rejoicing, ask blessings upon her,
   Who gave us for birthright so bounteous a part;
Our pride and our pleasure—our trust and our honour—
   The star of our memory—the hope of our heart!

The war-strains defiant have ceased from her towers;
   The sceptre lies hid in her Pendragon's grave;
But Melody moves us from Beauty's calm bowers,
   And Freedom sits guarded by mountain and wave;
And Peace plants among us a banner of brightness
   Which Wisdom and Mercy and Genius surround;
And strong in our union, and strong in uprightness,
   We, Britons, with Britons, defend British ground.

The wires that engirdle, and arches that span us,
   But Prejudice fetter, but Passion disarm;
Gwyllt Walia's old breezes unchangingly fan us,
   Health rounds the fair bosom, and nerves the strong arm;
And, oh! the dear speech of the Awen and Altar—
   The language we love as alone *it* can tell—
Shall never on lips pure and patriot falter,
   That *for* it and *with* it plead wisely and well!

          [1] The South and the North.

And still old Eryri's grey summits aspire :
　　In lonely Geirionydd the heavens still beam,
But over a kingdom bend, broader and higher
　　Than Arthur could win, or Taliesin could dream :
O Cambria's true sons, let us cherish that treasure !
　　O let us live worthy so glorious a part !
Be Cambria our love and our pride and our pleasure—
　　The Star of our memory—the Hope of our heart !

A SONG FOR ST. DAVID'S DAY.

Joy, joy for a morning that hallows existence,
    And wakens the soul from her visions of clay;
Sheds the light of the Past o'er the Future's dark distance:
    Our Day of Saint Dewi—our Cambrian Day!

Spring welcomes it now with her heavens serenest,
    And violets' sweet odour, and birds' gentle call,[1]
As if for his sake who loved highest and meanest—
    Lived holy, secluded, and grateful to all.

While far over oceans the Southern Cross beaming
    Lights the Cymro's glad steps where idolaters trod,
And Autumn well honours, by golden gifts teeming,
    Menevia's rich fruitage that glorified God.

One pulse thrills the people wherever is vital,
    The blood whose warm fountain is Cambria's deep heart;
Wherever is cherished that loftiest title
    To hold in her faith and her fortune a part:

For not the broad sweep of Missouri's proud waters,
    And not the warm glances of Aryan maid,
Can win us from Gwent's or from Gwynedd's bright
        daughters—
    Can hide the hill-streams where our Infancy played

Unfrozen and pure are those primal affections,
   Though rich be Australia, and Labrador bleak ;
And vivid and lasting those old recollections,
   Though Age touch the forehead, and Climate the cheek.

Joy, joy for this morn when the long disunited
   Are linked by the Spirit whose call they obey ;
When the far-scattered picture their heart's home delighted,
   And Day of Saint Dewi—their Cambrian Day !

But where can devotion rise truer or higher
   Than here in the land which his genius nursed ;
Where the mighty of old hailed the heavenly fire,
   And guarded the altars that glowed with it first !

Oh ! raise the glad song and the hymn of thanksgiving,
   Let Music's best melodies heavenward swell ;
Love weeps not his death who, immortally living,
   Yet blesses the Country he cherished so well !

See, bright on his brow, with the Isle's ancient splendour,
   The crowns of Cunedda and Arthur combine ;
And in his deep eyes, how majestic yet tender,
   The graces of faith and benevolence shine !

His heart as a lion 'gainst Error contending,
   The softest emotions could win and enthral ;
True servant of Christ, and true friend of Man, blending
   The meekness of John with the fervour of Paul !

His soul nurtured Wisdom, his mind mirrored Learning,
  And passionate Eloquence kissed his pure lips;
And sweet human Charity in his heart burning,
  No lust could enfeeble, no pride could eclipse.

Oh! witness fierce Boia's unhallowed aggression,
  Disarmed and transmuted by patience and prayer!
Oh! witness Caerlleon's victorious session
  When black Falsehood beaten crouched home to her lair!

Oh! witness the hearth of wan Misery brightened,
  The orphan protected, the outcast restored,
The faithful exhorted, the doubtful enlightened,
  By him who did all in the name of the Lord!

And now, wheresoever God's praises are chanted,
  And Cambria's prayers guard her unperishing tongue,
Let Piety think of the Churches he planted—
  Let Gratitude echo the psalms that he sung!

For are not those Churches among us still springing,
  Though arches can bend not, nor columns can climb
From the dust with the ivy of centuries o'erclinging;
  Their silence is voiceful, their ruin sublime!

Wherever rude tower relieve the wild mountain,
  Wherever fair spire ascend from the plain,
By seashore or forest, by river or fountain,
  Our Dewi has reared it, or blesses the fane.

And near the proud mosque : on the verdant savannah ;
   Where idols are bowed to abroad or at home ;
Resound yet the strains of that early Hosanna
   From lowliest chapel, from loftiest dome.

There Childhood can lisp them with accents angelic,
   And patriot Youth grow unselfish and warm,
There Age can enshrine, as the holiest relic,
   Calm trust in God's love, from life's infidel storm.

Joy, joy for this hour ! but be it productive
   Of more than the fiery emotion that burns
Like the sun of an April too bright and seductive,
   Till the evening of torpor its ashes inurns !

If princes of old thronged Rosina's far valley,
   To learn of thy wisdom, or bow at thy shrine ;
If once thy loved voice could the timid heart rally,
   And be for the valiant a watchword and sign ;

If, 'mid the rude conflict which Treachery nourished,
   Thy prayers and thy labours availed to afford
One quiet green spot where Humanity flourished,
   And Love worked to strengthen the Pendragon's sword ;

Shall *we* not live worthy of thee and the sages,
   The heroes and saints who ennobled the land ?—
We, we, on whom shine the beneficent Ages
   When Faith linked with Strength fears no ravager's brand !

When Liberty spreads her broad plumes like the eagle,
   Above our old mountains and wealth-laden seas;
When Justice, with power and majesty regal,
   Rules People and Throne by her Christian decrees!

And over the Islands lips faithful and fervent
   Tell hourly the truth to the peaceful and free,
And still to Menevia God granteth a servant
   Well worthy, great Primate, of Cambria and thee!

Such treasures surround us; O Dewi, inspire
   Right use and enjoyment, and as *thou* hast been,
May we, with pure motive and patriot fire
   Be loyal to Altar, to Country, to Queen!

May ever a ray of the light of thy spirit,
   Wise father! on ours increasingly shine;
May ever our hearts, tender pastor, inherit
   Affections as warm and unworldly as thine!

Oh then we shall cherish this radiant morning!
   Oh then its fair beams will perennially play!
High purpose exalting, sweet concord adorning,
   Our Day of Saint Dewi, our Cambrian Day!

WHAT WAS THOUGHT IN WALES,

A. D. 1859.

And is it then consummated and done—
 This newest work of heartless statecraft planned
Calmly before high Heaven and the sun,
 Against the altars of our mountain land ?
 Was 't not enough to flout, ignore, withstand,
And mock our speech, our history, and our song ;—
 Was sneering voice, or cold oppressive hand
Withheld, and dared they add this utter wrong,
To thrust 'tween God and us their impious will and
 strong ?

O shame ! O pity !—see her where she lies—
 The Cambrian Church, despoiled, degraded now,
Gathering her robe of many miseries
 To her cold breast—her queenly matron-brow
 Vacant of gems save one, whose primal glow,
Enkindled at the Cross of Christ, shall burn
 Before His Throne : her voice is faint and low—
Her bounteous arms droop pinioned— hoarse waves learn
Her dirge, and wild winds pause around her living urn.

Sadly to her of power and place bereft
    Come stately memories and immortal dreams;
Dubricius leads from Enlli's rocky cleft
    His saintly thousands; royal Lucius beams
    With Truth's perennial light; the hills and streams
Quicken and heave when Dewi comes, who blest
    Their gifts to Man : the Past with glory teems;
Where is the Present ?—they who should invest
Their Church with strength and love, and vindicate her
    best !

Alas ! her children hasten from her side
    As from a plague-struck mother ; she is mad
With mutterings strange—senseless to prompt or guide—
    Nerveless to feed or cherish ; dwells a bad
    And blighting spirit in her: would ye had
Prevented timely ! but ye yet may heal;
    Return from meaner worship—make her glad—
Unfetter, raise her, purify, unseal ;
Let tongues of fire now plead—let hearts of mercy feel !

O royal Lady of Earth's proudest throne,
    Defender of the Faith, we hail thee still !
So be thy mercy and thy justice shown
    To Cambria bowed 'neath one colossal ill
    Of English peer and bishop—they who fill
Her Courts with grass, her people's hearts with gall—
    The pompous parasites who starve and chill
The breast that feeds them like an idle thrall—
Alien in blood and speech, what other could befal !

When Dewi led the multitudes to God,
　　'Tis fairly fabled—who is he can say
What truth or fable be!—the spot he trod
　　Swelled to a mount with Spring's sweet honours gay
　　To lift him Heavenward: Is it thus to-day?
What prelate boasts of fruit, result, or sign—
　　God's favour, or Man's love? Again we pray
Thee, all-compassionate, to save each Shrine
Whose ancient aisles resound with blessings on thy line!

For we have reverend men among us, true
　　To thee and to the laws, while prompt to speak,
And think, and act, for Wales in all men's view,
　　With all men's love: Madam, thy Cymry seek
　　Support in these that make their state unique—
Tradition, custom, language; but their breath,
　　Arms, wealth, hearts, all are thine, sincere if weak;
Oh be to them who love thee unto death,
Their Helena anew—their bright Elizabeth!

But prayers to *thee* were vain, insidious Chief,
　　Who hold'st our Sovereign's power without her grace:
Idly we deemed that Cambria's trefoil leaf
　　Would flourish in thy keeping: it was base
　　To crush high hope with heavy commonplace;
Thou mightest truer love and ampler sway
　　Have won in justly dealing with our race:
But *this* thou could'st not rise to. Go thy way—
Go tread thy tortuous path, and live thy little day!

Cymry! the work is yours. Unite, arise—
    Before the Throne with peaceful protest come;
And heed not habit, sect, antipathies;
    Let love be eloquent, dissension dumb:
    Think how of old the Hierarchy of Rome,
Who warred 'gainst British right and conscience, quailed
    Before your fathers; and in Girald's tome
Read how the Norman power your Church assailed,
Nor till the sword grew sharp, through years on years, pre-
    vailed.

O brothers, doth not now a greater need
    Claim now a greater effort! By the child,
Vowed at the font to Christ in word and deed,
    Whose rosy lips have first in Cymru smiled—
    First charmed with Cymru's tones; by maiden mild,
And ardent youth, and feeble sire, who stand
    Troth plighting, faith confirming undefiled;—
By all I would invoke you—rise—demand
A Bishop of your own for God and Fatherland![1]

[1] Ultimately the next best step was taken in the appointment to the see
of Bangor of Dr. Campbell, whose residence in Wales, and knowledge of
the Welsh language and character, had endeared him to his people. But
the fact remains stronger than ever:—Government will not appoint a *Welsh*
clergyman to a Welsh bishopric.

If the Protestant Church in Ireland is to lose her rightful predominance,
and be deserted by the State in deference to that old falsehood, the principle of *numbers*, will not the Established Church in Wales have, sooner or
later, to bow before Dissent? How can Government avert a result which
its policy has so powerfully tended to promote?—(*May*, 1868.)

FOR THE CONWAY EISTEDDFOD, A.D. 1861.

Who said that the star of Gwynedd
    Hath paled its beaming ray,—
That the light of heroic Ages
    Grows faint and dull to-day?
Who said that the heart of Cambria
    Beats languidly and cold,—
That Commerce dwarfs the haughty,
    And Custom awes the bold?
That never again her children
    Shall glow with the spirit of yore,
Which taught and prayed in Gwent's fair shade,
    Or guarded Gwynedd's shore?

Answer, ye harps loud ringing,
    As across the battle blown!
Answer, ye lips, sweet singing
    Each old familiar tone!
Answer, ye bards of wisdom,
    Lords of the immortal tongue,
Which, old as the hoary patriarch,
    Is yet as the infant young!
Answer, ye thronging people
    Who listen and rejoice,
Whose eye is bright with feeling,
    Whose heart speaks in your voice!

What though your patriot princes
   Have lost their native throne,
Ye rule in the great *Unbenaeth*[1]—
   The Empire is your own!
What though your dragon standard
   Feel not the mountain breeze,
Ye have a part in the flag supreme
   That floats o'er the world's wide seas!
Not vainly on Dyganwy
   Your 'Island Dragon' stood,[2]
And flung the Mercian war-wolves
   To howl in Cynwy's flood:
Not vainly on those wave-washed crags[3]
   Your Gruffydd's blood was shed;
Not vainly through these halls was borne
   Llywelyn's wasted head.

For God's high dispensation
   Is never blind or vain;
He weaves the web of happiness
   From threads of grief and pain:
Sure, though unseen, Earth rolling
   Round Him her path pursues,
The rocks sustain her bosom,
   The tides her brow suffuse:
As sure and as resistless
   As rock, or wave, or wind,
Grows for the Eternal purpose
   The good of human kind.

[1] Sole Monarchy.   [2] Maelgwn Gwynedd.   [3] Penmaenmawr.

Gaze on your fields of Powys :
  Are they not doubly fair
Since War has ceased to trample them,
  And Peace has brooded there ?
Gaze on your stern Eryri ;
  Is he less wild or grand,
That the blood-red beacon-flames are quenched
  Which marked the foe at hand ?
Oh, free are the storied valleys :
  Oh, free are the circling seas ;
And many a Christian spire
  Gleams among Druid trees :
And the Saxon dyke is levelled,
  And the Norman fort is dust ;
But Friendship needs no barrier,
  And Strength is mutual trust !

Oh ! shame upon the Cymro !
  Let the loyal Cymry say—
Who would shake the noble pillars
  Of British strength to-day ;
Who with his English brother
  Would not march as brothers can,
Whether in Art's and Learning's train,
Or, if their Country call again,
  Firm in the battle van !

And shame upon the Saxon
  Who gives not Wales her due,
Who, loving well her glens and hills,
Loves not the kindred soul that fills
  Her tongue and people too !

Oh! shame upon the Saxon
　Who lightly deems or says
That noble things can perish,
　Born of the ancient days!—
That all the dreams of Theory,
　Or all the arms of Might,
Can take, or ought to take, from Wales
　Her heritage and right!
'Tis fair in the leafy valley,
　'Tis firm on the mountain head,
It flashes adown the cataract,
　It rests with the quiet dead;—
'Tis twined in the firs rock-rooted,
　'Tis deep in the heart of Man,
'Tis shed through the winds and waters:
　Remove it if ye can!

Joy! for the day is dawning
　When Faith and Love shall be
The only law for the Nation,
　The only bond for the free:
Witness, this ivied ruin,
　With shaft and oriel bowed,
Which never saw an hour more bright—
　A company more proud![1]
For here the blood is mingled
　Which erst was idly poured,
And the ensigns hang around us
　Of love that shames the sword.

[1] The Eisteddfod was held in the Castle.

FOR THE CONWAY EISTEDDFOD, 1861.

And, oh! of that love's gold fetter
  May never a link outstart,—
May Celt and Saxon firmly stand
Brothers, not only hand to hand,
  But brothers heart to heart!

ARMORICA, A.D. 1867.

READ BEFORE THE CELTIC CONGRESS AT SAINT BRIEUC,
OCTOBER, 1867.

Lone Genius of the Celtic lands! whom oft
   I seek by Cymric Enlli's sea-vexed graves,
Or pleasant Menai red with evening soft,
   Not Druid blood, or where the north wind raves
   O'er Môn's sad marshes, and the wintry waves
Beat on Aberffraw's ruins; or where far
   On Loegrian plains the Giant Circle[1] craves
Faith in its dubious megaliths whose are
Strange concords with the old world, and circling sun and star:

Nor less, O dark-browed Genius, dost thou sit
   In soaring camp and various battle-ground,
Whether in Powys holding closest knit
   The great Silurian's memory,[2] or around
   Strathearn's fair meads where living streams resound
The name of Galgacus; and it is thine,
   Patron and guardian Presence though discrowned,
To watch o'er choir and college, cell and shrine,
Where burned through centuries dark, Song, Learning, Faith
   divine.

---

[1] *Côr Gawr*, Stonehenge.   [2] Caractacus.

But chiefly 'tis across the narrow sea,
   Within our elder Britain, dear Arvòr,
That thou, sad Spirit, lovest most to be,
   And chiefly on the melancholy shore
    From Sena's Isle where whelming breakers roar
Around the Bay of Death,[1] to where the land
   Enlocks Morbihan with her history hoar,
And where far Belle-Ile looks on Quiberon's strand,
And by Biscayan airs the drifting dunes are fanned.

So, couched upon Saint Michel's storied Mount,
   My dreams have seen thee in the dawn-light pale,
Mournfully looking to the Orient fount
   Whence flowed thy people, and to where the wail
    Of Ocean testifies the latest tale
Of race on race through ages westward driven
   To those extremest bounds where yet they fail,
And having 'gainst assaults innumerous striven,
Seem now by subtler fates to slow extinction given.

Beneath thee Carnac spreads her little life
   Of field and cottage round the Christian fane
Of good Corneille; but all beside is rife
   With the dead Past, thine old Druidic reign
    Adumbrated in stone: athwart the plain
The solemn *Menhirs* stand in mystic rows,
   And fitfully upon the unequal train
Of gaunt grey columns in their mute repose,
The clinging sea-mist falls, and the clear sunlight glows.

---

[1] Baie des Trépassés.

Defiled, despoiled, for Want's ignobler ends,
   By the poor peasant-Vandals of the spot,
Less grandly now the rugged crescent bends,
   And the long issuing lines continue not
   Eastward as erst, by cromlech, caer, and grot,
To the drear gulf where brooding Ruin dwells —
   O Stones, in thousands gone but unforgot,
In thousands shall ye stand while Learning spells
Dark words, and Faith her beads of many colours tells !

Prone lies on Lokmariaker's old shore
   The mightiest Menhir, and the Carnedd's breast
Above is rifled of its sculptured store,
   And children play, and curious eyes invest
   The serpent tokens ; and all dispossessed,
Ménéhom of the Osismii looks forlorn
   Upon Douarnenez ; and on Michel's crest
A Chapel marks, of purer Worship born,
How by the exulting Saint the Ophidian creed was torn.

Yet, yet it perished not, the old belief ;
   Though, wove by Time, Truth's vestments must decay,
Truth still endures ; the meteor bright and brief
   That cleaves the midnight ere the dawn of day,
   Is not less *light* ; the living lips that pray
In the perfect faith of CHRIST, with knowledge filled,
   Are scarce more eloquent of GOD's high way
With Man, than were the Bards' for ever stilled—
The deep-voiced priests who graced Religion's world-wide
   guild.

'Good with the Gospel is the Stone,'[1] was said
  By those who cast their symbols at the feet
Of the fulfilling Word; the Druid dead
  Survive and speak around us, if 'tis meet
  To make love strong, peace broad, and virtue sweet.
Revolve high themes, assert the immortal soul,
  And trace the Almighty Archetype complete
From the marred human image; to control
Fate with Free Will, and shape Earth's course to Heaven's
    goal.

  Nor memories only of stern Worship fill
    This silent coast; with arms the air is loud,
  The waves are vexed with triremes, every hill
    Flames through the dark, and Celt and Roman crowd
    Tumultuous in the fight where Strength is bowed
  And Valour foiled on crimsoned Morbihan
    For hapless Arvor;—yet let Gaul be proud
  Of her fierce sons who circumscribed the span
Of the dread Eagle's flight, though Keris fell with Vannes!

  Who held through the long centuries, ever firm,
    Name, soil, and speech against each alien horde,
  Against apostate kin—by any term
    A foe—Norse, Frank, or Norman—well the sword
    Of Gradlon, Houel, Arthur, shining lord
  Of chivalry, and Nomenoë, kept
    Their cherished confines; well the prayers were poured
  Of Cadoc, Hervé, and each pure adept
Till Samson who afar in Cymric Lantwit slept!

[1] 'Da yw'r Maen gyda'r Evengyl.'

And now when arms have ceased, and with slow hate
   France meditates to quench the primal fire
Abjured from her own halls, that lingers late
   On Breton hearths, and Power will not tire
   Till the last accents of the old tongue expire
On Breton lips, and thou, their Genius, part
   From these old seats; what doth the hour require
Of thy diminished children?—Let the dart
Be hurled, and beaten back with calm and constant
   heart!—

Be beaten back, and back, as from sweet life
   Is many a harm by temperance and by will;
Till God's plain purpose interdict the strife,
   Oh let them not accelerate the ill,
   But strive as they who Fame's last annals fill—
Le Gonidec, Chateaubriand, La Tour d'Auvergne,
   Brizeux—and each who strove with strength or skill—
Each *Paotr kalet* of Arvor—in whose urn
A nation's ashes laid unquenchably shall burn!

And live there not of such a hundred more!
   Courson, De Gaulle, La Borderie, of wise name,
And tuneful Luzel, *bepred Breizad*, pour
   Their love, their learning, freely; and 'twere shame.
   To weep for Fatherland, for sure is fame
If doubtful fortune; nor omit we one
   In birth, life, labour, of thrice noble claim—
Villemarqué, in whose wreath, through shade and sun,
Laurels and bays shall twine while Ellé's waters run!

And shall not she, the Arvor of the Isles,
  Aid, love, sustain, her Sister elder-born,
Whom first she taught to rear the granite piles
  Of old Devotion's twilight, left forlorn
  In the sun to-day; whom, when the fuller morn
Arose for both, she guided to the Cross;
  With whom, when thronging foes had vexed and worn
Their race, she linked herself 'gainst pain and loss,
To curb the o'erweening steps which would the world engross!

Yes! Cambria's heart is Bretagne's, and the more
  When stricken now with Change, and Fever-pressed;
But Change that may not all their Past restore,
  Shall not divide their Future!—'neath the crest
  Of Snowdon Llydaw lies; her deep full breast,
Turbid anon with wintry snows, or bright
  With gleams of autumn stars, loves ever best
To mirror that proud Peak who, day and night,
Grows darker with her gloom, or gladder with her light.[1]

[1] This *Llyn* bears the Welsh name of Armorica, Llydaw.

55

A Breton Version of the preceding Poem. By the VICOMTE DE LA VILLEMARQUÉ.

ANN ARVOR ER BLOAZ 1867.

TROET E BREZONEK

HA KENNIGET DA GENVREUDEUR ANN EISTEZVOD KELTIEK,

WAR DON *ar re naanet.* (BARZAZ BREIZ.)

AWEN c'houeg ar Geltied! Te a glaskann bepred
War draez enez Enlli gand al lano gwasket,
War draez ar Menai ruziet gand ar c'huz-heol,
Na lavarann ket gand gwad ann Druzed lazet holl;

Te a glaskann war c'heun Mon, pe war zarz Aberfraw,
Pe belloc'h c'hoaz, war meaz meur ar vein hir enn ho zao
Hag a hanver *Ti ar gawr,* eunn ti kromm 'vel ar bed,
Ar bed koz, enn dro d'ezhan ann heol hag ar stered.

Hogen chom a rez ivez war al leac'hiou huel;
Chom a rez ivez, Awen, war meazou ar brezel,
E bro brudet a Bowys, bro ar Sellour distak,
Pe a-hed douriou Strathearn a wel ato Galgak.

Evid oud da vout tristik ha didalgen hirion,
Ouz it-te a zell difenn hor gwen hag hor giziou,
Ouz it-te a zell difenn kor ha skol ar Varzed
Ar skiant, hag ar furnez, ann Doue heb-ken, bepred.

Hogen enn tu-all d'ar mor eo gwell gan-ez beva.
Enn eur vro muia-karet, e tal hor c'hoar hena:
Adaleg enez Sizun ha Boe ann Anaon,
Tre beteg ar Morbihan e tired da galon;

Adaleg ar c'herreg gwez a lamm gant-ho ar mor
Beteg ann douar meulet gand ann dud a enor,
Tre beteg enez Gerveur, rag-enep Kiberon
Leac'h 'ma ann treaz gwentet gand awel ar mor don.

Eno ema da galon: ha me, o vale Breiz,
War grec'h Sant-Mikel konsket da weliz eur pe deiz:
Te droe da zaou-lagad war zu ar zav-heol
War zu ar vammen founnuz omp denet ont-hi holl,

Te gleve ar mor kanvuz a lavare 'nn he iez:
'Ac'hann tud ar c'huz-heol a lammaz a-liez!'
Te lavare da man, Awen: 'daoust ha gwir eo
E vez va gwenn diskaret, sioaz! gand ar c'hrign-beo?'

Setu ar ger a Garnak a vev e giz-ma-giz,
Enn hi parkou ha tiez, enn he c'hreiz he iliz,
Hiz kaer sant Korneli; hogen a dro-war-dro
Nemet traou ann amzer goz, nemet lion ar maro;

Da vrud zo skrivet ama, 'nn eul leor diaez da lenn,
- Eul leor burzuduz meurbed, peb eneben eur maen;-
Ann heol a lak da lintra enebennou al leor,
Ha gorventennou awel hen sar hag hen digor.

Meur eneben zo roget gant tud keiz ar barrez;
Ma ce'h ober traou iskiz, n'ed eo mui enn he bez:
Gwech-all ann neb hen lenne oa red d'ezhan redeg
Pell, pell, tre beteg ar mor, a garrek da garrek:

Kerrek brudet! Kouezet oc'h; ia, kouezet oc'h a leiz;
Med angoviet n'ed oc'h tamm, chom a rit enn hor c'hreiz;
Chom a rit soun enn ho sao; hag al lennek hello
Ober c'hoaz he arvaron, hag ar c'hroac'h he c'helo.

E tal Lokmariaker eur peulvan zo kouezet,
Hag eunn daol a-uz d'ezhan hed-da-hed zo faoutet,
Ar vugale a c'hoari dindan, hag al lennek
A zell gant preder mar gwel roudou ann Aer-vorek.

A-uz da Zouarnenez e sav ar Menez-c'hom
Ne azeuler mui eno pell-zo ann Doue falz Kromm;
Ha war grec'hen Sant-Mikel eur chapel a weler
A ziskouez eo diskaret kreden Ofiz, ann aer.

Hogen ar c'hredennou koz n'ho c'holler ket da vad;
Beo eo c'hoaz ar wirionez, nevezet he dillad;
Al lne'hedennig a red enn ear abarz ann deiz
A zo ar c'houlaouennik kannad ar goulou-deiz.

Beleien Jezuz ho deuz pedennou helavar
Ar wirionez e teskont enn eunn doare dispar,
Koulskoude ne oa ket gwan kanaouen ar Varzed,
Ne oant ket gwan kennebeut pedennou ann Druzed.

Ar Varzed a lavaraz gwech-all enn ho c'hentel:
Mad eo ar meaa, eme-z-ho, *mad gand ann Aviel*
Evit-ho da vout maro e komzont enn hon mesk,
Darn euz ar pez a zeskent, hon beleien hen desk.

Ar peoc'h hag ar garantez, ha leiz a vertuzo,
Peurbadelez ann ene a oa hetuz d'ezho;
Dione'h skouer ann den, ann den mad, ho Doue hi a eure,
Enn eur ziskouez ann hent eon, eme-z-ho, da bep re.

Ne ked ann traou-ze heb-ken, am laka da venna,
Nemet strap ar c'hlezeier ha trouz listri Roma ;
Peb menez a lac'h enn noz ; Galled ha Romaned
Eu em vesk, en emgann ; gwa ! gwa ! c'houi tud diskaret !

Ar Morbihan zo ruziet he zour gant poullou gwad,
Diwall a ra enn aner he vro peb kenvroad ;
N'euz forz ! grit fonge gant-ho, tud Naoued, tud Gwenuet,
Grit fonge gant-ho ! harzal ann Erer euz int gret.

Piou a ziwallaz ivez, bepred kre ha didorr,
Piou a ziwallaz hon iez hag hano bro Arvor
Oc'h tud estren pe drubard, Franked ha Normaned
Ha Danezed, a vagad a bep tu dastumet ?

Kleze Gradlon a oa vad, kleze ar roue Houel,
Kleze ar roue braz Arzur, brudet a dost, a bell,
Kleze roue Nomenoiou, pedennou sant Samson,
Sant Kadok, ha sant Herve, ha kant kristen gwirion.

Ha brema pa gouez ann trouz, pa ra ar pez a c'hall
Evit laza tan Arvor he amezeg Ar Gall,
O veza maro pell zo holl dan ar C'halloned
Hag o veza beo ato hini ar Vretoned ;

Brema pa droc'h goustadig Broc'hall teod ar Vreiziz
Ha pa da wask, Awen ker, vit ma 'zi war da giz,
Petra zo red da ober d'az pugale mantret ?
Derc'hel stard ha kalonek, moustra pa ver moustret !

Moustrit, ia, moustrit bepred ! gwall glanv eo hon mignon,
Klaskit louzou talvouduz da zistan he galon ;
Na loskit ked ar c'hlenved da wasaat bemdeiz,
Stourmit 'vel ho keuvrendeur, brudeta tud a Vreiz ;

Stourmit 'vel Ar Gonidek, ha Koret, ha Brizeuz.
Stourmit 'vel Kastelbriand, a oa eunn den mar 'zeuz.
Stourmit 'vel peb Paotr kalet, 'vel peb Breton dioue'h-tu,
A ra van da vout maro, hag a oar pegi du !

Stourmit 'vel ma ra Courson, Laborderie dale'hmat,
Charlez Broc'hall, Ann Huel, barz chouek, *bepred Breizad* ;
Pa ho gweler o stourmi, lenva n'ed eo ket red ;
Vit-hi da vout ezommek hon bro zo enoret ;

Stourmit 'vel ma ra'nn hini a garer enn Arvor,
Dre ma stourm tregont vloaz zo 'vit rei d'ezhi enor.
Dre 'ma o wea d'ezhi, gant lora ha gant frouez,
Eur garanen a bado 'tra redo dour Ellez.

Na te, Breiz Veur ann Enez, c'hoar iaouank Breiz-Izel,
Daoust ha na gari da c'hoar, na ri d'ezhi skoazel ?
Na ri skoazel d'ann hini a zeskaz d'id somma
E bro ann hany ar vein-heir, eunn deiz, eun eur gana ?

A zeskaz d'id goudeze sevel gant kalz a feiz
Kement kroaz Doue a weler o splanna e peb Breiz ?
Ha kleze ouc'h kleze lemm, ha kalon ouc'h kalon,
Ha breac'h ouc'h breac'h, troad ouc'h troad, a harzaz al Leon?

Ia, kalon Breiziz Breiz-veur eo kalon Breiz-Izel !
Ia, hirio gwell 'vit biskoaz eo red en em zere'hel !
Ia, hirio ann deiz pa dro ar bed war he c'hino,
Kaer en do ober troiou, tra n'hon diunano !

A-uz da grec'h Ereri ema Lenn ann Arvor,
(Lynn Llydaw a ra out-hi ar Vreiziz a dreuz mor)
Wechou 'ma louz gand ann ere'h, wechou sklear gand al loar ;
Wechou trist, wechou laouen, sellout ouc'h krec'h a gar.

CYMRU TO ARVOR

(October, 1867).

' Nid Cadarn ond Brodyrdde.'

Hail Sons of ancient Arvor !
  Hail Brothers of our race !
Whom long our love has cherished,
  We greet you face to face :—
Hail Land of truest glory,
  Of all-enduring name,
Of many-textured fortune,
  Of Christ-confessing fame !

We leave our hills and valleys,
  We leave our Cymric shore,
We cross the friendly waters
  Our fathers crossed before :
Around us spread the oakwoods
  With autumn splendours drest,
The moorlands bittern-haunted,
  The meres with sedgy breast ;
Drear beaches, wind-swept sand-dunes,
  Slow streamlets, granite mounds ;
All tell us we are parted
  From home's accustomed bounds.

But what though Nature vary
  Her many-jewelled robe,
The Celtic heart beneath it
  Throbs changeless o'er the globe !

We hear the fervid accents
    Of child and maid and man,
As Edward heard in Gwynedd,
    As Cæsar heard in Vannes ;
And as our grandsires spoke them
    Our grandsons still shall speak,
Hushed here and there, it may be,
    Or tremulous and weak :
But till the winds careering
    Grow mute 'neath Fashion's spell,
Till Power's jealous murmur
    The sea's deep voice can quell,
Till Art can train the thunder
    To tell the flute's soft tale :
The Briton's tongue shall cease not,
    Nor the Briton's lineage fail.

Again we look on Arvor
    Not unfamiliar now,
Dear sister of our Cymru
    Though sadder be her brow :
See, through the veil Change-woven
    The changeless Spirit burns !
See, through the mist of Ages
    The heroic Past returns !

From Penmarch's Point with sunset
    Golden, to brimming Loire ;
From Cornouaille's wave-washed granite
    To Quiberon's sand-ribbed shore :

From where world-weary Tanguy,
    On the lone foreland's rim,
'Mid driving foam and sea-shock
    Raised the rejoicing hymn:
To where by Aleth's ruins
    Rance glides to ocean-deeps,
And 'neath the Cross he honoured
    Sublime Chateaubriand sleeps:
Through all the land of Llydaw
    Our heritage we trace,
We read in all, emblazoned,
    The records of our race.
There rise the mystic columns
    Of the lore our Druids taught,
Who smote with light the Idols,
    And vanquished Force by Thought :—
Rude Stones, through the centuries stedfast,
    Rejoice, for the faith ye fed
Lives in the fair Cathedral
    Not lost but perfected !
Vorganium's battle relics,
    And Peran's dubious wall,
With all the Northmen's power,
    And all the Frankish thrall,
Vex not our peaceful Present
    With more than fleeting stain ;
But the light of God is o'er us,
    The signs of God remain.
Yes ! for we meet as brothers
    And gaze on all around,
Christians 'mid Christian worship,
    Britons on British ground.

Beside your Gouet's waters
   Our Brieuc came to dwell,
And reared his lowly Chapel
   By Orel's blessed Well:
And where that ancient City
   Lifts Heavenward still her eyes—
Calm lake near life's mad torrent—
   Our Paul of Léon lies:
And ours the warlike Samson
   Who gave her fame to Dol,
And ours the gentle Malo
   Whom love made strong of soul.
Even so, in mutual blessing,
   Your sons of saintly name
To Cymru's guardian mountains
   With princely Cadvan came:
And many a hallowed tower,
   And many a crag and *cwm*,
Sure spring, and lonely sea-marge,
   Their life and death illume.

Nor less before our vision
   The elves of Fancy dance,
And softly falls around us
   The roselight of Romance:
Enora, warm with beauty,
   To her lost love angel-borne,
Greets him with heavenly passion
   Heart-stirred, yet half forlorn:
And list!—in the summer gloaming,
   Through the dense leaves zephyr-fanned,
Comes the song of happy Vivien
   From green Brocéliande.

She kneels by the moss-lipped fountain
    Afar in the secret glade,
And fern and rose and lily
    Embower the stately maid :
No sound save the rill's low murmur,
    Or the nestward-fluttering wing,
No sign that a subtler Presence
    Lives in the enchanted ring !
But the oak of a thousand winters
    Spreads his broad bulk around,
And the ghostly forest-shadows
    Glide through the pines star-crowned :
And she chants—her white arms outspreading—
    And she chants—and her dark eyes shine
O Merlin mine forever !—
    O Merlin forever mine ! [1]

And Arthur ! whose name of wonder
    Like the rainbow's glory stands
Arching our British waters,
    Based on our British lands :
Who rose like a star in tempest,
    And scattered the Saxon horde
By the dread of his Dragon banner,
    And the force of his knightly sword :
Who in Caerlleon or Camelot,
    Unhelmed, led the minstrel's song,
And nurtured his shining Chivalry
    In hate of shame and wrong.

---

[1] I accept the Vivien of M. de la Villemarqué (see *Myrdhinn*), not the
Vivien of Mr. Tennyson (see *Idylls of the King*).

Dear Land! our hearts still trace thee
  Through all thy royal line—
Gradlon and Nomenoë—
  Conan and Constantine :—
Through all the war of races,
  Through all the growth of years,
Are linked with thee in triumph,
  Are linked with thee in tears :
For thy Past is the Past of Cymru,
  Thy Speech echoes Cymru's Speech,
And her's is thy Faith's foundation,
  And her's its Heavenward reach.
And now what fate soever
  Betide the Celtic name,
Our gain and loss are blended,
  Our destinies the same.
O brethren, the task is ours—
  Let none his part forget—
To stay the jealous billows
  Which coldly our borders fret !
Let them waft us Art and Commerce,
  Let them knit us in the bands
That make one sacred brotherhood
  Of Earth's divided lands !
But let not all their fury
  Our landmarks old efface,
Nor break one dear memorial
  Of our far-descended race !
Faith, Song, with all that the Ages
  Around our history wreathe,
'Tis our privilege to inherit,
  'Tis our duty to bequeath.

F

If the Speech which God hath given
    We consecrate to Him,
Our Speech shall never minish,
    Our light grow never dim.

By Plestin's strand, where wildly
    The Atlantic surges toss,
Conspicuous on Roc'hellas
    Saint Efflam reared his cross :
And while those arms of mercy
    Rise clear above the wave,
The traveller unfearing
    The Ocean's march may brave.
So, brothers, travelling onward
    Along the Nation's track,
Keep still the Cross before you—
    And fear no foe's attack :—
Keep still the Cross before you—
    Hope—strive—resist—endure ;
The battle may be stubborn,
    But the victory is sure !

VERSES WITH NOTHING NEW IN THEM.

Ver novum, ver jam canorum, vere natus orbis est ;
Vere concordant amores, vere nubent alites,
Et nemus comam resolvet de maritis imbribus,
                    CATULLUS, *Pervigilium Veneris.*

I HAIL thee welcome, spirit-moving Spring !
  Welcome again, thou Season fresh and fair,
Virgin and Love as now awakening
    From thy chaste bed of snows, and Night's cold care.
    Approach ! thy opening breast, thy flowery hair,
Thy fragrant breath, thy beaming eyes incline
    Kindly to his embrace whom life's harsh wear
Hath left, alas ! no solace sure as thine,
No love so unalloyed, no blessing so benign.

Meet me enamoured in thy nascent charms
  Types of all-perfect beauty, matchless they ;
Not the full kiss of matron Summer warms
    My bounding senses ; not the rich array
    Of Autumn's treasures brightening in decay.
Like thee, ambrosial Influence ! can impart
    That temperate joy which passeth not with May.
But lives a pleasure followed by no smart—
An ever-vernal bliss within the reposing heart.

F 2

All harmonies, all melodies arise
    With thee, and overspread the rejoicing earth;
Light glows in landscapes green, and laughing skies,
    And sparkling waters; air resounds with mirth;
    All loveliest hues and forms with thee have birth--
Sweet odours, gentle heats, and quickening rain;
    How many noble hopes and thoughts of worth
Thy smiles suggest! thou comest not in vain
To lighten Labour's steps, and smoothe the bed of Pain.

With rosy health thou tintest Woman's cheek,
    And fired by thee, her eye the brighter beams;
Thou armest Man with energy to seek
    The work-day duty that his lot beseems;
    And oft thy pure and happy face redeems
The wretch whom sin and misery bow down:
    While mirrored in the Poet's heavenward dreams.
What thronging shapes of thee descend to crown
His soul's far-imaged home, where fadeless peace is known!

Thou fructifiest latent thought and feeling--
    The infant owns thee on its mother's breast,
And Youth's quick pulses, variously revealing
    The pregnant will to do, and sweet unrest
    Of genial passions all thy power attest;
But kindliest fans thy breath the pallid brow
    Of him whom City sights and sounds invest--
Bind in the strife to live, and disallow
Lost time with sun or shade, clear stream or budding bough.

And one of many such, I learn from thee
   A deeper scorn of destiny and fate,
A multiplied belief that Man may be
   In measure as he wills it, good and great,
   A mind to frame and love that double state
Where thought with action, rest with labour blends,
   Where evening follows day to recreate,
Where music, poesy, art, flowers, friends,
Relieve and reconcile life's ruder, sterner ends.

And though obdurate Circumstance impede,
   Be ours to conquer and to realize !
For Will moulds Way, and Thought eventuates Deed,
   And less in outward things than in *him* lies
   Much that opposes Man : for me I prize
Doubly those moments that compelled they come,
   Which lead me on to learn of earth and skies,
Or shape sweet visions at the hearth of home,
Or far from towns for health and healthful thoughts to roam :—

Roam cheered and guided by thy happy smile,
   Of Nature thou the first and fairest born !
To mark the growing waves embrace the Isle,
   To breathe the bright and unpolluted morn,
   To press the grass, and touch the tender corn,
To thread the wood, and low-voiced dove to list,
   To trace the stream's smooth bank or channel worn,
To climb the mountain through the parting mist,
Whose head the new-sprung Sun rejoicingly hath kissed.

And whither can my eager footsteps bend
  For such, if not, dear Cambria, still to thee!
Where blessings manifold from Heaven descend,
  Where Beauty hallows mountain, vale, and sea,
  Where Nature's joyous bosom swelleth free
'Neath the glad Hours' ever-young embrace:--
  Alas! that here should human discord be,
Old faith decay, new fantasies have place,
And patriot ardour droop, and worldly lust debase!

Enough! for little verse of mine availeth,
  And headlong Passion's breath that dully stains,
As soon from off the mighty glass exhaleth
  Which mirrors the Eternal;—*she* remains,
  Calm Nature—faints not, wearies not or wanes;
Still is her torch undimmed, her portals wide,
  And I on Snowdon's crags, or Mona's plains,
Weep not for hopeless fame, or love denied,
While *she* is hope and love, joy, recompense and pride.

NANT FFRANCON.[1]

Now from the world of sorrows, shows, and lusts—
From the life-mine deep, hard, and cold, where Man
Must dig for daily bread that gives but strength
To labour on and ever on—I come,
A little while to know repose and truth,
To bend to Nature's fair and awful charms.
And win some pure emotions from her face.

Joyous, my footsteps press the winding road
Amid the hills uplifted; backward, sink
The gleaming Straits, the calm romantic Bay.
The far infinity of sunbright waves;
Yet soon to rise more beautiful, more free,
Again upon the vision, and around
The sterner scene pour liberty and light.

The Pass grows onward, glorious to behold,
And turning, shuts and spurns the beaten plain
Where Fashion struts, and Commerce buys and sells,
And Manufacture dins; but opes instead,
Dear Cambria's wildest vestibule and shrine,
Rock-walled, and mountain-shadowed, and stream-laved,

---

[1] The scene of this poem is the Pass of Nant Ffrancon (approached from
the direction of Bangor), the Fall of Benglog, the tarns Ogwen, Idwal, and
Bochlwyd, and the mountains Glyder Vach and Vawr. The time is the
evening of Christmas Day, 1854.

Where the poor task-bound senses may exult
In pliant freedom, and the languid veins
Throb with an influence new, and the hot brow
Bathe in the freshness of quick-rushing airs,
While circling silence thrills the deeper ear,
All eloquent, and love and wonder lift the soul.

Now dreadly hang above me Davydd's crags,
A terrace of convulsion, dark and vast;
Here curved and jagged and shattered, strewn along;
There in fantastic grandeur pillared high,
Or rounded to a storm-defying front;
Now like the mightiest fort of human hands
In granite solidness and turret mould;
Now crumbling down in hosts of savage shapes,
As when the throat of War has flamed destruction:
But idly Fancy summons human arts
To so compare, for where is he could frame
Such battlements, or where could overthrow!
That bulk outlaughs the Titan's fabled boast—
That height alone the warder eagle knows;
The elements have raised the mountain-wall:
The elements alone have changed—shall change:—
Look how the jealous clouds enwrap the steep—
Look how the vivid lightning wantons there—
Look how the virgin streams come dancing down;—
All tells of calm and unapproached repose—
Of Power that antedates the world, abiding
Sublime and still, until the world dissolve!

Beneath me lies the valley low and green,
Whose other verge the peakèd Glyder bounds,

As this, the Carnedd's crags—a sweet recess,
Which frowned upon by all around, above,
And girt by forms of terror, sounds of awe,
Gives back but beauty to their dark embrace—
Gives back but lightsome joy and vernal smiles :
For here the sun is wooed to linger long,
And here the breezes furl their mountain wings
And bend to kiss the grass ; while in the midst
Glides quiet Ogwen, smooth and brimming, by—
Glides quiet Ogwen now—but list the dash—
The deep and crystal dash of prisoned waves,
And mark the flood of spray that floats and sweeps
High o'er the chasm of dense and dripping rocks ;—
'Tis Ogwen falling from his mother lake
Set fair on high, the mirror of the hills—
With roar and bound and flashing tumult falling,
To know a quiet course, and meet the sea
In peace beyond Nant Ffrancon's level floor.

River of life, is this thy history too!
Emerging from some antenatal lake—
Dim dream-acknowledged source of daily being—
To meet upon the margin storm and woe,
And scattered, tossed, perplexed, through youth be driven
O'er shelving precipice, through winding ways,
Where countless forces wait to thwart and bend ;
Happy, if speed and strength and high endeavour
Can break through all, and know a calmer time !

Let me descend, and feel upon my cheek
The pure cold spray flung freshening by the wind ;

For Ogwen, after many a sullen plunge,
And involuted whirl, and headlong dash,
Falls volumed, massed, and foaming, at my feet,
In everlasting gleam and resonance
Reverberated by the hollow walls
Which, dark and still, contrast his life and brightness,
Yet lichen-specked, and diamonded with beads
Of dew, and ever bathed in crystal showers,
Stand fittest framework for a scene so fair.

Eternal waters and eternal rocks !
No transient thing may mingle here with you
Save yon bleak tree that o'er the mid abysm
Stretches its withered arms and naked head,
As if survived some Druid spirit there,
To guide and guard the river's deep-voiced psalm.
Eternal waters—mountains—rocks—how oft
The fiery sun hath lit ye festively :—
How oft the snows have mingled with your tide,
And filled your rifted steeps in feathery play ;—
How oft the rainbow with sweet vivid charm
Hath hung around ye, and the midnight moon
Shed clearer beauty from her pearly urn ;—
What storm and darkness have encircled ye
Since first your waves outwandered from the mere—
Since first your rugged pinnacles arose ;
And so again through time's repeated cycles
Shall these still wax and wane, when he that looks
And listens now, decaying, frail and mean,
While ye endure, shall moulder, pulseless, voiceless—
While ye endure—the same through all—to all !

Yet not—for one imperishable part
Brightening the complex dust, shall brightest grow
When death unbinds it, scattering wide that dust
Oh ! let me ever think—the vital sense
Which moves within me and impels me hither,
Enamoured of this ancient solitude
Of stream and rock, and wood and mountain hoar,
Shall thrill with double sympathy and joy,
And purely know, and purely feel whate'er
Is like itself good, great, sublime or fair,
When these slow feet have ceased their ministry,
And these dim eyes withdrawn their narrow gaze !

And if in Man's weak frame there thus may live
And *after-live*, so measureless a power,
Shall not the mighty heart of Nature beat
Reciprocal, and to the kindred soul
Intelligible revelations send !
Still—with the wisest, noblest that have felt,
Still would *I* feel how all her shapes and sounds
Have deep significance to eyes and ears
Undulled, and as within our human world
Doth beauty ever beauty seek, and love
Respond to love, and wit prompt equal wit;
So ever do the fair and great in Nature
Unite their essence to the same in Man—
So ever Nature's spirit may with his
Meet in communion—truth, and love, and beauty
Its seals and signs—and with material voice
That mystery is outspoken, in the sigh
Or swell of winds and waves—in the deep thunder
And whispering wood, and restless waterfall.

But day declines, and over Trivaen's brow
The frowning clouds are thickening : Horror sits
Stern on the topmost crags that meet around
And darken o'er the depth where Idwal sleeps—
Cold ghastly pool !—hence let me haste to gain
The mountain-crest and downward track to where
Llanberis shows her bright twin laughing lakes
That sweetly glisten like the eyes of Spring,
Beyond the wintry chaos of the Pass ;
While old Dolbadarn, grey and bowed and mute,
Looks fondly on their ever-vernal beauty—
On their rejuvenescence looks with years
On years the same, while he by time is made
A Ruin, yet how eloquent and fair !

Now southward as I tread the rising path,
December's dusk-red twilight briefly floats
Around the head superb of Glyder Vawr,
And faintly touches each discoloured peak
Outflung against the eve, and palely sinks
Within the water, latest lingering there ;
But every cleft and pillar and ravine
Looms massed in blackness, and one horrid chasm
Far through the mountain cloven, downward yawns
Precipitous, and nurses in its coils
A howling stream and dwelling-place of fiends.

Idwal ! cold, sad, and lonely lake that liest
Encradled high on Glyder's breast,
As in some outer world where never are
Glad sounds, warm colours ; whither still ascend
The fiercer elements to pour their rage,

NANT FFRANCON.

And vex thee into passionate unrest,
And wake and overcome thy sullen cry :
No flowerets spring beside thy stony marge,
Nor Childhood plays, nor Love reposes there;
No summer Zephyr kisses that dark brow ;
Within those frigid depths no Evening burns ;
But when the winter moon hangs high above,
And when the air is thick with driving sleet,
And north winds sweep convulsively athwart
Snowdonia's buttresses, and lightnings strike
Sublimely on each bold defiant crest—
Then art thou, Idwal, e'en a wild delight !

Murder hath stained thy waters, and there brood
Red legends over thee, voluminous ;
The far-off light of olden time remains
About thee; deeds of suffering and of strength
Rise dimly from thee in the midnight mist :—
The far-off light of olden time remains ;
Ghosts of a thousand buried years surround
Thee and thy mountains where the feet of Change
Which rapid trample out Man's haunts and Man,
Come not or slowly come—but all survives
Past ever Present—ever Then as Now !

Upward and upward o'er the craggy slope
Mid rocks edge-poised, columnar, pyriform,
Rude altars framed for rites invisible—
Rude fonts that lift their grey eternal urns
Fed with the ice-cold dews, and Memnons rude
Whom animate the wild winds' wizard tones.
Upward and upward where unnumbered rills

Mossed underfoot and plashy, steal adown,
Or tear tempestuous their resounding way ;—
Upward with beating breast and weary foot,
And eye deluded thrice by ridge o'er ridge
Expanding, until now I gain the brink
Of a deep-stretching *cwm* whose walls inclose
A night of dripping clouds—whence one steep ledge
Approaches to the mountain's secret brow
Far unattained above me and around.

Here gaze I backward through the darkening air
On gathered outlines shown sublimer so :—
On Trivaen's stormy front, Llywelyn's side
Rounded by bold impending Olea Wen :—
These lap fair Ogwen in their stern embrace
Whose river-child delights the eye afar,
Disporting through the crag-invested glen ;
And the white granite arch is seen which bears
That firm and graceful road—the boast of Art,
And bridging o'er the tortuous cataract,
With all the giant mountain massed above,
Stands perilled in its strength like liberty
Assailed internally by anarch force,
And overshadowed by a tyrant's power.
Nearer, on either hand, the gloomy tarns
Idwal and Bochlwyd rest, while not a sound
Save the wind moaning through the rifted rocks,
And—far adown—the sleepless waterfall !

And this is Christmas night ! of months and days
The holiest name, that blesses and embalms
The winter drear, a bright perennial time ;

When God's goodwill, and peace to mortal men
Descend from Him ' Who gives upbraiding not,'
And angels waft down Love's fair links of gold
Uniting heart to heart, and Earth to Heaven.

In this wild, silent, early home of Nature,
How swift Imagination now unbound
From clinging cares and visions of To-day,
Rends lightning-like the veil of centuries,
And listens—
          Hark ! from out the catacombs
Of many-templed Rome, a loud-voiced hymn
Yet glad and irrepressible, ascends ;
The Christians sing the birthday of their Lord,
And not the Afric lioness who waits
Famished and sullen, till to-morrow's sun
Shall in the gleaming circus see her rage
Upon their naked limbs, and not the steel
Of Cruelty, or taunt of lettered Pride,
Can once affright their souls whom love and trust
Sublimely temper or for life or death.

But list a stranger chant, a loftier tongue !
And forth from yon pine forest moves a band
Of white-robed Druids girt with evergreens
And mystic symbols of Truth's eldest creed :—
Within that temple of unsculptured stone
They gather, and a crowd of worshippers
Submissive wait their doubly sovereign will ;
When lo ! a shout—a tramp, a glittering rush—
And woman's shrieks and clamorous despair,
And rallying valour poured in stubborn fight ;—

The pampered eagles swoop upon their prey,
And priest and bard and chieftain forth are hurled—
On through morass—on through engulfing wave—
Backward to Mona's last and lone retreat,
Before the victor Roman's legioned might!

But turn to breathing life, and what and where
Is Rome? while that extreme, barbarian clime,
Conserving in its conscience and its laws
And in its arts and arms the Truth of truths,
Hath gained a wider, surer, deeper power
Than e'er with empire crowned the Seven Hills;
And o'er the Islands beautiful and free,
Village and town that hail Victoria Queen,
No people blend more piety with life,
Or make their lives more worthy of their land,
Or cherish humbler, higher faith in Christ—
Training their drooping language to His praise—
Than the poor simple peasantry of Wales.

Farewell my reverie! even now the night
Starless and cold is come, and with the night,
Behold careering from their secret cells
The elemental spirits hither throng!—
The wild Ellyllon—whom autumnal fields
Or level pastures, thymy, clover-sweet,
Or murmuring brook or quiet garden-plat,
See never—fair in sunny pleasantness—
See never—crisp with frost or dull with rain:
But on the rock-ribbed headland lifted broad
Above the storm-bird's wing and billows' roar,
Or mid the trackless deserts far recessed

NANT FFRANCON.

Around the feet of mountains, or sublime
Upon their congregated tops that, met
In majesty of council, interpose
An ambient zone of many-coloured cloud
Between their greatness and the smooth dull world:—
There, speeding o'er the chasm's toppling ridge,
Or in its viewless depths fierce revelling,
Or haunting, turbulent, the heaving lake,
Or where the tortured stream is foaming flung
Down from the bare cliff to the leafy vale—
The wild Ellyllon hold their midnight play;—
Their music and their might, the thunderbolt
Redoubling stern among the skyey rocks,
And smiting hail, and wide-enthralling mist,
And winds now monotoned with sullen plaint,
Now furious sweeping, with the note of war,
From peak to rival peak, the blinding snow.

These circle me, afflicting, as I press
Bewildered, pathless, down the hill of crags,
Unknowing whither, yet with hope to win
A peasant's kindly hut, and warmth and light;
Now falling bruised from point to point, the while
A treacherous mirage looms of lakes and glens
In unfamiliar aspect changing oft
And blended oft as by enchantment's work;—
Now sinking in the ever-dripping moss,
Where countless glowworms trim their tiny fires,
Bediamonding the ground; now pausing faint:
Now struggling slowly o'er the dashing torrent
And rugged breastwork of unchiseled stone;
Now clinging to the soil while onward dart

The mad storm-spirits whirling from the west
Where break the wavelets o'er the sandy Traeth,
Onward with gathered passion, to convulse
The wintry sea that bases Penmaenmawr.

Interminably down! for in the gloom
Level on level grows, and precipice
Surpassed, conducts to precipice again :—
And this is Christmas night when round the hearth
Of home secure, may throng congenial friends,
And urge the tale, the song, the buoyant dance,
With beaming looks and cordial words, and thoughts
Of kindness for the absent, e'en while I
Benighted on dark Glyder, wander lost,
And wrapped by rushing winds :—

                              Yet have I thus
A sympathetic joy more deep, more rare
Than home's becalmed and dull sensations yield,
And vulgar pain and soul-debasing fear
Mar not that pleasure passing eloquence.

And lo! the heavens are blue, the kingly star
Beams over Trivaen like a diadem,
And lo! swift sailing from the parting cloud
The crescent Moon comes brightening, blessing night :—
How beautiful! her presence is a calm
Transfusing all—as mercy after wrath ;
She touches tenderly the darkling lake,
And Idwal wanly smiles on her, like Sin
Whose death-bed Faith half softens and consoles:
The circling crags, from mist unrobing, feel
Her effluence mild assuage their frowning brows:

The guardian stars about her burn; the winds
Repressed, retire; the cold translucent air
Bathes earth and heaven with living purity;
And I with new emotions vigorous,
And guided steps, resume my way, and mark
The paly trembling shafts of light outpoured
Along the vale whence human voice again
Is audible—one effort yet and now
I hail a cottage nestling tranquilly
On Ogwen's side, engirt by all the hills;
And soon the melody of Woman's words
Delights me, and her kind officious cares,
And soon with wearied limbs and thankful heart
I sink to sleep and dreams felicitous,
In the great shadow of Pen Olea Wen.

LINES

SUGGESTED BY A NIGHT ASCENT OF SNOWDON, IN THE WINTER OF
1857, ADDRESSED TO FRIENDS WHO HAD SENT A WHISTLE TO
THE WRITER TO REPLACE ONE LOST IN THE EXCURSION.

Gwynt gwaedd feni
Galwawr Eryri. — TALIESIN.

TRULY 'tis a handsome whistle,
Kind inscription, kind epistle;
Just received and read and blown,
Perfect each in form and tone;
Like a finished Cambrian triad
Good and graceful:—Oh! that I had
Something of a poet's power
Skilled in Edeyrn Davod Aur,[1]
To express in nervous rhyme
Of the old Myvyrian time
All my thanks!—But do I need it,
For methinks you wouldn't read it?
Awdl of sublimest bard
Might you not pronounce it hard?—
Call it names like Bulwer Lytton
In the epic he has written—
So I'll venture this alone,
Diolch i chwi gyfeillion!
And—don't fling the paper down—
Yr ydwyf yn chwymedig iawn!

[1] Edeyrn the Golden-tongued, the great grammarian of Wales, in the
thirteenth century.

Oft shall I renew our trip
When I put my pipe to lip;
Whether I on sea-cliff vast
Call the spirit of the blast;
Or in waveworn cavern nigh,
Mock the startled guillemot's cry;
Or through valley pacing slow,
Tempt coy Echo hiding low;
Or, my foot on mountain crest,
Blow a pæan from full breast,
And the hills all stooping round,
Waken, ireful, at the sound!

While the Llechog ridge we crossed
Was my signal-whistle lost;
There with Æolus it lies,
Nor shall mortal find the prize,
Till, erect on donkey-back,
Stumbling o'er the stony track,
Or on tariffed wheels swift rolled,
Perfumed, prim, and parasolled;
Comes the 'Season' on again,
Troops of tourists in her train;
Or while yet the nights are long,
Till the wild Ellyllon throng
Round the Clogwyn's toppling crag,
And mine ancient whistle drag
From its place in mosses nested,
And some chieftain imp, storm-crested,
Seize the pipe for deeds of ill,
Breathe a note so keenly shrill,

That the elves recoil aghast,
And the over-sweeping blast
Pause to hear, and souls at sea
Sadden at the wizard glee,
Owls in Dolwyddelan tower
Shrink within their ivy-bower,
Trout in Coron's sedgy nooks
Dream of fryingpans and cooks!

Ever will this whistle new
Waken old emotions too,
With the tones sent down the wind
Through the night, which you behind
Knew were meant to make you hurry
Up the steep of old Eryri—
Old Eryri looking down
On the tired men from town:
Jove! but 'twas an hour of joy
Years of dulness can't destroy;—
Lo! from Nantlle's deepest valley
Out through Drws y Coed there sally
Four adventurers bold and free;
Day's last beams behind them flee,
And the night moves on before,
Blackening the mountains o'er:
Under Aran's island-pile
Now they urge their way; awhile
Close around them all the hills,
And the air with silence fills:
Now they climb the marshy steep,
Grows the hour more calm and deep;—

Heed not clouds that idly frown,
Or the torrent brawling down;
Night—brave Beauty—bends to meet you,
Waits with all her stars to greet you,
On the hidden mountain crest—
Spring exulting to her breast!
On! but look a moment there
Backward to the valley fair—
Fair no more but glorious now,
Palest twilight bathes the brow
Of the stormy Mynydd Mawr,
Sternest type of stedfast power,
While Llyn Cwellyn at his base,
Type of motion, life, and grace,
Broadly now his bulk receives,
And with waking winds upheaves:
Next—the valley's southern bound—
Silyn's crags are piled around,
Hebog stands athwart the skies,
Thence the mountain walls arise
Circling to the eastern side,
There is Aran in his pride.

See, huzza! his brightening brow—
See the Moon emerging now!
As to the *telyn* [1] comes the tone
Comes she to her Cambrian throne;
Calm, and eloquent, and clear,
Filling earth and atmosphere—

---

[1] Harp.

Rivulet in rocky bed—
Peak with cloud-encumbered head—
Crag sharp-outlined, storm-repelling—
Cwm, the elves' sequestered dwelling—
Hill's green bosom maiden-moulded—
Lake where ferns repose sleep-folded;
And the enamoured human heart
Purer in each better part,
Happier in each vivid feeling.
Wiser by each deep revealing:
Feels the all-transfusing might,
Owns the hour of love and light.

Upward—On! Hope leads the van
O'er the crags of Cwm y Llan—
O'er the vast Cathedral Cwm
Consecrate with light and gloom:
Lonely watcher, noon or night,
Bears it not its name aright!
Point the pile that haughty Art
Frames so grand in every part!
Space?—regard the emerald floor.
See the heavens bending o'er;
Strength?—behold the walls of rock,
Heed they time or tempest-shock?
Beauty?—let thy heart declare
When the young Moon worships there,
Touching all with tender light,
Made herself more holy-bright—
Like to virgin Womanhood
Bent before the sacred Wood.

Pure and peaceful in her flower,
At the solemn vigil-hour,
When by love received and given
Earth may meekly blend with Heaven.
Beauty? Worship?—say again,
For on the mountain thou hast lain,
And with the starlamps keenly bright
Watched the lapsing autumn night;
How through opal gates of dawn,
Up from Gwynant's verdant lawn,
Came the Sun with face benign
Into this eternal shrine;
Shedding purest glories there,
Waking voiceless praise and prayer;—
As some youthful patriot king
Great in empire, bright as spring,
Kneels in all his strength and beauty,
Humbly seeks to learn his duty,
Asks upon the altar-stone
Grace to fill his father's throne,
Rule the world with royal mind,
Just, beneficent, and kind.

Nor didst thou forsake the cwm
When December's midnight gloom
Passed upon it, and there rang
Fiercely out the north wind's clang,
And through aisle and buttress steep
Swelled the diapason deep
Of the far upgathered thunder
Till the valleys trembled under,

And the long-forgotten dead
Slowly came with muffled tread,
O'er their ancient hills to range
Changeless 'mid a world of change!
Who would give that stormy psalm
For the flute's enervate calm!
Who would miss those mountain graves,
And the wind that o'er them raves,
And the hour of wintry night,
And the crag's all-barren height;—
Church with ever-open door,
God's great presence shadowing o'er;
For the garden's fairest prime,
And the azure summer time,
And the City's formal aisles
Where Fashion struts, and Thought beguiles,
And Habit burnishes his chain,
And Misery scowls upon Disdain,
And Worship pines into a sound,
And Love droops pinioned to the ground!

Now ere Bwlch y Maen is crossed
Riseth long-reluctant Frost
From the upper rocks keen breathing,
And the rolling mists o'erwreathing
Meet us on that lonely height,
Saddening the brow of Night,
Veiling all before, behind—
Thus are hope and memory kind,
Veiled in the madness-clouded mind;
And with war-song wild, at length,
Comes the Wind in all his strength—

Aquilo with streaming hair,
As we front his ancient lair
On the Glyder rent and bare.
But in vain such powers combine
To divert our high design;
Though the anger-laden blast
Rave and beat, the ridge is passed;
Though the clinging mist enthral,
Eye of Will can pierce its pall:
And behold in airy fight
Cloud and Wind at last unite!
Now retreating, now returning,
Eddying, circling, closing, spurning,
Till the baffled vapours glide
Sullen down the mountain side,
And afar the clouds are driven,
And the Moon through lucent heaven
Treads the deep cerulean floor,
Brighter, happier, than before.

Shrinks the Wind within his lair,
Sleeps the cold and stainless air,
And the world of hills and vales
Cynthia's beaming presence hails,
Cwellyn calmed her smile reflecting,
Eilio his clear crest erecting,
Peace and Silence, sister-forms,
Crowning the shepherds' ' Hill of storms;' [1]
Fair beyond, the twin lakes lying,
Each with each in beauty vying,

[1] Carnedd y Gwynt, part of Glyder Vawr.

Further yet, the island-shore,
Spirit-shadows brooding o'er;
Near, the matchless hollows meet
In the ridge beneath our feet,
Thence their outlines vast expand
Prominent on either hand;
Each, an ebon casket, holds
Gems of pure water in its folds,
Pearl-like *here* the tarns upgleam,
Flashes *there* the diamond stream;—
But of all things whereon now
Bendeth Night's triumphant brow,
What shall match the rocky cone
Rising in its pride alone—
Snowdon's Peak, ' Conspicuous ' named,
Triple-buttressed, history-famed!

You, Companions, I invoke
Oft to spurn the City's yoke,
Oft ere grow the senses dim,
Ere inaction cramp the limb,
Ere routine consume the heart,
Ere the higher instincts part
Wholly from you, and give place
To the selfish, dull, and base.

Come where common life is sweet,
Where unfevered pulses beat,
Where the eye grows bright and strong,
And the spirits mount in song;
Where the bounteous nights and days
Chill not hope with cold delays,

Mar not sleep with visions vain,
Load not memory with pain,
Vex not industry with loss,
Plant not thistles, heap not dross!
Come! and whether Sunrise glow
On Spring's maiden cheek, or throw
Life along the mountain snow;
Whether yet the matron Moon
Soothe the ardent breath of June,
Or the autumn meteor-star
Shoot from peak to peak afar;
Whether to banks of holy Dee,
Or where sweet Dovey weds the sea,
To Snowdon's crag, to Conway's hall,
To wood, or lake, or waterfall;
By the scene and hour arisen
On you, you shall disimprison
All the faculties innate
Pressed beneath the City's weight;—
Pure emotions that have lain
Fettered by Convention's chain,
And the power and will, aright
To use the new-evoked delight—
Learn from mountain, valley, sea,
What is simple, great, and free,
Lead a life—for *that* bestowed—
Nearer to Nature and to God.

A SONG OF THE DEE.

Oh! blessèd be the Power
That oft remits an hour
From the far and wide enthralment of the world's nets ever
    spread ;
And tenderly unsealing
The founts of light and feeling
Revivifies the dormant heart, and clears the troubled head '

Be mine to clasp the pleasure,
To use aright the treasure,
Enjoy the golden season ere its April brightness fails ;—
Renew the old emotion
Of mountain, vale and ocean—
Of *el mental* liberty that cannot pass from Wales !

From cottage walls retreating,
When night and day are meeting,
I seek the sinuous margin of Deva's holy stream ;
Where vernal boughs embracing,
And lightly interlacing,
Involve the fitful star and the moon's translucent beam :

Where purest dews descending,
With heat prolific blending,
Deck Spring's triumphant feet with the hyacinth's fair bells ;—
Cowslip, child-wept when perished—
Anemone song-cherished,
And violet, stainless beauty of the Naïad-haunted dells :

Where the old historic River
Flows on, flows on for ever,
Bearing his ancient tribute to the mightier stream of Time :
But here no ivied ruin,
Or work of man's renewing,
Shows stateliness or loveliness less perfect than its prime.

Glide the waters still serenely
Through meadows lying greenly,
Which render back in beauty the bounty they receive ;
Or surging on and singing
Through white rocks midway springing,
Bent, broken, yet unchanging still, their rapid way achieve.

With vital force eternal,
Fed by influences vernal,
Rolls the pure and living stream as it rolled ere mortal gaze ;
And summer languors press it,
And autumn leaves caress it,
And winter with long wreaths of snow and feathery frost
arrays :

And all the free winds sweep it,
And all the Genii keep it,
Whose guardian presence o'er the land the secret heart may
know ;
And Time and Nature ever
Breathe on the wizard river,
The interfusing charm that links To Day with Long Ago.

Mark, from their lonely dwelling
In Aran's shadow, welling,
Two rivulets emerge, but seek each other as they flow:
Like friends whose troths are plighted,
And hearts and lives united,
And kindling with exalted hope to meet the world who go!

Through fair Llyn Tegid gliding,
Unmingling, undividing,[1]
They pass, one current, self-assured, in self-reliance strong:—
O brief but sweet existence
While in the rosy distance
Love fondly shapes a quiet course where no distractions throng!

And now such calm attaining,
No obstacle restraining,
Flows the stream beneath the willows, cool and crystalline and
deep;
Awhile it bends to dally
In Edeyrnion's green valley,
And lave the lily blossoms that hang in mirrored sleep.

To Corwen soon advancing,
Behold it broadly glancing,
Baring its placid bosom to the genial summer sun;
So far in life's progression
Love's mutual fond possession,
And Fortune's all-prevailing hand, a golden course have won.

[1] Assuming that the Dee passes through Bala Lake as the Rhone does through Lake Leman.

But now ungently falling,
Rude stony shapes enthralling,
It runs the race of passion and lifts the voice of pain ;
Yet to endure is glorious,
And joy to rise victorious,
And sweet the hope of pressing through to tranquil hours
again.

And as those waters surely,
Beneficently, purely,
Move ever on their varied way from mountain unto sea ;
Let the life of firm affection,
Resigned to Heaven's direction,
Be happy, and *make* happy, whate'er high Heaven decree !

But O, beloved river,
Forgive me that I ever
By emblem weak imputed aught of suffering or of wrong !—
No ! all thy moods delight me,
Thine aspects all excite me,
Love—beauty—blessing flow with thee—joy triumphs in thy
song !

More rugged streams high gushing
From rock-walled tarns, and rushing
Smooth o'er the pine-clad precipice with deep and solemn
sound ;
Thence down the valley springing—
Loud-murmuring, foam-flinging,
Have won my heart's communion, and my restless spirit
bound.

H

And not the gentle Clwyd
Rich with memory of Druid
And battle-field and fortress, hath a softer calm than thine;
Though—all the rest transcending—
One starry name[1] be blending
Its brightness with the woods and waves—meet Genius for
such shrine!

No more the hues of slaughter
Profane thy crystal water—
Albeit with love and reverence paused and bowed the fiery
ranks—
No more the lurid flashing
Of flames to heaven rushing,
That rose from altars reared upon thy oak-embowered banks.

For Peace and Truth most holy
Have trod the valley slowly,
And stilled the strife of races, and banished cruel creeds:
And in thy breast, fair river,
The stars untroubled quiver,
And Quiet broods upon the hills, and Health frequents the
meads.

Now loveliest colours blended
Glow o'er the sun descended
Where Llantisilio's pasture-glens reflect the ripening day;
But night through heaven flitting,
Comes, shade to shadow knitting,
And all the rosy-streaming bars melt momently to grey.

[1] Felicia Hemans.

Above the eastern mountains,
See from her clear cold fountains
The Moon suffuse Eglwyseg's sublime embattled crest;
And on Llangollen's cluster
Of white walls pour new lustre,
And wake the darkened water to a magical unrest!

Happy, whose heart, the Spirit
Of Night can all inherit,
Unsighing, unencumbered, with pulses beating free;—
Fearless of puny danger,
O'er ocean paths a ranger,
Iona's graves, Helvellyn's crags, or by the banks of Dee!

Happy, who bold pursuing
The matchless Beauty, wooing
Her varying moods and changing charms with all-congenial
breast,
Can win her love ne'er cloying,
And taste the deep enjoying—
Now lifted on the wings of storm—now lapped in lowly rest!

To him, a sister soothing,
She comes, the vexed brow smoothing,
Gives the anodyne of quiet, and hope's sweet sovereign
balm;
To him, a friend beguiling
The world's neglect by smiling,
And teaching what the world is worth, and what contentment's
calm.

To him, a Muse unsealing
The Past's great book, revealing
The doubt of human history, the depth of human heart;—
Prophet, to whose clear seeing,
Becoming flows from *Being*,
And future paths diversely from life's present highway part.

Poet of truth, enlightening,
Revolving, clearing, brightening
Emotion, thought, and enterprise that stir us in the day!
Poet of fancy, breathing
Celestial air, and wreathing
Flowers whose hues and odours sweet exhale not or decay!

Poet of nature, mating
With earth and heaven, creating
What best belongs to them of free, of silent—awful—grand—
For him she loveth loosing
The eloquence transfusing
Wood, mountain, planet, wind and wave, which few may
          understand!

I feel her now before me,
For midnight closes o'er me,
And locks all breathing life in rest or feverish or deep:
Hushed is the bird's late singing—
Hushed the bell's festal ringing—
And hushed upon Moel Geraint's side, the cry of wayward
          sheep.

But the fitful wind is waking,
    And 'mid the branches making
A harp-like music many-toned, that tells of old lament;
    And the river low is calling
    Responsively in falling
Adown the rugged ledges which its rapid course indent.

    While the moon supreme presiding
    In heaven's court, is gliding
Slow o'er the azure floor, the shifting shadows throng;
    And all the hills that bound me,
    Seem closer to surround me,
And press their pæan of old fame, their monody of wrong:—

    Press on the ear ideal
    With voice as silence real,
Nor only relevant to works and record-rolls of Man;
    For each enduring feature
    Glows with the dawn of Nature,
When all unkenned the sun revolved, unheard the river
        ran.

    Superbly Dinas standing,
    The lowly vale commanding,
Lifts his fantastic coronet of gray and gaping stone;—
    Young, in spring's green renewals,
    And autumn's purple jewels,
Old, in the mist-clad memories that gird his stedfast throne.

The power hath left the palace—
The wine drained from the chalice—
The wind raves through the portal—the storm beats on the
floor—
Valour's bright sword is broken—
Beauty bequeathed no token—
The banner spreads not to the breeze—the harp resounds no
more !

Yet wherefore trite reflection
Or mournful recollection ;—
Unseen, not perished, are the things oppressed by Time and
Death ;
Not the first state and splendour—
The fair, the grand, the tender—
Can match with what the musing mind conceives of bloom
and breath !—

The sacred Vale where nestle
Tombs, arches of Egwestl ;[1]
Where Beauty broods in sadness, but Faith still keeps a
shrine :—
All Cambria's blood yet vital,
Shed for her glorious title,
To Glyndwr last and stormiest chief of the great Llywelyn
Line :—

[1] Valle Crucis Abbey.

And strength that knows not ruin

In earthworks of Caer Drewyn[1]—

In Arthur's turrets[2] raised by Him who formed the clinging

cloud ;—

Signs of the old prevailing

'Gainst foreign arms assailing,

As it shall yet again prevail ere Britain's front be bowed !

Old Llywarch,[3] lonely weeping

For all his brave boys sleeping,

Whose necks unbent, the golden torque of Cymru's princes

bore :—

Eliseg[4]—what though broken

The Cross, love's fitting token,

His mightier race guards mightier faith—TRA BRYTHON still

TRA MOR ![5]

And Deva's queen, Myvanwy,[6]

Like the flower of Dyganwy

Which Nature's happy poet-child, and poet-loved hath sung :

---

[1] Opposite Corwen.

[2] Craig Arthur on the Eglwysegs.

[3] Llywarch Hên, Prince and Poet of the sixth century. Of his twenty-
four brave sons, *Eurdorchogion*, one, at least, lies in Llangollen; 'Bedd
Sawyll yn Llangollen.' And another near to it ; 'Bedd *Gwell* yn y Rhiw
Velen.'

[4] Of the seventh century. His well-known pillar gives name to the Vale
of the Cross.

[5] Taliesin's words, ' *Tra mor, tra Brython* ;' ' *While the sea will be, the
Britons will be* ;' or ' While there be sea, while there be Britons ;' co-
duration being clearly intended.

[6] Myvanwy Vechan, the celebrated beauty of the House of Trevor, who
resided in Castell Dinas Bran in the fourteenth century. The ode of her

For round that ruined tower
Twines her beauty's deathless flower,
And hers the deepest eloquence poured from that stony
tongue :—

And hers the light that flashes,
As an eye beneath dark lashes,
From out the sombre shadow of the dreary wind-swept wall;
Morn's fragrance sweet ascending,
And midnight's stars o'erbending,
With *her* are redolent and bright—*her* life to ours recall.

Now in her home of power
Sits she at festal hour,
Mistress of many a faithful heart, of many a flashing sword :—
Hark to the song ascending,
The rose and laurel blending,
For Trevor's fairest maid whose guest is Gwynedd's bravest
lord !

Now in the glowing pages
Where live the vanished Ages,
Immortal Arthur fires her breast, or Hywel good and wise;
The legend now securing,
More eloquent, enduring,
Beneath her ardent fingers see the tapestry-colours rise !

lover, Howel ap Einion Lygliw, comprises all that is known of her. See
Evans's *Specimens of Welsh Bards*, p. 14. A fragment of an inscribed stone
has been found in Valle Crucis Abbey, which would indicate that she was
buried there.

Now by the stream she ponders,
Or on far summits wanders,
Where yet may white Craig Vorwyn keep her virgin heart
and name:
And now she seeks sedately
The Abbey fair and stately,
And humbly bends before the Throne whence birth and beauty
came.

And the vesper-hymn she hearkens
While the mountain shadow darkens
Around her sires' honoured graves where time will spread her
own—
Look! what dim Shape went flitting
Where the Past's grey ghosts are sitting—
There—where the wan and yellow moon streams on the broken
stone!

But now, of state denuded,
Behold her sit secluded,
High in her turret-chamber at quiet eventide;—
Her scarlet robes neglected—
Her jewels all rejected—
And doth she put the *woman* on, and hath she done with pride?

Ah no! her cheek's pure blossom
Unchanging glows; her bosom
Heaves not in sweet suspense; her eyes are ever calm and deep:
She listens coldly heeding,
While comes her lover speeding
With heart in flame, on foaming horse, up Bran's resounding
steep.

She opes the casement—higher
Ascend those hoofs of fire,
Till dies the rugged sound beneath her lonely taper's light ;
And now the bard upturning
A face with passion burning,
Outbreathes his soul as love compels, and poesy, and night.

Is it the night-wind flutters
Her bosom while he utters
The lay that wafts its sweetness still across the wastes of
time ?
A moment only tender !
He shall not lightly bend her—
She lifts her downward-verging heart to compass the
sublime !

Shall *he* presume to love her !
She scans the heavens above her ;
Nor heeds the access tremulous of love's refulgent star :—
Her heart and eye of eagle
Seek Jove serene and regal,
And mighty suns which sweep through space immeasurably far.

And the languid airs that dally
With rose-odours of the valley,
With child-entrancing music, and with minstrel's selfish
sighs ;
Reach not *her* brow raised boldly
To bathe in winds which coldly
Speed, pure and wild and vigorous, athwart the upper skies.

Linked with no feeble rhymer,
Her life shall grow sublimer,
Firm in that highland fortress with Beauty, Strength, and
    Will ;
And haughtily repelling
Youth's currents inly welling,
Shall like an ice-isle indurate, bright, terrible, and still !

Was this well done, Myvanwy ?
For marble towers can we
Forget what Womanhood may give—what Poesy may claim?—
But such regret were idle
When an eternal bridal
Unites the crowns of love and pride, and thine with Howel's
    name :—

When springs a greater glory
From Dinbrain's classic story
Which, save for *that*, nor song could boast, nor history could
    disclose—
E'en as the cataract's power
Outlives the summer shower—
E'en as the statue white and calm transcends the blushing
    rose !

FROM CARDIGAN BAY.

I RISE to meet the glowing sun, and look
With him on earth's most bright responsive face,
As on a cherished life-consoling book,
Which oft at dawn secluded we retrace,
Ere the heart's founts with mid-day dust are dry,
Or the world's lures distract the temperate eye.

Great wordless volume from the Almighty hand,
If unto me 'tis bountifully given
To turn thy Cambrian pages fair and grand ;
Inspire O still my praise and prayer to Heaven,
That ever I may mark and use aright,
A lore so deep—a loveliness so bright !

Thy noblest characters address me here ;
Ocean uplifts a pleasure-murmuring voice
And breast broad beaming ; mountain-brows austere,
Unveiled and calm to meet the day rejoice ;
Rocks stand impassible, and swift and slow,
Through mead and wooded valley rivers flow.

The landbird with short flights and broken song
Is restless in her joy ; the seabird sails
Silent and high on snowy wing along ;
The breeze a vital purity exhales ;
Clouds from the opal east float softly by,
In ether melt, or lightly fleck the sky.

And glorious Morning blesses all, and brings
New form, new voice, new being to the air,
The earth, the sea ; living and lifeless things
More strong, more pure and eloquent and fair,
Grow, as with pristine excellence beneath
The loving Spirit's recreating breath.

With impulse keen the senses bound and meet
The outer world which kindred sense contains ;
With added energy the pulses beat,
E'en as the blood revives in Nature's veins ;
Strengthened, refined by all, like all, the soul
With clearer ken surveys and sums the whole.

Time shows us death and darkness, and his wings
Chase woe and change and ever-eddying cares ;
But is he not an angel too who brings
Recurrent hours when the future wears
A golden aspect, and clear light is cast.
To bless and guide the present, from the past !

Eve wakens memory and delicious sadness;
Night thrills the being with celestial call;
Morn renovates with hope and buoyant gladness :—
But glorious, beautiful and good are all,
And blent and varied as the varying heart
Reflects on each a character and part.

Glorious indeed and beautiful and good,
When Nature's frame harmoniously inspiring
In such a scene as this! for hither could
The student come, from words and forms retiring,
And win, unchilled by doubt, unchecked by pain,
Knowledge that is not objectless or vain !

Here the cold mocker of a holy creed,
Or colder votary of decorous rites,
May learn a lesson suited to his need,
And scrutinise high truth by vivid lights :
Then home return the human world to scan,
With dawning faith in God and love for Man.

And is there one to whose world-wearied breast
Friendship comes not, or comes to falsely mock :
Where love oft bidden will not be a guest,
And whose vexed bark is broken on the rock.
Seeking a haven; let him hasten hither
Ere feelings indurate and senses wither !

For Nature's friendship what shall e'er estrange,
If he but knit in true congenial bands,
His heart to hers! and though her aspects change,
Each, new delight, new sympathy commands ;
Unfailing as intelligible, each
Can soothe and stimulate, inspire and teach.

And who the rarer depths of love can measure
Hid in the loyal heart that owns her sway !—
Who tell the augmenting and unwasting treasure,
Her gift to men perchance of meanest clay !—
Poor human beauty fades and passion stains.
She ever fair and calm and good remains.

Divinest joy ! supremest consolation !
Whom Wealth can purchase not, nor haughty Birth
Inherit only, nor aspiring Station
Command ; whose bright and beauteous form of Earth
To all belongs, irrevocably given,
Who seek the spirit there all eloquent of Heaven !

TO CYTHNA.

Mynnu ddwyf draethu heb druthiad na gwyd
Wrthyd haul gymmryd, gamre wasdad!
HOWEL AP EISION LYGLIW (*circa* A.D. 1350).

I CROWN thy beauty with a Cambrian wreath,
I praise thy dearest name to Cambrian ears;
Not for the grace that moulds, or pride that rears
A queenly form; nor virgin bloom and breath,
Nor e'en the dark Silurian eye beneath
Lashes that tremble with the heart's true tears:
Or softly dreaming over shadowy years,
Or scorning with sweet ardours change and death:
No! 'tis that unevoked in these there lies
A love more passionate, a power more grand
Than ere could glow with lighter sympathies,
Than ere in lighter conquests could expand;
Such love, such power, claim I from thine eyes,
To serve the Land of Song—my cherished Mountain
    Land.

What though thy stately steps were guided first
Through the smooth pleasures of an English lawn,
And round thy maidenhood were greenly drawn
The elm's broad arms and trellised vine sun-nursed:
Though thou hast watched the amber splendours burst
O'er pastoral meads, and wake the frolic fawn;
And loved to see light's starry second dawn
Folding thy cherished flower-cups athirst

For dewy sleep; and though in tranquil pride
Thy summers still have led thee; though admiring
Fashion solicit thee, and Flattery glide
Around thee; thou art calm and undesiring
Of such, and canst adorn a nobler side,
And measure rarer joys, to loftier heights aspiring.

And thus then I invoke thee!   I would teach
Thy earnest brow to scan the Cymric scroll
Unblotted yet; to mark Time's billows roll
The Past's rich relics on the narrowing beach
That girds the Present, and discern in each
Some sign to chasten, stimulate, control;
Oh keep inviolate with stedfast soul
Old faith and form, tradition, learning, speech.
As each is stamped with Truth's eternal seal!
Oh lead the wavering people on to win
Cambria's own good in Britain's commonweal—
Rights from without by duties from within;
And fervently with purest lips reveal
Peace to all hearts made deaf by Trade's mechanic din!

Thou glorious maiden! rise, and put to shame
Those alien daughters careless of their line
And language, weaving with a poor design
Their life's pale colours on an English frame;
Not their weak limbs but weaker hearts I blame.
And dull, dull eyes that see no beauty shine
In lake or valley, save a landscape fine—
Feel not the sun-glow on the hills of fame:

O come, my Cythna, plume thy spirit's wings,
The mountain waits thee with its lichened walls
Of crag, its grassy depths, its bubbling springs,
Its wind-swept crest ; the sea enamoured calls :
And sweet for thee the bird of twilight sings
In Worship's voiceless fanes, and Power's slow-
    crumbling halls !

The ghostly Carnedd shrouded in the waste
Of towering peaks, silent through sun and snow.
Mid funeral silence, save when keenly flow
The hail-floods on its granite, or in haste
Come the wide-wheeling pinions hunger-chased ;
The dark memorial-stone where Mayflowers blow
By singing streams, and Valour long ago
Died in the arms of Love ; the camp high-placed
Graving its history in unfading lines ;—
They wait thee, lofty Heart, they welcome thee ;
And Nature, too, in fairest lap enshrines
The Past she nursed, and decks immortally :—
Ah ! speaks she not *in us* by kindred signs,
And knitting both to her, knits she not thee to me ?

TO CYMRO,

AN OLD MOUNTAIN DOG IN WHOSE NAME WAS SENT TO ME A
PRESENT OF FLOWERS.

THANK you, Cymro, for the flowers
Gathered in these wintry hours
From your favoured garden-bowers!—

Many treasures choicely set—
Rose of beauty blooming yet,
With my darling violet;—

Gilly sweet, and intertwining
Mosses silky, soft, and shining,
Fresh and fair and free combining—

Mosses that to memory tell
Of their nestling-place so well
In the Oread-haunted dell;—

In the wooded valley steep
Where the river's foamy sweep
Ends in one resounding leap;—

Of the upper mountain-crest
Where the sun embrowns their vest,
Where the storm invades their rest;—

I 2

In the *cwm* where moonlight falls
Lighting up the fairies' halls
For their secret summer balls ;—

Or in home's delightful bound
By the Churchyard's hallowed ground
Girt with guardian hills around.

Did you, Cymro, cull them there
At the old tree-shaded chair
Where we met the morning air—

You and I, while mistwreaths curled
Slowly o'er your valley-world
River-vocal, dew-empearled ?

Long shall I remember you
As a Cymro honest, true,
Brave and swift, and handsome too !

May you long your life enjoy,
Care, privation, and annoy
Never shadow or alloy !

Free to course before the gale,
Where the crags command the vale,
Where the white Cloud spreads her sail :—

Free to range the woodland warm
When the dove her deep-voiced charm
Utters, and the wild bees swarm ;—

TO CYMRO.

Frolic in the feathery snow
When the northern ice-winds blow,
Birds are mute, and streamlets slow ;—

Bask in Autumn's noontide heat,
While the Hours with lingering feet
Glide around your garden-seat ;—

Stretch your limbs before the blaze,
When Home's social sun its rays
Scatters 'gainst November's haze.

And when nights are long and dark,
Be your honest eye and bark
Prompt to warn and keen to mark !

Little reason though there be ;
Love and Virtue keep the key,
Rests the treasure safe and free.

Light and grateful are the tasks
Cymro's mountain mistress asks—
Happy life that bounds or basks !—

Happy Cymro to abide
By the young Eilnned's side—
She the kind and gentle-eyed !

Catching from her loving face
Something of its thoughtful trace,
Something of its inner grace ;—

TO CYMRO.

Mad with joy, when bounding blithe,
Treads she laughing, flushed and lithe,
July's fields that wait the scythe.

And when dear Euronwy strays
By the Pymrhyd's winding ways,
Musing on the ancient days;

Where by old Tydecho's bed
Aran veils his haughty head
With a tempest overspread;

Or within that sweet recess
Which the secret fairies dress,
And the softest winds caress;—

Where, through green embowering leaves,
Cowarch playfully receives
On his breast light's vivid sheaves;

There shall Cymro's steps be staid
Near the earnest British maid
Mourning patriot love decayed;

And his instinct half shall know
Hope upon her poet-brow—
Hope and faith that inly glow;—

Joy for what remains behind—
Many a heart sincere and kind—
Many a high unyielding mind;—

TO CYMRO.

Will, to cherish in her breast
What is noblest, purest, best,
And to leave to Heaven the rest.

Faithful Cymro! nor alone
Faithful to the ladies shown,
But when dark December's zone

Binds the vale, and watchlights burn,
Warm fires glow, and warm hearts yearn
For the master's quick return;

You shall meet him ere he come,
On the bleak road white and dumb
Bring the first delight of home.

But, old Cymro, I refrain
From this too protracted strain
Lapsed into a tedious vein.

Thank you for the pleasant flowers
Gathered in these humid hours
Interposed mid sun and showers!

I shall keep them, love them, long,
Hope and memory and song
In their faded petals throng.

*   *   *   *   *

I am gazing in the fire,
And my thoughts like flame aspire
With a dominant desire.

TO CYMRO.

I would nurse my spirit's dreams
In the Vale of 'spreading streams'
Rich with unforgotten themes.

I would see the Morning wake
O'er the hills, and Evening make
Twilight long for Beauty's sake.

I would watch the stars ascend,
And the Moon her sphere suspend,
And the vivid rainbow bend;—

Wander where the shrouding snow
Wraps me, and the winds of woe
Chill the ghosts that glide below;

Then with pale cheek rushing down,
Win the wild enthusiast's crown—
Win Eiluned's archest frown;—

Study then conundrum-wit,
Puzzle o'er the answers fit,
Laugh at each unhappy hit;—

Wake the song, or turn the page,
Mingling with the Middle Age—
Bard and chronicler and sage;—

Task our Ovateship to shine
In more worthy native line
Than that graceless triad mine—

TO CYMRO.

Tri chariadau Cymry: Telyn;
Coffadwriaeth llew Llewelyn;
(Goreu oll) hen Gwrw melyn!

And when Spring's delicious skies
Light the maiden violet's eyes,
And her buried sisters rise;

I would mark each one unclose,
Till the perfect beauty glows,
From the snowdrop to the rose.

But, alas! desire is vain,
Reason tightens Fancy's rein,
Duty's path is straight and plain.

I must press the iron track,
Be the earth and heaven black,
Gold will gild them—who would lack!

Tethered to the central stake,
Though you short excursions make,
Firm the bonds—your *heart* may break.

In the ever-rushing street
Swerve a moment—myriad feet
Trample you to ruin meet!

Yet 'tis something to retain
Feelings that relax the chain—
It shall perish, *they* remain!

TO CYMRO.

Thus these simple flowers tell
Of the vale I love so well;
I can love them nor rebel.

All that they denote to me,
Virtue, grace, and purity,
Kind affections, fancies free;

Such, I trust, with life may last,
Though the symbol's bloom be past,
Leaf and stalk in ruin massed;—

Though I wander nevermore
In that vale, or see that door
With its roses clustering o'er!

ELLEN EILÙNED.

Sweet Ellen Eilùned! oh who would not love her,
  Who loves what is fairest and holiest and best—
Skies, waters, woods, mountains, around and above her,
  Have moulded her beauty, and live in her breast!

The breeze that exhales the pure freshness of morning—
  The whirlwind of midnight that sweeps the dark pines—
The daisies those greenest of meadows adorning
  Which margin the river that sings as it shines:—

The snow-wreaths that with the bleak mountain-crests dally;
  The grain lowly nestled till golden and warm;—
All shapes and all sounds that descend on the valley,
  From moonlight to noontide—from slumber to storm;—

Are gathered to *her* with most gentle affection—
  Are mirrored in *her* with intensified hue;
Oh never may aught come to mar that reflection
  Of lofty and lovely, of tender and true!

Oh never may birthdays rose-garlanded, bringing
  New grace and new beauty, more honour and sway,
Break that first vivid charm to her childhood long clinging,
  Or snatch that supremest attraction away.

But let the meek virtues, dear Ellen, for ever
   Your maidenhood cherish, your womanhood hold;—
Be happy and wise, if not brilliant and clever;
   Be loving and gentle, not stately and cold!

Oh better—believe me, Eilùned—far better—
   In freedom of spirit and quiet to live,
Than wear the uneasy though flowery fetter,
   Which Fashion and Worldliness mock while they give!

Let talents be hid not, nor study neglected,
   Seek lofty-browed Science, or soft-smiling Art;
But learn first each duty by Heaven directed,—
   Each line on Life's stage of the heroine's part.

Then lightly will sorrow and suffering pass o'er you—
   Then amaranth blossoms your head will entwine;
And Friendship will follow, and Love will adore you,
   Yet brighten, not darken, so spotless a shrine.

And though the swift stream of eternal mutation
   Bear you far from the mountains and vales of your youth.
Oh cherish for ever the old inspiration—
   The early simplicity, candour, and truth!

And thus, sweet Eilùned, and dear beyond measure,
   Wherever your footsteps may rest or may roam,
We fondly shall hail you our pride and our treasure—
   Pure Lily of Dyvi, bright Star of your home!

WENEFREDA.

SONG WRITTEN FOR AN OLD WELSH AIR.

WENEFREDA, white and holy,
  Lady of the Fountain-shrine!
Teach us, friends and lovers lowly,
  Teach us faith and love like thine;
More than thine our earthly pleasure,
  Life is free, and love secure,
Yet oh add thy richer treasure,
  Ever growing, ever pure!
      Give the love
      Born above,
      Hallowing breath,
      Spurning death,
Light not from earth that springs,
But shed from seraphs' wings.

Love not only household-bounded,
  Instinct's law and habit's chain,
Love not only joy-surrounded,
  Perishing by doubt or pain;

WENEFREDA.

But the love of nobler passion,
   Charity's sublimer glow,
Fearless love which smiles at fashion,
   Conquers fortune, tempers woe :
      Sweetest calm,
      Softest balm,
      Fairest flower,
      Firmest power,
Though bloom and strength depart.
Though mirth forsake the heart.

Wenefreda, white and holy,
   It is good that Love divine,
Ordering life for us so lowly,
   Gave a bliss denied to thine ;
Yet oh guide us in our going,
   Not by Self's dull torch alone,
But the reflex clear and glowing,
   Of the light before the Throne !
      This is love
      Born above,
      Love unsighing,
      Love undying,
The stream like thine still sure,
The fount as deep and pure.

TO A COTTAGE GIRL OF CLWYD.

Dearly I love thy native land
  For all that bounteous God hath spread
Imperishably fair and grand
  From ocean-floor to mountain-head;
Rock, waterfall, wood, vale, and sea,
Are blest and beautiful to me.

Nor only in their hue and form,
  And light and motion love I them,
And haunt the sources of the storm,
  Or quiet fields which flowers begem;
But that the undying Past broods there,
And sacred spirits throng the air.

For as the light transcends the lamp,
  Or as the voice excels the lips,
Or e'en as Heaven's mighty stamp
  Impresseth silence or eclipse;
I seek to know and feel aright
The inborn eloquent and bright.

And such spring amply from the scene,
  On every hand, at every time,
And many an hour my heart hath been
  A pulse of pleasure, and sublime
Hath soared my newly-winged thought,
And soft emotions tears have wrought.

And I have marked, dear maid, the daughters
　　Of thine old fatherland, and thee
Their type, like thine own mountain waters,
　　Melodious, pure, secluded, free;—
Have marked, as well as alien could,
The beauty born of hill and wood.

I gaze upon thy young sweet face—
　　No art its clear expression hides:
I mark where glows the Cymric race,
　　And where the Saxon blood abides;
If such the union, never be
Their equal charms compared by me!

'Twere hard for painting to define
　　The modest roses of thy cheek,
Or eyes where happy feelings shine,
　　Or mouth whence only truth can speak;
What spirit-guided pencil gives
The soul that in the features lives!

And 'tis not, Mary, idle praise
　　I offer to your beauty now;
I frame no tributary lays
　　To Hebe-lip, or Pallas-brow,
Nor seek I to mislead your heart,
And play a poor unworthy part.

Love may I feel, but 'tis, perchance,
　Not such as you conceive; I look
Upon you with a quiet glance,
　As on a limpid, lucid brook,
Much pondering what its course will be
Ere it attain the far-off sea.

Sweet girl of Clwyd, my love beholds thee now
　Formed by each influence that haunts the vale;
The placid hills fair outlined in the glow
　Of sunset, guardians true of town and dale,
The river in its pastoral dress, which glides
Embraced by mead and wood, and swelled by freshening
　　tides:

E'en the bowed Castle and the mournful Marsh
　Reflect the pensiveness, the shade that lies,
Without a trace of querulous or harsh,
　In the deep lustre of those earnest eyes;—
Long may such beauty-giving shade remain,
But no sharp sorrow the fair eyelids stain!

Long may the hills, the woods, the vales, the streams,
　Preserve the freedom that endears them now;—
Long move the heart and quicken noble themes,
　And give sweet health to bless the cheek and brow
And fostering simple wants, may long withstand
Encroaching Pride, and Trade's all-grasping hand!

K

And never may the brightness of your youth,
  Dear Mary, change to any shape less fair:
May all the virgin innocence and truth
  That fills your heart, be ever vivid there—
Show to congenial eyes with added grace,
And fix perennial beauty in your face!

Live so, sequestered here as birds or flowers,
  And know existence in its better part,
Not in its vicious moods, or frantic hours,
  Not in the idler's hall, or trader's mart,
But near to God 'neath Heaven's purer dome,
Girt by the loves and blessings of your home!

Yet not all passionless; the heart's deep strings
  May vibrate soon to stern affliction's touch,
Or rare emotion lift you on its wings
  To heights where much is seen, and suffered much:
Drink, then, from founts whence mingled waters flow,
And know what all Humanity must know.

But as the mountain which black clouds array
  At midnight, glows sun-diademed at morn,
As from the valley storm-embraced to-day,
  To-morrow beauty manifold is born,
As thunders rock, and winds enrage, the sea,
And leave it yet more calm and fair and free;

So will you meet the passions and surpass,
  If only you be simple, truthful, wise,
And like the breath-stain transient from the glass,
  Shall fade each stern emotion from your eyes,
And native peace succeed that brief unrest,
And native joys spring quenchless in your breast.

And I again may come from life's rough ways
  To consolations old that never mock,
Where the bright matron mountain-queen surveys
  Her valley-realm, or where the castled rock
Looks proud upon her, and my heart may swell
Again by Elwy's banks and blessed Well.

And then, dear maid, my deepest joy will be—
  No wife's, alas! or sister's love is mine—
To learn simplicity and peace from thee,
  Heal my vexed spirit with the balm of thine,
Hush the world's discord with thy low sweet song,
Nor hurt thee by one word or thought of wrong.

SNOWDON.

Ar oer garreg Eryri
Mae ged vawr, lle magwyd vi.
RUYS GOCH ERYRI (*circa* 1380).

A TREE-CROWNED, grassy, undulating hill
   Sloped pleasantly toward the sunny weather :
Whence musical glides down the pebbly rill;
   Where the brown bee exults among the heather.
   And rural lovers rest or stray together,
And quiet cattle feed, and birds rejoice
   While the soft west wind ruffles scarce a feather :
Whence the fair fields and white walls of your choice
Are seen, and heard around is cheerful Labour's voice.

Such, haply, dost thou know, and hath thy heart
   Grown tame and passive many sweets among,
And rarely mayst thou feel emotions start,
   Secluded far from worldly woe and wrong ;
   Thy pulse beats calm, thy measured sleep is long,
Thy feet glide willing in the path of right ;
   Thou lovest placid mirth and gentle song,
And leafy lawn, and terraced garden bright,
And Beauty's mild blue eye, and warmth and ease and
   light.

But hath the spirit's harp one only chord —
 One only refrain of a flute-like tone;
Doth Nature's mighty cabinet afford
 One tint of rose or emerald alone!
 Hence! let thy energies o'er life be thrown,
Oft high desire impel thy voice and hand,
 And trace the scenes where kindred signs are shown—
The wild, the stern, the beautiful, the grand,
Where rise in ancient strength the mountains of our
  land.

Let others rove from foreign spot to spot,
 As Fashion bids, or Novelty grows old,
And throng to gaze, perchance discerning not,
 On storied shows and scenes of giant mould;
 Can such read Nature's mightiest book unrolled,
Or e'en to thee can Alp or Andes rise
 Revealed in all its bulk?   Oh be consoled,
And first the hill-page lit by British skies
Interpret with deep heart, and scan with earnest eyes.

Ben Nevis know, on whose surpassing crest
 White Winter sits defiant of the sun;
Helvellyn, dear to every poet's breast,
 For streams of song that from its fountains run;
 Green Cheviot, and romantic Mangerton;
Plinlimmon bare, and forest-girt Cairngorm;
 And Snowdon all unmatched, whose crags upon,
The immortal Past endures, and whose great form
Rose at the birth of Time from Chaos and from Storm.

Assume the glance of that unvanquished bird
   Who made Eryri once his home of pride;
Behold the hills when autumn rain has stirred
   The air, and Morning's fingers parted wide
   The horizon-bounds; from where Dubricius died
In holy Bardsey, on to Penmaenmawr
   Far eastward planted bold against the tide,
See sweep fantastic, or sublimely tower,
Caernarvon's mountain boast, and record-roll and power!

And midmost, Snowdon rears his triple head,
   And holds his court: around him and below,
The subject hills, yet scarce outrivalled, spread
   Their giant limbs, and lift their rugged brow;
   Llywelyn, Glyder, Hebog, Eilio,—
Names memory-stamped with Man's or Nature's might,
   The elements come up to them, and lo!
The mingling and the lapse of day and night,
Of worship, council, wrath, disdain, repose, and fight!

But now approach him; the dark summit crags
   Stand sharp in ether blue, and the young Day
Darts eager glances where yet Shadow lags
   Deep in the hollow sides, and ray on ray
   Explores the stony mysteries till they
Gleam broadly desolate and all unveiled:
   And in the nested tarns the heavens play,
And peaks which late the midnight storm assailed,
Now first in tranquil rest the glowing sun have hailed.

And here where still the hardy sheep maintain
    Scant life, once bounded the broad-antlered deer;
The Cambrian goat an unapproached domain
    Possessed; the golden eagle plumed him here,
    And the dark Druid pine-trees waved austere;
And pregnant with the changeless still the scene;
    A wealth of metal lurks in chasms drear,
    And Flora's Alpine offspring sit serene,
And spread to nursing storms their many-tinted green.

Profound the silence grows, and more profound
    While slow you traverse the encumbered steep;
Hushed in the clear calm air, the hills around
    Seem, fancy-scanned, to listen or to sleep;
    Not so of old when Dolwyddelan's keep
Saw waving spears and circling beacon-flames—
    To battle saw the shouting Cymry leap,
    Led by the prince whom Clio proudly claims,
Llywelyn, first amid his land's heroic names :

When Gwynedd's chiefs in festive triumph stood,
    Or worn and weak, their patriot blood outpoured;
And rock and llyn and waterfall and wood,
    And bardic song and human heart have stored
    Memorials of high sage and mighty lord :—
What else ? a dubious cairn, a toppling tower,
    Perchance a golden torque or broken sword
    Remains, interpreting old strife and power,
Less than the battle-field's corse-nurtured fruit and flower.

Such trophies leave to microscopic minds,
  Such links of rust exhumed by time or toil,
For that unseen but perfect chain which binds
  The Past around the people and the soil;
  This not the lapse of years can dim or spoil,
It flashes freely to the summer sky,
  Tradition bathes it as with freshening oil,
Nor shall it cease to be a nation's tie,
Till Cambria's hills decay, and Cambria's language die!

Behold a relic truly! piled above,
  The granite summits stedfast evermore,
Rare trophy for the virtuoso's love
  To teach him surer truth, sublimer lore;
  These rocks of eldest time saw silent shore
And sunless sea with shell and weed and bone
  Of darksome life, slow rise through ages hoar,
And slow retire through added ages grown,
Themselves unwasted still, unlinked to Change alone.

Now press the tortuous track; see Wyddfa's ridge
  Upheaved immense on adamantine walls;
Pass thither by the crag's aërial bridge;[1]
  With guarded steps when clinging mist enthrals
  Snowdonia—then he perishes who falls —
But sunbright yet, magnificently lying
  Beneath your feet behold those mighty halls,
Far piercing down to depths which undescrying
The eye pursues, and whence the shepherd's song comes
  dying:

<hr>

[1] Clawdd Coch.

Far sweeping round with myriad shapes indented—
 Ledge, buttress, pinnacle, and chasm deep—
Within the eagle winged his flight contented,
 The clouds roll midway curtaining the steep,
 And on the ever-verdant floor they weep
Their purest tears, and wizard colours glow,
 And funeral shadows throng, and lightnings leap
Transverse, and rise the sounds of war or woe
When the careering Winds their stormy trumpets blow.

From central Wyddfa's cairn-crowned summit part
 The mountain pyramid's deep curving lines;
Of Cwms that matchless triad—Snowdon's heart—
 And peaks whereon the golden morning shines;—
 Crib Goch, Crib Ddysgyll, bare with stony spines,
Grey Lliwedd's side majestically sheer;
 These gleam all changeful, but when day declines,
Their giant images fling broad and clear,
And shed o'er half the East their beauty grand and drear.

But who, from these great crags though long beholding,
 Can tell aright the infinite display!
One nearest zone all Venedotia folding
 Which Loveliness and Terror both array;
 Then myriad circles widening away
O'er rural levels, forest, river, plain,
 And teeming city; o'er the bending bay,
And o'er the sparkling waters, till again
Within each kingdom's bound they touch a mountain
 chain.

All objects merge compressed within your ken,
    All distance now enchanted semblance knows,
The winds have accents which the haunts of men
    Hear not, and heaven a holier repose;
    The sea uplifted near you swells and glows,
The hills bow prominent on every side,
    And Mona full her storied islands shows,
One gleaming fair where Menai's currents glide,
One paled by twenty leagues in mid Saint George's
    tide.

And mark, around the mountain's rifted base,
    The shining lakes in varied shapes expand;
Now deep-embosomed lies their liquid grace,
    Now brimming high as in a giant's hand;
    Sweet Gwynant here begems the vale's green band,
Llanberis there her fairy waters holds;
    And open Cwellyn's crystal face breeze-fanned,
And loveliest Nantlle e'en mid beauty's moulds,
And winding Llydaw laid in dark Cwm Dyli's folds.

Come hither from the world! Ambrosial Spring
    Quickens the breast of Nature, and thy veins
Throb warm and generous: though no linnet sing,
    Or garden-bloom, or joyance of the plains
    Invite, yet here the vernal Spirit reigns
Matchless in azure sky, reposing sea,
    And clouds, the wild winds' image: Who remains
On this proud peak with him, and cannot see
A spring o'er Cymru fall, broad, beautiful, and free!

The spring of truest liberty and light,
    Of victory over prejudice and wrong,
Of high dominion ;—what though Arthur's might
    And Rhodri's sway no more to her belong,
    Nor in her halls resounds the prince-bard's song ;
Yet God protects, and who shall quite destroy !
    Taught, chastened by the Past, more wise, more strong,
The Future she shall fill; not tool or toy,
But Britain's Muse, and Hope, and Counsellor, and Joy !

Come hither from the world !   Sweet Autumn brings
    Clear temperate day, and night for starry dreaming,
And now one last and crowning beauty flings
    O'er earth and sea and sky : As love late beaming
    In proud and arid hearts, the grey rocks gleaming
With purple lights incline their lofty breast :
    Low to the vale with warmth and colour teeming
Darts the full stream ; fair-woven boughs invest,
And soothe with weeping charms, the cataract's unrest.

Come hither when the ardent summer Sun
    Springs in full strength above the Berwyn-steep ;
His circling course from hill to hill is run,
    In many a lonely lake his splendours sleep,
    In many a streamlet flash, and broad and deep,
Far crags and chasms touch with chequered play—
    Arenig, Aran, Idris' giant keep,
Eifl's mute camp of stone,[1] till slow away,
In beauty blending all, they die in Arvon's bay.

<hr/>

[1] Tre'r Caeri.

As when the Roman oft at vigil-time
　　Gazed from Segontium after doubtful fight —
Gazed on the crimson-bannered West, the clime
　　Beyond his ken, beyond his eagle's flight :
　　Where now his own imperial City's might !
Where now the hosts that wrought at Cambria's chain !
　　The Norman eagles crown yon turrets' height ;
What strength hath sunk—what glory shone in vain !
Still bend the beaming heavens ; the mountains still remain.

And ever glows the quenchless light from God,
　　Religion, spirit-beauty of the land ;
This wreathed with myrtle many a tyrant's rod,
　　This joined the Saxon's with the Cymro's hand,
　　This fired the Muse, trimmed Learning's lamp : how grand
The victory by the chained Caradoc won,
　　Binding the Roman in a golden band :
For what fair Eurgain's blessed heart begun,
Kindled the conquering Cross of queenly Helen's son ![1]

Star-wooed, cloud-wrapped, the gentle Moon comes gliding,
　　Yet evermore the Sun's pale path pursuing,
Like Woman's love for some bright Fame, abiding
　　Hopeless, untold, intense, her life's undoing ;
　　Yet Dian soon her virgin pride renewing,
Looks o'er this rock-realm like a fairy-queen,
　　Her magic shafts fantastically strewing,
And mixing ebon shade with pearly sheen,
Till kindling Fancy hails the wild and wondrous scene.

---

[1] Eurgain the daughter of Caractacus, is said to have introduced Christianity, with St. Ilid, into Britain, on her return from captivity in Rome.

But when the fair young Moon—sweet Promise—bends
   Upon heaven's verge all twilight-veiled and low,
And timorous of those diamond halls, descends
   Throneless till majesty shall grace endow ;
   Then come the stars in faint and fervid glow
O'er-arching ; midnight deepens round the Pole ;
   No breath of care or passion from below,
No earth-bred damps their influence control,
But clear their lustre beams, their harmonies deep roll.

Who hath not felt Light's sphered spirits fill
   Earth's dark gross frame, and plant a passion there,
In wood and sea a mystic life instil,
   Give meaning to these crags so dumb and bare,
   Bind good with all ; see Cytherea fair
Quiver o'er Silyn, and Jove's burning car
   Roll o'er Llywelyn through the azure air ;
And know how strength—joy—beauty—doubly are
Linked to those glorious forms, the mountain and the star !

But would'st thou feel the mountain-glory fold thee ?
   When purblind Luxury to cities goes,
When not a foot will trace, or eye behold thee,
   Come hither fearless in the time of snows :
   When to a hundred peaks in white repose
The faint cold flushes of the dawn return,
   When Nature like a classic marble shows
Her inmost form, until the bosom burn
With rapture that the world's poor painted toys can spurn.

Elen, or Helena, a British princess, was the mother of Constantine, whose
vision of the Cross, and the ' In hoc signo vinces,' is well known.

And I have couched above the broad abyss,
    On the rock's jagged marge, when cloud o'er cloud
Dark-massing quenched the brightness that did kiss
    Lone Llydaw far adown : then crashing loud
    Came the wild hurricane ; the sky was bowed
Upon the hills, and floods of loosened hail
    Smote the unyielding crags ; while wrath-endowed,
The winds swept seaward rending spar and sail,
Or round my head intoned their long unearthly wail.

So lapsed the night ; a sea of mist upsurging,
    Cut by the sluggish lines of chilling rain,
Holds the sad dawn oppressed and unemerging,
    And drifting columns pass in spectral train ;
    Till, as the sickly shapes that cling to Pain
Are chased by rosy Health, the vapours glide
    Before the strengthening Beam, and now the plain
Rejoices, and the beauteous bow hangs wide,
Arching from Aran's head to deep Cynghorion's side.

Then come, vain youth, who indolently wearest
    Queen Fashion's livery ; daylight mummy rolled
In Form's strong swathings, come, for yet thou bearest
    Within, a source of joy untried, untold ;
    And come, thou poor mechanic slave of Gold,
And bring thine own pale slaves, nor let them steep
    In Lust's mud-lethe the few hours doled
For breathing-time ; come all, and drink ye deep
From wells that purge the heart, and break the spirit's
    sleep !

Yet flock not hither as to city show,
    Nor herd carousing like a Bacchic band,
Nor weakly prate of sentiment ere glow
    Inward the image of the fair and grand ;
    But on the mountains reverently stand,
Most holy by the Briton once confest,
    And holy are they still, for hand in hand,
The Muses yet the favoured ground invest,
With Heaven's Angel-forms that quicken themes more blest.

Alas for me who use a stranger tongue,
    And touch with erring hand a humble lyre,
When Cambria's harp for Cambria should be strung,
    And vibrate to her native words of fire !—
    Oh that the lay could like the thought aspire,
That so my gratitude I might record
    For hours of health and peace and pure desire,
And weave a song from all my heart hath stored—
Such song as Llywarch loved, or high Taliesin poured !

WAR VERSES, 1854.

ODESSA falls. Sunk ship, dismantled mole,
    Wide-flaming arsenal, and shattered tower,
Massed in the mocking waves that o'er them roll,
    Mark the base crime and well-avenging power!
    No more a pirate-nest where dastards cower
To sweep the Euxine when our flag is far;
    No more a sustenance for battle-hour
To nurse the frenzy of her maddened Czar;
She lies beneath the feet of mighty Western War.

Odessa falls, as momently may fall
    Sevastopol with all her armies girt;
But justice-winged upflew the fiery ball,
    'Gainst one alone its quarrel to assert,
    The armed imperial foe, nor carried hurt
To peaceful arts and homes; not ours to bend
    A Nation's hosts to wrong, or so pervert
The spirit of our better Age to rend
A second Magdeburg, or raze a new Ostend!

For as our War is nobler in its aim,
    Thus be it ever nobler in its course!
No province do we steal, nor fealty claim,
    Nor treaty break, nor fraud maintain by force:
    With mercy let us use the last resource,
Our prowess old, and science-doubled might,
    And show ourselves through all this dread divorce
Of States, to those unarmed whom battles blight,
Magnanimous as strong, firm arbiters of Right!

To rural uplands, mist-wreathed, glides the morn,
  But pure and brightening, till with waving gold
Gleams the brown ripeness of the unsickled corn,
  And myriad sheaves recline in graceful fold ;
  Then Labour's sweetest, only task of old
Invites ; song-urged, moves on the harvest-wain ;
  Day glows and sinks ; the kingly star behold
Beam o'er the village gleaners' humble train,
And Innocence and Mirth, and Peace and Plenty reign !

Light struggles sullen through the poisoned air,
  And sulphurous mist above the bastion spread ;
The work is done, the citadel lies bare,
  And blood-stained ashes wrap the legioned dead ;
  Havoc exults, and Carnage full has fed :—
But hark !—the clang—the tramp—the boom ; again
  Upleap the flames—the driving steel drips red,
Till Night's pure eyes look shuddering on the plain
Where mingle Famine, Death, and Misery and Pain !

God's truth is broad. Let each September story
  The bosom's noblest sympathies excite ;
Be ours alike the hate of War's false glory,
  And of his infamy who fears to fight :
  Still pray that Time War's upas-tree may blight,
Art bloom, and Heaven's blessings crown our need :
  But when our cause is Liberty and Right,
Come Battle's horrors ! Let us bear and bleed
Till peace be battle-won, which shall be peace indeed !

L

MEDITATIONS.

'Tis the calm of July midnight, and the world around me
    sleeps,
Save where Wealth's pale priest Labour a fiery vigil keeps ;
And the gleam from his iron altars o'er the placid sky is
    flung,
Ever of human sacrifice telling with blood-red tongue.
But I turn to the southern planets that in purer air outbend,
And I hear the breeze soft-flowing from their lucid founts
    descend,
While I lie with cheek moss-pillowed, plaided 'gainst dewy
    harm,
Waking the old dream-spirits by the well-remembered charm :
So have I pressed the mountain when the beating blood in my
    veins
Throbbed over silent clouds and crags and glimmering lakes
    and plains,
Till that pulse seemed the pulse of Nature, and her silence
    and her glee,
Her beauty and power and passion, were upgathered into me ;
Then down the shelving granite through the mountain roots
    I would glide —
Down where blind Earthquake nestles—down where the
    Gnomes abide—
Down to the glowing chambers where the giant work is done
That shall whirl in the crowning Ages Earth's fragments
    around the sun :—

Thence forth to the ocean-gardens, to the tideless hyaline,
Where mid the mazy corals the lights of emerald shine—
To the ghostly shell-paved cities where never may footstep
  tread
On the spoils of human grandeur, on the bones of human
  dead :—
And upward yet to the noonday, and upward thence afar,
Till upward and downward be not, but only ether and star,
Till I saw earth sphered and convex in her steady courses run,
And the first pale solar glory strike on her bosom dun.
Then drooped weak Fancy's pinions, and a loftier Spirit came
Who lifted my heavy eyelids, and lighted a purer flame ;
I looked on Life's narrow purpose, on Pleasure's phantom
  goal,
I looked through the circling Infinite on the birthright of the
  Soul,
I saw the dust-bent foreheads grope with the flickering torch
  of Time,
And I prayed for the light eternal—the path and the faith
  sublime.
The vision faded from me, but I bore to the world a boon
Which, long as night can awake it, shall never be quenched
  by noon—
Sweet hope for the clouded heaven, sweet calm for the hour
  of strife,
And an ampler rule of Duty, and a larger view of Life !

    *   *   *   *   *

    Day after day the Sun's old splendours still
    Rise opaline, and fall in golden flame :
    The Moon puts on her beauty's changeful robe
    In sure recurrence, and the solemn stars

Watch o'er the city's throng as erst they watched
O'er scattered shepherds couched on Asian plains:
Earth spreads her lap to all the elements,
And flowers and fruits, and dews and rains, and snows,
O'erfill it; still her mountains stand, her rivers
Run ever, and her immemorial seas
Gird her, and cry with choral monotone;
And she with all her life and wealth and beauty—
Parent and child as well as world and mother—
Obedient sweeps around the central Light,
While hours feed years, and ages centuries grow.

Man alone changes; not alone with change
From frail to strong, from misty morn to noon
Of shorter shadows; not as grows the boy
To his full heritage of nerve and brain,
Or as the savage comes from tangled woods,
And sluggish meres, and idols fire-enshrined,
To kneel upon the marble floor beneath
The Cross of Christ, and in the forum stand
Pre-eminent in letters, arts, or arms:
Such increase is all good, such change is glory,
Effulgence born of the Promethean spark
To light and lift the world.   It is not this
That moves to tears or scorn the heart which love
And exultation ought unmixed to fill;
'Tis the dark shade where plants unlovely spring—
The Vice that trampling Virtue's fair white robe,
Puts on a gaudy veil and struts absolved;
It is the lusts, lies, follies, sins and shames,
That grow with Man's advance, and day by day
Warp him the more from what he was when near

To Nature he was nearer God;—Oh why
Should Civilization, bringing precious gifts
Of knowledge, wealth, ease, beauty, power, bring too
What turns them all to lures and counterfeits!—
Why set up idols false and frail as clay
To sit like adamant upon the heart—
Fashion, Convention, Habit—all that stands
Between us and our Maker!   Why with wants
And cares and aims innumerous oversow
The field of fellowship till man to man
Is enemy!   Why knit Earth's utmost bounds,
Yet dig a gulf within the walls of home!

Alas! we walk amid the flood of light
Darkling, with footsteps base and foreheads bent,
Seeking some pleasure's gaud, or folly's toy,
Some golden profit, or some fortune-charm—
Selfish the search, and selfishness the end;
We will not lift our eyes or lend our ears,
Though Nature from the circling universe
Call with her many voices grand and sweet;
Though borne on Time's swift car there pass us by
Great Destinies and lofty Needs demanding
Achievement at our hands, and human Love
Pass sorrowing, and Love divine reproach
In pity our lost worship;—what to us
The old faith, and simple aims, and childlike trust,
And patriot virtue, and firm brotherhood,
Patience and self-denial!—they are *names*;
Their substance would but choke the stream of
    life,
Let them then leave their semblance here and go!

Yet—yet, not all is fled, for though above
The smooth false levels of our social state,
Some crime colossal deep-engendered there,
As rise the corals in Pacific seas,
Rears oft its head to startle and annoy;
Still see colossal Virtue rising too!
Witness his honoured name[1] who in a day
When Poverty is Vice, and Gold is God,
Stripped him of half his wealth's rich robe to clothe
His naked brethren: little need he care
For prudent tongues that mid the forced acclaim,
Whispered—'Tis strange—'tis foolish—he is mad.
And he too, foremost hero of our time,
Hero of Aspromonte not the less
Than of Marsala; they adjudge him mad,
The man of calm clear mind, because he went
Straight to his heart's pure purpose, heedless all
Of Statecraft's rule and Priestcraft's interdict;
Because he trusted to his fellow-men,
Declared their right, and bade them but assert
Their power to have whate'er their right comprised:—
Go, measure then the Sun's ecliptic path
With your base ell-wand ere you measure him!
Great now as ever when you deem him fallen;—
He falls, and doth Italia rise? Ye fools
Who sigh for Venice—Rome, yet dare not let
Your pulse beat warm enough to nerve your arm,
Talk on—wait on, poor diplomates, and dream
That to your feeble heads there will be given
What with your craven hearts ye could not win!

[1] GEORGE PEABODY.

TO GERTRUDE, ON OUR BIRTHDAY.

I.

Sunset's ruby flames are glowing
   In the tall and leafy limes,
While the south-wind softly flowing
   Brings the Convent's vesper-chimes.

Sleep is nestling in the flowers,
   Coolness fans the level lawn,
And a veil of happy hours
   'Tween the night and day is drawn.

Fair the morn will be to-morrow
   By the evening's rosy sign;—
Let us put by gloom and sorrow,
   'Tis our birthday, thine and mine!

'Tis our birthday! we will make it
   Bright with song and game and glee;
What's good for thirteen, I take it,
   Isn't bad for thirty-three.

I must have them all about me—
   All the rays that grace the Gem;
Well I love my G.—don't doubt me—
   And we both love E. and M.

Esther with that pretty fashion
    In her looks and words and ways ;—
May those Norman eyes long flash on
    Fair, if changeful, future days !

Mabel, sterling little Saxon,
    Quiet, loving, arch and kind,
She will bear Time's worst attacks on
    Life, with calm and cheerful mind !

They shall come, and all the others,
    Yours and theirs of home's sweet ring—
Good Papa, Mamma, and brothers—
    I, alas ! have none to bring.

Hail our Birthday ! we will show it
    For a day of happiness,
And the marmalade shall know it,
    And the ivory keys confess !

II.

'Tis indeed our birthday, dearest,
    Gertie, faithful little heart,
Here our lines of life run nearest,
    But from hence how wide they part !

From the summit of existence
    Granite-bare, I look around ;
Thou art in the purple distance
    Where the lilies deck the ground.

I can see, where nought can hide them,
    Peaks that lured me from the plain ;
Passion's mist had magnified them,
    I have scaled them—they are vain.

Soon must I with swifter motion
    Downward bend, and humbly go
To that shoreless silent ocean
    Where is never ebb or flow.

Thou, fair child, shalt journey gently,
    Only good as fair remain—
Only heed not too intently
    Flowers of pleasure, thorns of pain.

Though our destined paths divide us,
    Brighter, surer, still be thine !
And the love that once allied us,
    Long shall shed its light on mine.

III.

It is midnight ; clouds are flitting
    Over heaven's sepulchral deep,
And the Moon, pale Witch, high sitting,
    Counts the shadows as they sweep.

See, she calls them to their places,
    Gliding ghosts of buried years,
Dim but unforgotten faces
    Gay with smiles, or dark with tears !

Little Clarrie, little Clarrie !
   Come from midst them—it is thou ;
Thou wast angel here, or fairy,
   Hardly more thou canst be now.

Oh those golden curls o'ershading
   Dimpled neck and forehead white ;
Oh those eyes which, all-pervading,
   Awed us with their mystic light !

Oh that cheek's too changeful blossom,
   Where the quick blood mantled wild,
As the restless little bosom
   Heaved too proudly for a child !

Well I loved thee in thy laughter
   When the amber tresses shook,
Marking well, to mimic after,
   Stranger's song, or speech or look !

Well I loved thee in thy learning—
   Loved that high and longing glance,
Still from Fact's cold noontide turning
   To the twilight of Romance !

Oh I loved thee beyond telling
   When thy Genii from afar
Bore thee sleepbound to their dwelling,
   Ocean cave or summer star !

Little Clarrie, little Clarrie,
  Dost thou now unsleeping stand
Where the white-robed children tarry,
  Leaning on their Father's hand ?

Where is light to fill thy vision—
  Where is love to bless thy heart—
Beauty, like thy dreams, Elysian—
  Joy that knows no after-smart.

IV.

Life, warm human life, is nearest,
  And I clasp its ties again,
Clarrie lives in Gertie dearest,
  And this birthday is not vain.

Year on year the summers golden
  Bear her with them as they run ;
Hardly heeds she memories olden,
  She is blooming twenty-one !

Fair to gaze upon, but fairer
  In the meaning of her eyes,
And a beauty subtler, rarer,
  Every feature underlies.

Earnest-hearted, simple-minded,
  Purpose pure, and speech sincere,
Not a word leaves pain behind it,
  Not an action prompts a tear.

Loving still the dear ones round her
  Deeply as their sacred due,
Home affections do not bound her,
  Kind and Country loves she too.

No vain talent in her fingers,
  No light skill of pen or tongue,
Marring life's matureness, lingers
  From the days when life was young.

Well and early hath her spirit
  Drunk of Art's unsullied springs ;
Genius through the fields of Merit
  Bears her on with broadest wings.

Gloom and glory of the mountain
  Feed her with ethereal fire,
While, as from some wood-screened fountain,
  Comes the influence of her sire.

All that music subtlest, finest,
  All that song's sweet accents can,
Useth she for ends divinest,
  Praise to God, and peace to Man.

Noble girl ! erect in duty,
  Gathering still, as seasons roll,
Grandeur, melody, and beauty,
  From Creation to her soul.

Now in all her birthday splendour,
　Virgin-vestured see her stand,
Modest, candid, true and tender,
　Mid the friends that press her hand!

Be she always as this hour,
　Wise and simple, pure and good—
'Tis the never-failing dower,
　Strength and charm of Womanhood!

So shall birthdays ever-glowing
　Bathe with light the Past's grey urn,
So through change and fortune flowing,
　Happier be in each return!

A TRIAD.

Liebe, Licht, Leben.
(On HERDER's Tomb.)

I.

HAIL to the Life, the Light, the Love, that flows
Through eloquent marble, from the mute repose
    Around the poet's grave !
A triple amaranth to wreathe his name—
Beacon for Time's dark stream—pure guiding flame
    O'er the eternal wave !

Oh, beautifiers of the mouldering dust—
Oh, calm interpreters of joy and trust
    From night to battling day !
Still let us seek them though we never find—
Still let us woo them to our heart and mind,
    And shun—not dare—the fray !

Happy who can ! on whose sustained desiring
Possession waits—to meet whose high aspiring
    The Empyrean bends :—
On whose first fervency, no growing chill—
On whose deep sense of good, no quenching ill—
    As age on youth—attends !

II.

Life! for the poor and mean a pregnant soil
Of weed and bramble—many-textured toil
  To wring out daily bread;—
Wring out what serves but as the needed fuel
To wake again in ever-fixed renewal,
  The power of arm or head.

Life! for the rich and proud, a gilded net
By lust with suavities empoisoned set
  To lure and leave the soul;—
A morning's flirting with bedizened Fashion—
A noon's libation at the shrine of Passion—
  A midnight's deathbell toll!

Life! ardent essence poured into each mould
Of pleasure, knowledge, glory, art, or gold,
  The choice or chance of all:
Ah! none can satisfy and none can last;
Who doth not hate the idol he hath cast,
  And fret from thrall to thrall!

The tender heart soon breaks, or hardens soon;
The mind nods idiot-like to any tune,
  Or maddens in resistance;
Nerve, pulse, and bloom, an hour may blast or chill,
An atom blind, an inhalation kill;
  And *this* makes up Existence!

III.

Yet Wisdom's fair imperishable glow ;
The world without, the world within, to know—
  The depths of Being sound !
Alas ! Light's high advance is Love's decrease ;
The more of eminence the less of peace,
  Hushed voices breathe around.

What though some reflex of the mighty flame
May grace a brow and consecrate a name,
  Some saddening shade it bears :
Oft the unearthly radiance waneth out,
Dimmed by the damps of uncongenial doubt,
  Stifled by sordid cares.

Who points enraptured gaze the tube along,
Where growing stars on stars to meet him throng,
  Soon the strained eye must rest ;
Who climbs above the clouds on mountain-steep,
Amid emotions manifold and deep
  Draws pain with labouring breast.

IV.

Be Love then all our hope and best reward—
The one pure well, the harmonising chord
  Linked with our dissonant strings ;—
A low-voiced teacher of the golden mean,
A saving shield to lift in battle keen,
  Or balm that healing brings !

Ask the warm Poet—he hath wrought the spell
That binds such beauty to our souls so well—
    What is his own awaking
From rosy dreams of sympathetic bliss
Meet for the pure and delicate sense—it is
    To feel his vexed heart breaking!

Ask the high flaunter of ancestral blazon,
Who turns from Nature's solemn diapason
    To Folly's tinkling strain ;
What knows *he* of the love that cannot palter,
Whom policy leads scheming to the altar
    To meet a bride as vain !

Still, though with diamonds, orange-flowers, crests,
Love simple, single-minded, rarely rests,
    It lights the humblest lot !
No ! envy, hunger, disappointment, debt,
Are clouds o'er many a home so densely set,
    Love's beams can enter not.

Remain they then in middle paths that go,
Nor falsely great, nor languishingly low,
    And Love to such may cling :—
But theirs the lifelong, headlong chace of gold,
And Love were welcome to be bought and sold,
    But else an idle thing.

Yet blooms a time when every girl and boy
Is firm in faith and prescient of joy ;—
　　The heart Love's spring-tides lave :—
Ah surer still there droops an aftertime
When Life's repulsive wrecks and ooze and slime
　　Mark the receded wave !

V.

Alas ! o'er these fair words the cypress weeps,
Nor thus can retrospect from him who sleeps
　　Survive of *earthly* hours ;
The fruit was there, but with the worm destroying :
The gold was there, but with the dross alloying ;
　　And weeds oppressed the flowers.

Ah no ! with higher hope the legend burns,
And, as a talisman thrice holy, turns
　　The Tomb to Heaven's portal ;
Where Love shall be one Catholic embrace,
And Light enkindled from the Giver's face,
　　And Life intense, immortal.

VI.

Yet—beautifiers of the mouldering dust,
And calm interpreters of joy and trust
　　From night to battling day ;
Still let us seek them though we never find ;
Still let us woo them to our heart and mind,
　　Nor wholly shun the fray !

Still let us live to learn, and learn to live ;
Still of the kind affections freely give—
　　Requited well or ill ;—
And shape some end beyond our fireside bound,
And break the chains of Circumstance around,
　　With pure and lofty will !

And strip Pride's rags, and purge besetting Sin,
And fondly, reverently, guard within
　　And nurse the undying germ ;
And seek Creation's many-lettered lore,
And work, and rest, and suffer, and adore,
　　Gentle, and wise, and firm !

So may permitted storms of Fortune beat,
And Error's clouds perplex awhile our feet,
　　And Disappointment sting ;
With inborn force the outward counteracting,
From roughest herbs some anodyne extracting,
　　And clearing each dark spring ;

Live we undauntedly the life of years,
And while its eternal home the spirit nears,
　　Let it grow pure in *this ;*
Until at last, the sad novitiate ended,
Itself with Glory infinite be blended,
　　Omniscience, and Bliss !

LOVE-RHAPSODIES.

From the quiet little chamber where I sit the most in summer,
    Whence field and wood beneath me spread southward fair
        and free,
Where the pure winds cross my forehead, and the lark, a
        frequent comer,
    Pours out his soul's deep lyric, I unveil my heart to thee.

Last night I met the darkening face of Auster in his anger,
    When he whirled the sleet before him, when he chased the
        spectral Moon
Through her multiform cloud-caverns, as Strength oppresses
        Languor,
    As demons drive some piteous ghost from Mercy's blessed
    boon.

E'en such hath been the oracle of inauspicious seeming,
    Forever when I would unlock Fate's lips or Fortune's hand—
The thunder-throe of mountains, and the keen blue fire-bolt
        streaming,
    Or the sea's hoarse booming laughter on the drear death-
    jagged strand :

Or the mocking cry of nightbird athwart the forest wheeling,
    Heard shrilly through the tumult of the old Druidic pines,
Or the mist that swathed my spirit with a cold and corpse-
    like feeling,
    Or the rain that smote my eyelids with its dull and rigid lines.

But O impartial Nature! who hast answered me austerely,
    When with yearning strong I prayed to gain good omens
      from thy smile,
These grandeurs were a recompense won willingly though
    dearly,
    And Thought hath risen clear and cold from Passion's
      funeral pile.

And gently now thou soothest me with e'en a show of gladness,
    And pointest to the promise of the hour newly born,
For Peace has stilled the weary lips of elemental Madness,
    And Light has kissed away the tears from the clouded eyes
      of Morn.

From the pale green of the meadow to the azure of the zenith,
    Through twig and bud and brooklet—through every sen-
      tient thing,
Is shed the vital fervour of the season that beginneth,
    The first self-conscious flushing on the maiden cheek of
      Spring.

O thou who art my better Spring, my newest hope and nearest,
    Who breath'st thy beauty through the heaven, and o'er the
      earth around,
In whom I sum up all delights—O Cythna, ever dearest,
    Without *thine* influence vain to me were vernal sight or
      sound!

Without thee, June's meridian glow were Zembla's arctic
    morning,
    Without thee, Autumn's lavish feast were Nubia's desert
      bare;
What were the queenly diamonds some festal hour adorning,
    If on *thy* breast they sparkled not, nor gleamed within *thy*
      hair!

See from his fleecy couch of cloud the ardent Sun-god
    springing,
  Withdraws the filmy curtain of day's ethereal dome,
And downward to the earth's pale floor his shafts of glory
    winging,
  Smiles on the spot most dear to me, the white walls of thy
    home!

Alas! no glad responsive smile on that lonely mansion sitteth,
  But mute and wan and cold, it meets my oft-directed gaze;
A Grief is brooding over it, a dark-plumed Memory flitteth
  Ever around the rooftree of the undivided days.

Oh would that I could comfort thee in this thy recent sorrow,
  Could calm thy mind with lofty aims, and give a wider scope;
Could bring thee consolations thou from kindred canst not
    borrow,
  Could soften for thee memory, and brighten for thee hope!

Oh would that to my bosom, sweet Flower, I could fold thee,
  That while, as roseate leaf by leaf, the life-joys droop and
    part,
Watched, tended, blessed and blessing, Change and Fortune
    should behold thee
  Expanding still to happier bloom from thy glowing central
    heart!

I know not what I write or hope—some witchery is o'er me,
  And thoughts that once untrammelled roved, around the
    enchantress throng;
I summon the severer Muse, but thou art still before me—
  I turn from life's free paths and aims, a thrall to love and
    song.

It was not thus when long ago the fair false Dream, Ambition,
  While the City roared beneath me, to my midnight chamber
    came ;
With burning eye and tempting tongue she shaped a gorgeous
  vision,
  And filled my sight with fantasies, and fed my heart with
    flame.

And Woman feared or mocked me then ; I paid her back by
  scorning,
  And worshipped an Egeria long, in secret and afar,
Whose bosom was the swelling hills, whose breath May's dewy
  morning—
  Whose voice the streamlet's softest flow, whose eye the
    twilight star.

And yet there came a gentle girl, a little while to be an
  Inspirer and consoler from the vineyards of the South ;—
Her form matured to perfect grace in the mountains Euganean ;
  And sweetest were the liquid tones breathed from her rose-
    sweet mouth.

She passed ; and do my eyes grow dim before a second vision,
  And deeper harmonies of love around my spirit roll ;—
Ah shadow vain and vacant as the offspring of magician—
  Ah mocking music stifling not the dreary death-bell's toll !

For what art thou, whom, smitten with the glorious name thou
  bearest,
  I Cythna call, and fondly clothe with all her light and grace ;
Say canst thou show the nympholept his deepest, subtlest,
  rarest
  Conceptions of true Womanhood reflected in thy face ?

Art thou not moulded by the World, and tutored by Conven-
    tion—
    Bound by the laws which Folly makes, and Fashion coun-
        tersigns;
And could thy being ever know the soul's sublime ascension
    From Life's debasing social flats, and weary level lines!

Dost thou believe, and speak, and act, unshrinkingly appealing
    To God's eternal truths in *thee*, as all Creation, set?
Or dost thou take for arbitress of daily deed and feeling,
    That haughtiest, falsest, meanest, of Man's idols, Etiquette?

But oh I wrong thee, wrong thee thus; what sullen cloud
    was hiding
    Thy clear calm face that comes to me a blessing of the night,
Where, fair as Dian mid her stars, is Womanhood presiding
    Over the linkèd Spirits twain of power and of light.

Ah Cythna, with the introspect of love's quick looks of fire
    That hardly dared meet thine, I long have marked thy
    nature well;
I know thy patience and thy faith, thy genius to aspire,
    Thy sweet affections to endear, thy talents to excel.

I read thy love of noble things, thy prescience of all duty,
    Thy will that moulds and conquers all, nor feeble nor
    austere;
These are the themes, and for the type have I not all thy
    beauty
    Whose exquisiteness renders them thrice eloquent, thrice
    clear!

What is't to me if brighter eye have traced these living pages—
   If worthier heart have thrilled at them, if wealthier hand
     have turned;
Could *I* complain that other love thy queenly breast engages—
   That deeper passion was outpoured—that better vows were
     spurned!

I say not I am worthy thee, for thou art best and highest—
   I deem not I can win thee yet, for Fate is yet unkind;—
But oh believe that whatsoe'er of great and good is nighest
   Thy life and faith, around *my* heart with kindred growth is
     twined!

To search with me the mystic laws of Destiny and Being—
   To tread with me familiar paths of Nature, wide and far—
To know the Almighty Infinite, indwelling, overseeing,
   Alike in wood-anemone and world-composing star;—

To range with me through vanished Time, whose teachings
   vanish never;—
   Through Poesy's Elysian fields—through Wisdom's purer
     part—
Is what I ask thee, Cythna sweet, that mind with mind may
   ever
   Be interfused in growing light, and knit us heart to heart.

And knowledge comes by love, and joy of God's own good
   bestowing,
   And, fanned by love, life's folded powers and instincts
   chilled unclose,
E'en as to Zephyr's dewy breath, and June's caresses glowing,
   Responds, with all her inmost charms, the Spring-neglected
   rose.

PRÆLATA PUELLIS.

No starring charm in Beauty's list—
   No meretricious grace,
But unpretending loveliness
   Lives in her form and face.

Her mouth transparent candour marks,
   Her eyes good humour's light ;
She only utters what she feels,
   And only feels aright.

A soul from Nature fair and true,
   To love the true and fair,
To shine in Art, yet value not
   Its tinsel and its glare.

Knowledge more deep than loud, and wit,
   But tempered to be kind,
And will to do Life's earnest work,
   And Duty's straight path find :

With sympathy and sorrow there
   For those that fall or flee ;
A heart whose love for all the world
   Deepens its love for me.

Dear friend and love! whom once to know—
   Whatever then betide—
Through life, through death, is still to keep
   Good angels at my side.

TO CYNTHIA.

Cynthia! for thus I name thee, fair unknown,
  Binding a double glory round thy head—
  This from an ever-brightening memory shed;
That from the soul's expression all thine own,
If well I read it in those calm eyes shown ;—
  Comest thou to my heart, a garden dead,
  With perished buds and wild weeds overspread,
As cometh Spring with hope of flower and fruit ?
Com'st thou to wake in me the music mute,
  By true love's touch, and while my spirit's bark,
Wearily tossing on a changeful sea,
  Helmless and aimless drifteth through the dark,
Lured by false lights; arisest *thou* to be
  A bright and blessed star to guide it to its mark ?

Ah me! for what am I that know thee not
  Save as a star is known ; nor word nor sign
  Hath made thee conscious yet of me or mine,
And I am alien to thy loftier lot ;
  And thou perchance art other than I deem,
And could'st not wear the wreath my fancies twine,
  Nor fill the Ideal of Youth's golden dream
That missed the human, shaping the divine :—

No! I will trust thee; and as mountain grot
  Embosoms some pure source, which soon, a stream
Of breadth and beauty, bids the world behold;
So shall my secret heart thy name enfold,
  And love thee, though thy smile on others beam—
Love thee unknown and mute, yet with a joy untold!

Vain, vain the utterance! thou art still before me,
  Statelier and sweeter in thy sombre dress,
  For all it adds of inner loveliness—
Ever a presence like the sky bent o'er me,
  With more, alas! of shade than light: I press
Gloomily on for life's most sordid needs,
Or haply rush to far off river-meads;
  To valley nestling deep; to headland stormy;
To savage mountain where the icewind speeds:—
  In vain! 'tis not enough that thou art there
  A brooding Thought, a goddess of the air;
Passion for love unveiled and human pleads,
  And Nature's lips are dumb and offerings bare,
Without *thy* mind to note—without *thy* heart to share.

But when the clear and choral hymn ascending
  From holiest House asserts the holiest Day;
  When outward cares and pleasures fall away,
And purely longing, inly comprehending,
  The soul may catch one empyrean ray;
  Then, Cythna, thou art near me, and we pray
Meekly before the common Father bending:—
  Oh quicklier then Devotion's pulses beat
  That thou art near! since o'er the Mercy-seat
Of God, immortal Love's wide wings extending,

Draw heart to heart, and Earth to Heaven;—and thou
    Wilt love, I feel, where love may be most meet—
Wilt tread calm Duty's heights, nor disavow
The pure within thine eyes, the noble on thy brow.

ON REVIENT TOUJOURS.

THE eve is come with glories bright
    Of wave and cloud and star;
The ship pursues her path of light;
    The winds are hushed afar;
Mirth treads the deck, and Pleasure calls
    Across the charmèd sea;
But unresponding sinks my heart,
    Saddened for love of thee.

The morning glows on gorgeous Seine,
    On palace, bridge, and tower,
And wakes the world of joy again
    In hall and street and bower:
I listen to the eager speech,
    And seem to share the glee,
But cold and calm my spirit sleeps,
    Lonely for love of thee.

The noon is shed through arching boughs
    In silent Fontainebleau;
The deer flit forth across the glade;
    The shadows come and go:
The rocks in wizard forms are spread;
    The hills stand solemnly;
I lie mid Nature's lavished wealth,
    Careless for love of thee.

Night steals through dim cathedral panes
　On saints in sculptured sleep,
And arch and oriel bid the eye
　To visions far and deep:
But marble floor and blazoned vault
　And golden shrine to me
Nor charm the sense, nor lift the heart,
　Restless for love of thee.

ROBERT LUCAS CHANCE.

Not often, mid the ebb and flow of men,
  Dies there a man like this: nor life nor death
  Holds many such, in whom his Maker's breath
Was honoured, passing e'en familiar ken,
And all of him—heart, hand, voice, purse, and pen—
  Obedient still to what the Master saith—
  Work, pray, love, bless: *this* is the gold of Faith,
And all else dross! Weep him who bear his name;
He built your House erect in honest fame;
  Weep, and forget not: weep him with true tears,
Children twice orphaned now; ye sick, forlorn,
  And fortune-stricken: weep him, friends and peers:
Yet, yet rejoice the good old man is born
  To his undying youth, and his Lord's Well done! hears!

March 7, 1865.

x

ON THE EVE OF A REFORM DIVISION.

GLADSTONE! reflect, repent; the hour is brief
   Which brings thee shame or glory; scorn to bask
   In passionate Folly's smiles, but earn and ask
Love from the Nation's heart that owns with grief
Thine errors. Wouldst thou be her Council's Chief?
   Tear from thy darkening brows the graceless mask
   Of right; address thee to a loftier task,
With purer eyes; and Time thy laurel-leaf
   Will keep for ever. What! when justly planned.
As boldly ventured, for the common weal,
   Reform awaits their voice, shall Faction's sand
Engulf it! Shall not statesmen own the appeal
   Rock-based on Concord, nobly hand in hand
Crowning their work, and setting-to their seal!

  April 18, 1867.

THE LAY OF THE OLD STONE.

(Inscribed to A. A.)

An old grey stone near an old Church-tower.
　In a pasture-mead, by a brooklet's brink,
With nothing of service or beauty or power,
　Has little to waken one's interest, you think :

And heedless we see it, when east winds blow
　The factory-smoke from our winter air,
Lying formless and folded in unsmirched snow,
　Or black on earth's bosom frozen and bare.

And heedless too in the golden time
　When populous grows the meadow-path,
When round the rude angles June's wildings climb,
　Or the clover-sweet wealth of the after-math.

Yet though all unnoted, uncared for, lone,
　In our Vulcan-vowed district, and 'practical' day,
There's something about this incongruous stone
　That wit might guess at, and reason weigh.

How came it hither ?—the valley slopes
　Upward and south to the woodland crest :
Downward and north to the streets where mopes
　The poor little stream by bricks oppressed.

N 2

Sunrise and sunset show nothing clear
  Of quarry or hill to help our pains;
No ice-rolled boulder rests, I fear,
  Pace our Pastor, on Midland plains.

Well, was it dug from beneath the loam
  When the land was levelled, or bounded, or
    ploughed?
Some relic of building or battering Rome
  Among the Cornavii might be allowed.

But never a mark of chisel is there,
  And fancy *ballistæ* for such a ball!
Each *Her* is dumb, and these fields are bare
  Of tomb and trench and mound and wall.

Did it come from the Moon? Has she fires enough
  To hurl, with a thousand Etnas' force,
The glowing granite from crater or trough
  To the point where Attraction inverts its course?

Or was it an Asteroid's shattered shell
  That launched it afar in its flaming flight,
Till thundering and hissing to Earth it fell
  Stunning the ear of our calm Midnight?

But if it came thus from above or beneath,
  Why did not farmers clear it away,
Or *savants* impound it, and duly bequeath
  Some certified note for the men of to-day?

A boundary-stone? But the rivulet there,
  As old as it, runs shining and straight—
A market-stone? where the people in fear
  Of plague or ravage were wont to wait.

Yet History fails, and Evidence quite,
  And all that Tradition has to say,
Is that *two* horses brought the Stone in the night,
  And *twenty* couldn't take it away!

A marvellous pebble for growth, no doubt,
  Like the three in Idris' the giant's shoe,
Who, finding they hurt him, kicked them out
  To lie near grey summits and waters blue.

Or rather, when all was the Briton's land,
  And Archdruid ruled, and Pendragon led,
Here did the gold-wreathed chieftains stand
  To swear swift doom on the heathen head?

And what if no mystic Stonehenge be here,
  No Carnac's megaliths whose grey ranks
Rise like a ghostly phalanstere,
  Veiled in the fogs of Biscayan banks!—

Yet kneeling here may the white-robed priest,
  When solstice or equinox marked the time,
Have turned his deep-browed eyes to the East,
  And offered a prayer to the Name sublime.

Or while May-fires gleamed on the uplands gay,
  And the harp rang clear to the nodding wood,
Was the Stone flower-decked for the festal day,
  And ringed by a joyous multitude?

Or marks it a spot which Battle shook,
  And a warrior's rest, who, perchance when he fell,
Thirsted, but shrank from the blood-red brook,
  Till Death poured him Heaven's pure œnomel?

A glorious purpose! but 'Omne,' 'twas said,
  ' Ignotum est pro magnifico,'
And vulgarer uses come into one's head—
  Though time has hidden them, time may show.

Perhaps 'twas flung from the dried-up mere,
  And left as a worthless and harmless thing;
Perhaps—but I whisper you softly here,
  'Tis a secret, this, for the innermost ring—

The fields are quiet when midnight rules;
  The fields are dim 'neath the summer stars;
Shovels and picks are convenient tools;
  Good at need are ropes and bars;

Nobles or guineas would still suit me;
  Gems—worth a hundred settings—suit you;
Old plate becomes an old family—
  (N.B. For your Marriage we'll melt it anew.)

If you mark what these propositions show,
 Let us prove the reason of my rhyme,
And the *buried treasures* of long ago
 Shall flash in the sunlight of our time !

Ah well ! the old Stone is a sad one withal,
 Discoloured and vexed by sun and storm—
No *lotus lapis* to make us recal
 The Statesman who *didn't* give us Reform :

And ' Story, Sir '—it has ' none to tell,'
 Like Canning's knifegrinder, but what of that !
Its teachings are sound if you heed them well,
 Though common—as life and death—and flat.

It has seen the pageant of Man pass by,
 Joying and sorrowing to its goal ;
It has seen the pageant of the sky
 Reflecting in airy types the whole :

It has seen Trade's temples cumber the ground,
 And servile Poverty's pallid brood,
For ever launched in a vicious round
 Of Food for Work, and Work for Food :

It has seen the graves thicken where corn waved wide,
 And the fields grow hallowed with praise and prayer,
And many that kept their tryst at its side,
 And gathered the hay at its base, lie there.

Seasons and cycles and moons have rolled,
Circle on circle evolved and done,
The Past still locked in the Future's fold,
For ever finished, for ever begun.

Let Nature be!   In the world of Man
Is no mere reproduction hopeless and dim,
But circles widening and widening in span,
Till they touch the eternal Heaven's rim.

And we thank thee, old Stone, for thou tellest not ill
Of the passing time, and the coming end;
And we muse, while thou liest cold, changeless, and still,
Whence are *we*, what are *we*, and whither we tend.

AURORA.

This world has no perdition, if some loss.
Casa Guidi Windows.

No fond conceit of old funereal strain—
   Dirge, requiem, threnody—for thee we raise :
No lily weep we, bowed by winter rain,
   Or dawnlight missing the meridian blaze :
   Death seals thy life's completeness ; love and praise
Wait thee through all humanity, all time ;
   What though the flower from scent and bloom decays—
Fair springeth Egypt's lotos from her slime,
But fairer, surer, springs on Egypt's shafts sublime !

Full-statured Poet ; voice supreme of Art ;
   And crown of Womanhood ! thy tale is told ;
Thy noble work is done ; the harpstrings part
   No other hand may sweep : thou dost enfold
   Thy being in Heaven's glory, having rolled
Earth's languors from thy spirit pure and white,
   And wreathed the amaranth around the gold :
Yet mid the choral spheres of thy new sight,
Thy breast beats earthward still—love grows intense with
    light.

Aurora ! imaged by the mystic Sea
    Self-poised, unfathomable, vast and wild ;
With giant march and prophet monody
    Surging o'er countless Æons underpiled ;
    Yet glassing the cloud's bosom where have smiled
Red Sunset's amorous lips, as where in awe
    Dark Thunder's feet have passed, and flowing mild
On smooth-ribbed sands which lapping wavelets draw,
And gravitating still to God and central Law.

Aurora ! on thy youthful brow was flung
    Light from the Phidian marbles ; thy quick ear
Caught the great wood-god's music ; and thy tongue
    Touched with Hymettian sweetness, warbled clear
    The thunder-tones that else had been austere :—
Our nobler Sappho ! it alone was thine
    To wreathe Dione's rose round Ate's spear ;
To fill with holier names each empty shrine,
And show of templed Greece how much is still divine.

Nor less the Ausonian glory moved thy verse,
    And fired thine eye, but what Lucretius sang,
Or Seneca, became thee to rehearse,
    And stainless thoughts in faultless accents rang
    Through Sirmian ode as Tusculan harangue :—
O rare interpreter of **Arts**' old charm—'
    Of Life's old meaning ! who without the pang
Hast seized the pleasure, and with pulses warm
Poured the old œnomel, nor mingled loss or harm !

Thence down the lustrous Ages thou hast passed,
    Drawing their light to thee, till Petrarch's fire,
And Camoens' grace, and Dante's gloom were massed
    In one Immortal; but thy soul's desire
    Was not alone to sound a sensuous lyre—
Was not for wine or roses, though they be
    Of Chios or of Pæstum;—higher, higher,
Thou soughtst o'er golden land and purple sea,
The beauty crowning all—a People one and free!

And this hath been thy weak hands' latest task—
    Thy life's maturest purpose; even this
Hath dimmed thee to *their* eyes in ease who bask,
    Non-interveners, whom the serpent's hiss
    More than the serpent's wisdom, suits.   It is
A glory and a joy that thou hast stood
    In Casa Guidi when the near hour of bliss
Struck not; and from the heights of womanhood
And song, hast poured thy wrath's and pity's lava-flood.

So in the triumph of the aftertime;
    Statesman's not less than Bard's, thy voice was heard,
When Florence told the world by shout sublime,
    Babe Freedom in Italia's womb had stirred;
    Thine was the loftiest, purest prophet-word:—
And art thou dead by Dante's Stone!—Oh sure
    As Dante's be thy fame! A glorious third,
Live thou with Garibaldi and Cavour,
Deathless while Adria flows—while Apennines endure!

And hath not England too a claim in thee,
   True English Heart, and Queen of English Song!
Loud-echoing from the Isles secure and free,
   Unnumbered lips thy eulogy prolong:—
   Yes, we are free, but Error, Pain, Lust, Wrong,
Walk ghastly with us, and intrepid, thou
   Hast dealt them anger high, and satire strong—
Hast plucked the social mask from Falsehood's brow,
And broken Fashion's wand, and laid Oppression low!

Nor didst thou, hating more, love less, than she,
   Felicia, thy sweet sister, but thy prayer
Rose ever thus—Let man and woman be
   Gentle, unselfish, pure, that earth and air
   Blush not for their weak lords! O Spirit fair,
Still as the suffering children's choral cry
   Rings to the Mercy-seat in long despair,
Be thy most anguished pleading heard on high—
Be thou in angel-robes sent down to soothe their sigh!

Yes, it will come! the day for each and all—
   For nation as for child; though Misery's weeping
Blur yet the apparent dawn; and Doubt's cold pall
   Would veil it; and the Spheres sublimely sweeping,
   Curving round God in music, find us sleeping,
Rocked on our petty groovelines to and fro:—
   Yes, it will come! and thou, great Poet, keeping
Watch on the crystal towers, shalt joy to know
The triumph thou hast helped and heralded below!

AFTER CHRISTMAS.

TAKE the decorations down!
   Finished is the sacred show,
Leaves are limp and berries brown,
   Christmas waned a month ago;
Dim the Altar's blazoned dyes,
   Dumb each monogram and scroll,
Stars no more detain our eyes,
   Crosses move not now our soul.

As the symbols fade or die,
   Fades their symbolism too;
Heaven's shadowy pleasures fly,
   Faith is old, but Fact is new.
So to the irrevocable years
   Let our Christmas vision pass;
Breath of storms, and blur of tears,
   Fleet not faster o'er Life's glass.

Mid the lapsing rains and snows
   Lapseth our high Festival;
What to soul and sense disclose
   Changeful moons, succeedeth still;
Violets deck the Easter-time,
   Roses warm the Whitsun days,
Duly with the accustomed chime
   Rise the accustomed prayer and praise.

Christmas cometh once a year,
    Wide-acknowledged as the Lord's,
Twines the holly-garland dear,
    Tunes the anthem's subtle chords,
Lifts the rustic carol's plaint,
    Fills the winecup, feeds the flame,
Leads, in Fashion's robes of saint,
    Her whom Charity we name.

It is acted. *Ilicet!*
    Take the decorations down;
Have we not devoutly met,
    Owned the Cross, desired the Crown;
Scanned our duty, mourned our sin,
    Made our Christmas peace with Heaven,
Blessed our neighbour, loved our kin,
    Warmly wished, and freely given?

Now again in levels low,
    (Who may bear the heights sublime!)
Chase we shapes that beckoning go
    Down new vistas drawn by Time:
All the brood of Business wait,
    Interests plot, and Passions burn,
Life delays not, Work is Fate,
    Feasts and Fasts will have their turn!

Would an Angel might descend
    To our heart's weed-tangled pool!
Well it were the proud to bend,
    Punish knave, and quicken fool:

Better, better were we stirred
    From that state than Lethe worse,
Whereon the Almighty Word
    Launched the Laodicean curse!

Neither hot nor cold!—Alas!
    'Tis the distemper of our time;
What though ancient bounds we pass—
    Sound Earth's deeps—mid Planets climb:—
Are we nearer central God,
    Or by devils less enticed;
Tempt we not His fiery rod,
    Keeping Christmas, spurning Christ!

Keeping, for Convention's term,
    Festively those hours august;
Grafting pale Religion's germ
    On the blooming tree of Lust;
Spurning in the world's wide camps,
    Footprints of the feet Divine,
And with Passion's gaudy lamps
    Colouring the Light benign.

Steeped in Habit, swathed in Form,
    Ever from our babehood's bands,
When do aspirations warm
    Bend our knees or clasp our hands!
Saintly windows stain the East,
    Music's faultless notes enthral,
Languidly the white-stoled priest
    Breathes his frigid rhythmic drawl:

Unacknowledged idols plan
　　This our worship dim and pale,
Thrusting between God and Man
　　Rite on rite, and veil on veil.
Ah the solemn Litanies
　　That but choral lessons teach!
Ah the prayers that cannot rise
　　Fettered at the gates of Speech!

What though holy signs be worn—
　　Frontlets to the world professed!—
Darker characters are borne
　　On our bosom's palimpsest.
Brain and heart we duly bring
　　To the temples Mammon rears,
In God's House but offering
　　Curious eyes and itching ears.

If mid consecrated walls,
　　O'er the Bible's open page
Rarely light of Heaven falls,
　　Pointing depths pure thoughts may gauge;
Little force in house or street,
　　Dustbound and unused, it hath—
Flickering lamp unto our feet,
　　Doubtful light unto our path.

Half the Master's words we learn,
　　Slip from life like nursery rhymes,
Half, we dare to deem, concern
　　Other peoples, other times:

Rendering them in every speech,
   May we not interpret too—
Persons, nations, each for each—
   What to credit, what to do?

Letter here, and spirit there;
   Human gloss, and text Divine;—
Who shall purify and clear—
   Who shall fix and disentwine?
Though we heap our virtues high,
   Circumstance the measure strikes;
Hearts may yearn toward the sky,
   Feet are cramped mid Fashion's dykes.

Peace! for what avails to fling
   Censure at Convention's face;
Let the crowd dance round their ring,
   Swell their chorus—run their race:
Be it ours to stand aside—
   Not as stood the Pharisee—
Ours to make the Christmas-tide
   One with life, whate'er life be!

Valley, which green hills invest,
   Crags and summits tempest-torn;
River, from their twilight breast
   Falling southward to the morn!
Haunts of voices manifold
   Loud where human lips are dumb;
Heights, whence pure eyes may behold
   Ages vanished and to come!—

I have loved you long, nor less
    For that in your midst there stands
One grey lowly Church to bless
    Aran's legendary lands :—
Nestling 'neath the hill's sharp crest,
    Girt by yews in solemn form,
Offering peace and faith and rest
    In the solitude and storm.

When the summer cloud sailed by
    O'er the mountain's purple bloom ;
When the tender April sky
    Drew wild flowers from each green tomb :
It was good to worship here
    With the simple-hearted throng,
Whose glad voices rising clear,
    Met the lark's descending song.

But when Winter's seal was set
    On all life save Dovey's flow,
When the midnight clouds were met
    O'er the league-long wastes of snow ;
Gathered, braving toil and harm,
    Dame and grandsire, youth and child,
From each far-off cot and farm,
    Through the dark, across the wild !—

Gathered where the glimmering lights
    Marked the expecting Church, and where
Voice the holiest that invites—
    Rose the bell on the troubled air.

'Twas a joy to enter then—
   What though faint and travelworn!—
In His Name, Who died for men,
   Who to-day 'mong men was born.

Earnestly the pastor spake,
   Earnestly the people heard,
And all Nature seemed to wake
   Heedful to the Angelic Word:
There no reason-maiming rite,
   Soul-suppressing monotone—
Luxury's lures of sound or sight—
   Ushered Sin before the Throne.

There no courtly Folly stalked,
   Scowled not Envy, crouched not Pain;
There no vows to Mammon balked
   Prayers perfunctory and vain.
But the loud responses rose,
   Where the heart responded first,
And when came the appointed close,
   Every voice in carol burst:—

Singing mercies manifold,
   Christ the crucified and crowned;
Singing on through gloom and cold,
   While the frostwind sang around.
What if verse and tune were rude,
   More sublime the disaccord;
All the theme was gratitude,
   All the song was to the Lord!

AFTER CHRISTMAS.

And when now, the Vigil done,
    Ere they trod their homeward way,
Joined in greeting every one,
    On the happy Christmas Day:—
Greeting, not Decorum's vest,
    Not the mask of Selfishness,
But inspired by Him Whose best
    Blessing is the power to bless.

Musing then I closed my eyes—
    How these mountain children kept
Christmas in that simple guise,
    While the City danced or slept:—
How, evolved from daily life,
    And impressing life again,
'Twas no transient spirit-strife,
    No excitement vague and vain:
Not the gala-fire exhaled
    From Earth's darkness, dying soon,
But the Star the wise men hailed,
    Rising to perpetual noon.

BARDSEY.

BEYOND the extremest bound of Arvon lies
Enlli, the Island of the Bards, the grave
Of saints and princes of the heroic time ;
Parted from Lleyn by seas that heave and pour
Implacable, and parted from our life
By the stern centuries' ever-restless flow.

It is a sad and lonely islet, girt
Westward with many a gaunt outlying rock,
Whose slimy clefts the seething waves o'erleap
White-crested, wearing slow with hungry rage ;
And, pierced by many a cave, its wasted sides
Resound through night and day and moons and years,
Still wasting ; while to east and north the land
Is gathered to a mountain whose sheer steep
Defies the ocean, and whose stone-crowned head,
Though lashed by rain and smit by lightning, looks
Calmly across the Sound, as friend scans friend,
On the great cliff that guards the sombre shore,
The Cangan Promontory of old fame.[1]

[1] Braich y Pwll, the most westerly point of North Wales.

Few be the tenants of the soil, and few
Their needs; plain speech and simple ends, and light
To use the Present which God gave, and trust
To Him the rest, unquestioning, content,
Is theirs.   On the hill-slope their cottage walls
Securely nestling bound their utmost wish;
And Nature satisfies from earth and sea
Whate'er of daily human wants she wakes;
And at the last their bones in faith are laid
At Aberdaron, and their island home
Holds scarce a trace of them or of their work.

Enlli is not to these, but to the dead,
The innumerable dead who crowd her shore;
Who speak from the rude circle earthfast yet,
Of rolling spheres and circling Deity;
Who tell from daisied barrows of their fame
And honour, chieftains of the old battle-time;
Who write their legend on the abiding stone
Of sweet asylum, and of praise to God;[1]
Who throng above the sea-marge where the waves
Have bared the immemorial cemeteries,
And people our new day with storied shapes
Of monk flame-chased from books and cells; and maid
Flying from Lust's swift feet, and childless sire
From trampled home; and patriot overborne
By heathen hosts; and interdicted bard;
All finding sanctuary and solace here,
And recompense; all mingling here their bones.

[1] As appears from relics in my possession.

But most from midst the ruined Abbey set
On the green hill in Mary's blessed name,
Come to our soul those voices eloquent :
What if the sea-storms maddening insult
The roofless Chapel, and the rising sun
Shine sadly on the degraded altar-stone !
Yet, hallowed once, the desert spot remains
Holy for ever; and who bends him now
In faith and love shall hear the matin-bell,
And the quick hastening feet, and then the psalm
High rolling, and the interceding prayer,
Mixed with the deep-toned cadence of the sea.
And clear across his vision there shall pass
The old heroic founders of the pile,
The lifelong guardians of the Faith it kept ;—
Einion the prince, who laid his coronet
Before the Lord with prayer for grace and light ;
Cadvan as nobly born, who from the towers
Of kindred Arvor led her valiant sons
To plant new Churches on the Cymric soil,
Strengthening by holier ties the ties of blood ;
And Dyvrig,[1] great Archbishop of the West,
Who having ruled in Llandaff's primal seats,
And ruled in Roman Caerlleon's Christian fanes,
Silenced Heresiarch, and fought for Truth
As stedfastly as Arthur, whose dear head
He crowned mid sounding harps and clashing arms ;
Passed hither to the lonely island's peace,
And thence passed gently to the peace of Heaven.

[1] Dubricius.

Then came the long procession winding down
From Llëyn's unpeopled ways to Daron's strand;—
Came ever winding through a thousand years.
From farthest Alban and Ierne pressed
The pilgrims.   On the beach their tents were white;
Their sails thronged all the bay till east winds blew:
And mid Saint Hywyn's columns rose their prayers,
And in Saint Mary's mountain Chapel[1] hung
Their offerings, and before the expectant Isle,
On the great headland flashed their beacon-fires.

O ancient Abbey of the Sea! 'twas thine
To enshrine and tend the sacred flame from God,
And dedicate its beams to distant hearts,
And rescue darkling lives, even as the Light,
The kindling eye of Science at thy feet,
Looks stedfast from its tower, in our time,
On far-off ships across the sunless waves.
Oh that my wandering steps might here be stayed—
Life's broken circle be completed here!
That I might render back at last my soul,
Wiser, maturer, holier, to its Source:
That I might watch the process of the stars,
And tempests' birth, and flight of wings, and flow
Of many-coloured waters round my feet,
And the long lapse of seasonable change;
Learning from all how all are part of Man,
Attuned to sense, and interfused with mind,
Formed for his good, and tempered by his will!

---

[1] Eglwys Fair.

And here the sweet magic of my books should bring
Upon the mirror of the Present, stained
No more by Care's ignoble images,
A lucid reflex of the Past, and dim
Presentment of the Future, brightening still
As eyes grow purer; and with these should come
A deeper knowledge, and a loftier hope.
Far, far from seats where wolf-eyed Vice exults,
And Folly in the dust her idiot trail
Makes and remakes for ever, I would rest;
And far from regions where distempered Man
Draws o'er him smoke-clouds drear, and the swart earth
Vexes with passionate hunger for its wealth,
Or with dull apathy and silent hate,
As Circumstance hath made him slave or lord.
Yet not from Love's sweet sympathies remote
The hours should lapse: my fitting task were here,
A man of Enlli, to sustain my kind,
To mitigate for them laborious needs,
To help their interludes of harp and song,
To teach the youth their country's annals fair,
And what the double duties which beseem
Cambria's true children, and Earth's citizens;
And prompt the old to gild life's narrowing track
With the near glories of the larger World.

Alas! it cannot be.   The Isle remains
A pleasant Autumn-memory, and no more.

Yet tempered was that pleasant Autumn-tide
By other themes than joy and holiday :
One left us then, stricken with languid death,
O'er his famed task of bardic study bent.
AB ITHEL! sure no meeter soul than thine
The bright consummate Gwynfyd hath attained !
A true embodiment of all of high,
Fervid, and pure, which Druid Culture held ;
A Christian priest clean-handed, self-restrained ;
Wise antiquary, stedfast patriot, bold
To speak, not less than generous to feel :
While Fashion piped her cuckoo-plaint, he tuned
His life to nobler harmonies ; when modes
And systems ruled by turns, he pleaded still
For changeless Law and archetypal Truth.
He should have slept in Enlli with his race
Whose earnest life he lived, whose speech he shared,
Whose learning he inherited.   But no !
More fitly rests he where the Sabbath bells
Call his familiar people to their Church,
Who point with love and pride his plain headstone.
That love, repaying his own love, may yet
Pass with the generation whom he blessed :
That pride shall live while CYMRU keeps her name —
While the broad wave of Celtic Scholarship
Rolls over Europe backward to the East !

'Tri pheth sydd ymgadarnâu beunydd, gan fod mwyaf yr ymgais attynt: Cariad, Gwybodaeth, a Chyfiawnder.'[1]

Cyfrinach Beirdd Ynys Prydain.—TRIAD 43.

THE following Articles are intended to illustrate the facts, or amplify the opinions, advanced in the preceding Verses. Most of them are extracted and re-arranged from my 'Life and Writings of Ab Ithel,' a portion of which has appeared in the 'Cambrian Journal' of 1862, 1863, and 1864. The letters on the Welsh language and Welsh literary Societies were addressed by me to the 'Caernarvon and Denbigh Herald' in 1858.

---

[1] Mr. Matthew Arnold would have done well to add 'Justice' to the 'Sweetness' and 'Light' of his perfect Humanity, and so to reproduce the better formula of this Triad.

ART AND SCIENCE OF THE BRITONS.

'And Science then had half unveiled her face.'—PAGE 4.

THE speculations regarding the autochthonal settlements of the Cymry in Britain, and the accounts of the Druidic and Bardic systems may, or may not, seem reasonable to the modern historian; and the authenticity of such documents as the Triads and *Iolo MSS.* may, or may not, be convincing to the modern critic.

But whatever may be said of the more recondite portion of the themes traversed by such writers as Ab Ithel, there can be little question of the genuineness and interest of his *Annals* when he tells of the rural and civil arts of the Cymry; and it is these that I would more particularly commend to the calm attention of the English student.

Whatever may be thought of Tydain and Brân ab Llyr, as to when they lived, or whether they lived at all, there can be no doubt of the poetry and of the warlike valour of the sixth century; and however much the faith or practice of the Druids may be distrusted or defamed, it is certain that pure Christianity, at first blending with it, and at last displacing it, was maintained in these Islands with more or less lustre, through four hundred years preceding the Saxon invasion. Again, the legislation of the wise Alfred, founded upon that of Ethelbert and Ina, endeared him to his people, and is remembered wherever the Saxon race prevails.

But the laws of Hywel Dda, derived from sources long anterior to the rule of the Romans, and expanded from statutes binding among the Cymry from times when the ancestors of Hengist were rearing idols in the Germanian forests, are yet nobler than the laws of Alfred, and enter more largely into the living jurisprudence of Britain. To adopt the words of a learned writer,—'The Triads and the Laws of Hoel are as superior to the Anglo-Saxon Institutes

as the elegies of Llywarch Hên and the odes of Taliesin are to the
ballads of the Edda.'[1] It is indeed interesting to observe how
much of the code of Hywel, especially in the law of property and
of evidence, remains in familiar practice. The mode of trial by
Jury, for which the Anglo-Saxons generally get exclusive credit,
appears to have been applied by the Britons, in all its fulness, to
nearly every description of civil and criminal procedure.

The industrial and material resources of Ancient Britain are
exemplified in the Annals by well-chosen excerpts from classical
not less than from native records. Strabo says of the Island that
'it produces corn and cattle, and gold, and silver, and iron; which
things are brought thence.' Pliny gives like testimony.

Herodotus refers in a celebrated passage to the exportation of
tin from the Cassiterides. Cæsar, along with numerous allusions
to the intellectual training of the higher classes, speaks of the
agriculture of the Britons, and of their war chariots, of which
Cassivellaunus alone had 4,000. Carriages imply roads and an
advanced state of handicraft in wood and metals. Propertius
sings of the elaborate form and device of the British harness, for
the Britons were noted for the breeding and management of
horses, as well as for chariots. Cicero in his letters to his friends,
who were in Britain with Cæsar, bears witness to the mechanical
resources of the natives, when he speaks of the *mirificis molibus*,
with which the harbours were fortified; and I need hardly name
the great megaliths of Avebury and Stonehenge as works of a
more difficult class.[2] The Tre'r Caeri on the Eifl mountains in
Caernarvonshire, the finest existing type of a British fortress, may
also be mentioned. Wind-mills and water-mills belong probably
to a later date, as do the gay dresses, and golden armour and
ornaments, the glass drinking cups, amber beads, and instruments
of music, so freely named in the poetry of the sixth century.
A Bard was prohibited from three things—mechanics, war, and

---

[1] Flintoff, *Rise and Progress of the Laws of England and Wales*, p. 45.
Sir Francis Palgrave, in *Rise and Progress of the English Commonwealth*,
p. 37, adopts almost the same words.

[2] While I admire the learning and acuteness of Herbert, I must
utterly dissent from the theory in his *Cyclops Christianus*, that these
monuments are the production of a race posterior to the Romans in
Britain.

commerce;[1] but he was permitted to hunt, and cultivate his land, five free acres being presented to him by the country in virtue of his office, and testimony of his worth. These regulations show at once the exalted conception entertained by the Britons of the bardic dignities and duties, and the existence of a high material civilisation.

I may glance also at medicine, in which it is certain that the Druids were proficient—at least as regards the use of herbs. Pliny particularly mentions the mistletoe as being called, in Druidical language, *omnia sanantem*. It is curious that *oll iach, heal-all*, is a modern name of this plant. In the traditional accounts, too, of the use of letters, and of the *Peithynen*, a wooden book, or system of movable framed bars on which the letters were cut, whence the alphabet was called *Coelbren*, or 'wood of credibility,' there is a curious expansion of the well-known statement of Cæsar respecting the literature of the Druids. And as a proof of the singular richness and refinement of the early British tongue, I may notice its power of expressing high numbers by vocables evolved with accumulative force from the primitive roots, in which it as far surpasses the English as the English does the Polynesian.

In the most exalted subject of human investigation, astronomy, the details of the Cymric study are full of interest, as witness the names given to the constellations, and the celebration of the 'three blessed astronomers, Gwydion, Idris, and Gwyn.' Cæsar says of the Druids, that they taught 'multa praeterea de sideribus atque eorum motu.'

The word for *time, am-ser, about the stars*, has an excellence both in philosophy and philology, hardly approached by any other tongue, ancient or modern: as similarly, the etymon *Duw* (Dy-yw) intensifies the Name of the Divine I AM in a manner not to be paralleled in any language nearer to us than those of primeval origin.

---

[1] Two, however, of the most eminent bards of that time, Aneurin and Llywarch Hên, were warriors, though they fought not so successfully as they sang. Later names also are closely associated with lays of battle. But the bards of the Druidic system were teachers and philosophers, not merely poets.

ANEURIN AND THE GODODIN.

' The battle-harp of Bard, the torque of Chieftain free.'—PAGE 8.

THE great name of Aneurin will suggest itself here. The battle of Cattraeth, which he celebrates in the *Gododin*, was, indeed, fought at about the same time as was Arthur's fatal battle of Camlan.

The *Gododin* is hardly yet known as it ought to be to English scholars. Ossian rests upon nothing older than Macpherson. It is a work essentially and substantially of the eighteenth century, for no sufficient account has ever been given of its origin, and no MS. ever produced to justify its pretensions. As a modern poem the work is *sui generis*, and deserves, perhaps, its extraordinary popularity; as an ancient specimen it is well nigh worthless. On the other hand the *Gododin*, in its rudeness and fragmentary state, and in its native original tongue, presents the best claim to our acknowledgment of it as a true poem of the sixth century—unquestionably the oldest in Europe, since the brilliant roll of Latin classics was terminated by Clemens or by Claudian.

The earliest MS. existing of the *Gododin* is on vellum, and of about the year 1200. This is of course a transcript of other older transcripts, and the effect of these successive copies is plain in the textual obscurities which prevail; while the loss before the thirteenth century, of perhaps two-thirds of the poem, renders the remainder very unconnected and abrupt.

But fragment though it be, it is a noble fragment. It stands alone, a monument of the heroic Muse of Britain at the darkest period of her history, stemming the oncoming tide of oblivion which was soon to quench the voice of song on her lips.

The name of Chaucer is an immortal name, and the father of English poetry is in some respects the father of English civilisation: but, 200 years before Chaucer, when the Saxon had yielded to the

Norman after one battle, and the old Teutonic tongue was breaking up, the Cymric tongue rose to its highest development; and nurtured by a people's struggles and aspirations, which years were needed to repress, and which centuries have not yet extinguished, this tongue became the mighty exponent of martial prowess, of social affection, and of religious fervour. Thus has it ever remained down to the present day, and the mountaineer of Glamorgan or Merioneth can still enjoy the glowing effusions of Cynddelw and of Gwalchmai, while Gower and Chaucer are sealed books even to Englishmen of learning and taste. Yet although the Augustan age of letters in Wales be more closely connected with the present age, we turn with deeper interest to the old Bards who laid the foundation of it five hundred years before, and think how from the time that the verses of Ovid and Virgil ceased to be the delight of the student of Caerlleon, and the solace of the legionary on the Northern Wall, down to the day of the great princes Alfred and Hywel Dda; no poets save those of Celtic blood broke the savage silence, or relieved the thick gloom.[1]

---

[1] Perhaps I ought to except Cædmon.

(The two best—and indeed the only complete translations of the *Gododin* are both of our day, being respectively the work of M. de la Villemarqué and of the Rev. John Williams ab Ithel.)

THE EISTEDDFOD.

And in their great Eisteddfod to honour Art and Song.'—Page 22.

The bardic session, or congress, called the Eisteddfod, descends, it is believed, to the Cymry of to-day, from the period of Owain ap Maxen Wledig, or Owain Vinddu (the Blacklipped), who, according to the Triads, was elected to the chief sovereignty of the Britons at the close of the fourth century. The Eisteddfod has always been devoted to the study and practice of the poetry, music, and literature of the Cymry, to the preservation of the national language and usages, and to the promotion of patriotism and independence in the sons and daughters of the soil.

Associated with the Eisteddfod, and having a yet remoter origin, is the Gorsedd, which is more exclusively a convention of the bardic fraternity (in the larger sense of the term *bardd*), who were the depositaries of all poetic knowledge and historic tradition, the preservers of genealogies, the directors of religious culture, and the teachers of technical arts.[1]

Thus the Gorsedd is virtually the ancient assembly of the Druids, tempered by the holier principles of Christianity, and enlightened by larger secular knowledge.

It cannot be doubted that, with such functions, the Gorsedd and

---

[1] Properly speaking, the Eisteddfod is derived from the Gorsedd, as is that branch institution the *Chair*, which is appropriated to certain divisions of the country, as the Chair of Powys, of Gwynedd, of Morganwg. The well-known passage of Lucan pleasingly refers to one practice of the Celtic bards :—

Vos quoque, qui fortes animas belloque peremptas,
Laudibus in longum, Vates, dimittitis ævum,
Plurima securi fudistis carmina Bardi.

P

the Eisteddfod acquired a considerable social power, and perhaps played an effective part in certain critical epochs.

Fostered by the native princes, and loved by the nation, these institutions helped to maintain both the power of the ruler and the integrity of the people. When the great Llywelyn line passing into the Tudor branch, proved rather England won than Wales lost, the bardic congresses were well supported by the two Henries and by Elizabeth, and they have been continued, though under more adverse conditions, down to the present generation. One of the earliest meetings is that recorded by Iorwerth Beli, which was held upon the hill of Dyganwy, in the sixth century, by Maelgwn Gwynedd, perhaps after he had triumphed in battle in the marshes of Creuddyn.

Cadwaladr, who much improved bardism, held a celebrated Eisteddfod in the seventh century. Bleddyn ap Cynfyn and Gruffydd ap Cynan made further modifications, in the eleventh century. They enacted that no person should follow the profession of bard or minstrel but such only as were admitted by the Eisteddfod, which was to be held once in three years. In 1176, Rhys, Prince of South Wales, convened at Aberteifi, after formal notice of a year and a day, a very complete Eisteddfod, the particulars of which have been recorded. The prizes for poetry were here won by North Wales, and those for music by South Wales—a distinction that has been maintained even to our day. Another great Eisteddfod was held at Caermarthen in the fifteenth century. The town of Caerwys in Flintshire had long been famous as one of the chief seats of the Eisteddfod, and in the fifteenth year of Henry VIII. a meeting was held there at which the ancient bardic laws were confirmed. But the greatest was held in 1568, under the direct authority of Elizabeth, who acted with characteristic sagacity; and the proceedings of this Eisteddfod—which is the last, I believe, held at Caerwys save one—have been also recorded with minuteness.

In the beginning of the second half of the eighteenth century the Cymmrodorion Society was organised to promote Welsh social and literary interests, and later on, the Gwyneddigion, Cymreigyddion, and other societies co-operated in the work. Under the auspices of these bodies, which numbered some of the best scholars and ablest men that Wales has produced, many Eisteddfodau took place, the most notable being Caerwys in 1798,

Caermarthen in 1819, Wrexham in 1820, London in 1822, Welsh-pool in 1824, Denbigh in 1828, Beaumaris in 1832, Cardiff in 1834, Swansea in 1842.[1] In the following fifteen years there does not appear to have been any Eisteddfod of note except Aberffraw (1849), or Rhuddlan (1852), and except the brilliant meetings of the Cymreigyddion of Abergavenny; the chief causes being the growing rivalries and dissensions of the parties into which Wales is unhappily divided upon almost all questions, literature not ex-cepted, and the growing pressure of the demands of business-life upon the middle classes. Whatever was done was upon a local and sectional, rather than on a national and comprehensive scale, and was in little harmony with the typical idea of an Eisteddfod.

The Rev. John Williams ab Ithel conceived in 1857 the idea of restoring the old Eisteddfod, and giving it place as a permanently recurring festival. He found able and willing coadjutors in a small group of clergymen, his personal friends, and it was deter-mined to hold an Eisteddfod on the largest scale, in the following year, at Llangollen.

The result was a festival which will long be remembered by all who witnessed it—by the Welsh as a bright resuscitation of the past, and an auspicious earnest of the future : by the English as a rare example of genius and ability, hitherto unsuspected or denied, and of deep-seated and compact nationality unparalleled under the British Crown.

The great feature of this festival, however, was not the bards,

---

[1] These gatherings were distinguished by the presence of many emi-nent men in rank and talents, by the excellence of the compositions invoked, and by the general attention excited. Mrs. Hemans wrote some beautiful lines for the London Eisteddfod of 1822. Professor Rees' celebrated *Essay on the Welsh Saints* was produced at the Swansea Meeting. The Princess Victoria took part in the proceedings of the Beaumaris Eisteddfod. Peers and prelates enrolled themselves among the Cymmrodorion; poets, antiquaries, and philanthropists gave them sympathy and support. The Eisteddfod became, in the slang of the present day, *respectable*. Yet we do not find in it any statistics, or 'social science,' or encyclopædiology, or educational parade. Can *our* Eisteddfod attain so brilliant a *status*, and grow in popularity without declining in nationality? It is the problem which the new Permanent Committee have to work out.

or the musicians, or the orators, or the visitors, but the audience, the four or five thousand crowded within the spacious tent.

That a few enthusiasts should meet together to rehearse the ancient ceremonies of the Gorsedd, or invoke the competitive Muses of the Eisteddfod, is perhaps neither surprising nor important. But that thousands of the Welsh *people* should come from the plough, and the loom, and the forge, and the shop, from distant homes and daily duties, with little money, and with the certainty of inconvenience and expense, in order to take part in a celebration which, to an English understanding, offers little more than a concert mixed with recitations and speeches, is indeed a convincing proof of the depth and extent of nationality in Wales. As each vehement address was delivered, or clever *englyn* exploded, or well-contested prize adjudged, the appreciation of the audience was emphatically marked; nor seemed there less interest manifested, though it was of a calmer sort, in the essays, poems, and adjudications read. But it was when the harpists struck together some endeared household melody, some ravishing strain of a thousand years ago, as Gray said; or when the master-hand among them evoked some plaintive refrain of afflicted love or despairing valour; and chiefly when the trained singers of the Principality greeted their countrymen and country-women in songs where all Eisteddfodic elements were blended—poetry, music, eloquence, wit—it is then that the vast assembly seemed to throb with one pulse, *calon wrth galon*, heart to heart, and to glow with the inextinguishable fire of the Cymric race.

The effect of the Llangollen meeting upon Eisteddfodic progress was prompt and emphatic.

Stimulated by the unqualified success of Ab Ithel's great experiment, the other leaders of Cymric literature and song proceeded to organise and perpetuate the old Institution thus auspiciously revived. Denbigh, Conway, Aberdare, and Caernarvon Eisteddfodau were the result, together with a multitude of local ones; and at length a measure, much discussed and often postponed, ripened into attainment, the establishment of Yr Eisteddfod on a permanent basis in Wales, subscribed to by a large and increasing list of adherents, and managed by an experienced and energetic staff.

But dear as was this object to Ab Ithel, the administration of the Eisteddfod by the Permanent Committee—so far as it has proceeded—would hardly have realised his conceptions, or satisfied his desires. The idea of the Eisteddfod pure and simple, a congress for the promotion and practice of the Welsh language, literature, oratory, art, music, and song, has been largely sophisticated by an admixture of subjects and pursuits foreign to its character, and inconsistent with its aims. It has been thought right to graft on it the functions of a Mechanics' Institute, or even of the British Association, and to dilute it unsparingly with English studies, English methods, and the English language. Such an Institution may mean well and work well, *but it is not an Eisteddfod.* I demur most heartily to the innovation. Eisteddfodau are not schools for polyglotism and philosophy, or offices for industrial training. To divide the proceedings into 'sections,' and to read 'papers,' never occurred to the Cymmrodorion. To substitute English for Welsh, to a larger extent than is plainly necessary in the conduct of the meeting, and in the language of the prize subjects, is only worthy of Welshmen who are ashamed of their name, their origin, and their mother-tongue. No reasonable person would hesitate to encourage the Welsh youth to attain as large a measure of English knowledge as their opportunities will allow, or to arm themselves with as complete an experience of the practical as their vocations require. But it is still to be shown that the Eisteddfod is the only possible place for such education, and that the perpetuation of the Eisteddfod in its genuine and legitimate character will in any degree impede the moral or material advancement of the people; make them less clever, rich, happy, and loyal—less devoted to their families, less true to their faith.[1]

Ab Ithel's Eisteddfod of 1858 was, with one or two blemishes and drawbacks, a true and good model of an Eisteddfod for the people. It had few aristocratic supporters, and in no respect courted them. It provided in its prize scheme a sufficient range of *practical* subjects, and it gave ample scope to the national genius, and paid due respect to the national sentiment. Its faults are not difficult to avoid, its excellences not impossible to attain. As a splendid fulfilment of what it was designed to be, it must take rank with the best of its predecessors, and far above any that have followed it. Its good fruits are even now manifest, and its reputation will grow as it recedes into the past.

[1] The multiplication of literary Societies and middle-class schools is an improvement of the right kind in the right direction.

In speaking of the Eisteddfod I include the Gorsedd, which, having no longer any political or judicial functions, but only the control of the Bardic Order, and the enunciation of the principles of progress and peace, may well be associated with the Eisteddfod in all worthy operations and aims.

I earnestly recommend the Committee of Yr Eisteddfod to support wisely and heartily these ancient institutions; to endeavour by them to move and stimulate, as well as to instruct, the Welsh people; and while adding to them what may be needed in form and substance, according to the lights of the present day, to take from them nothing of the time-honoured character that has descended to us, through so many eventful centuries, from our foremost Princes and Bards.[1]

[1] The most recent Eisteddfodau held under the auspices of the Committee have been still further attenuated and distorted by the copious introduction of English singers and English music, with the object, or at least the result, of making the meeting *pro tanto* a fashionable concert. It is quite time that the real Eisteddfod were again revived, and supported by the real Welshmen of the land.

WELSH STUDIES AND ENGLISH CRITICS.

'Was't not enough to flout, ignore, withstand,
And mock our speech, our history, and our song!' —Page 40.

It is a singular but well-ascertained fact, that critics and archæologists who depreciate and ridicule British (and especially Cymric)
antiquities, are almost to a man unable to read, write, or understand three words in any one of the Celtic dialects, and are utterly
incompetent to form an original opinion on the date, character, and
authority of any Celtic MS.; on the use of any difficult Celtic
relic; or on the prevalence of any Celtic custom or practice; so far
as these points may be illustrated by the historical and legendary
materials available in Britain and in Armorica.

On the other hand, it is equally true that those scholars and
archæologists who have in the course of general study found it desirable to acquire the Celtic idioms, have reported in very favour-
able terms of the contents of the museum which this key has
enabled them to unlock; and in the key itself they have discovered
beauty, strength, and value, where deformity and worthlessness
had been imputed. I would point to the little work of Mr.
William Barnes, 'Notes on Ancient Britain,' as an excellent
example of what may be done by the knowledge of language.
The author says in his preface of six lines—'If I have cast any
new light on the subjects under hand, it has been by a careful use
of my little knowledge of the British language, which, I believe,
antiquaries have too often neglected.'

> To study tribes without their speech,
> Is to grope for what our sight should teach.

In the pages of Turner, Pictet, Villemarqué, Nash, Borrow, and
many others, the same results are evident; and we see also that

not only is the Cymraeg, as it were, a good telescope to make clearer and more intelligible to us, some of the remote antiquities of Western Europe, but also, as it were, a good microscope to give us a new insight into the sterling literature and living speech of the day.

I challenge the most abusive *Saturday* Reviewer, or the acutest article-writer of the *Times*, to explain, without reference to Celtic etymology, certain Shakspearian phrases, certain household words, and common street sayings; and I challenge Dr. Giles, Mr. Thomas Wright, Mr. John Evans, and all who have compiled *adversaria* on this subject, to show that there is not, internally and externally, sufficient evidence of the genuineness of the old Triads and the old Laws of Wales, to justify our acceptance of the illustrations they offer of the ancient history, manners, coinage, and religion of our land. They may be assured that all the sarcasm and ridicule which has been heaped since the time of Ritson upon those writers who have advocated what is called the Welsh point of view, is of little avail to overthrow it. The greatest respect is due to the authors, whether English or Welsh, who, having furnished themselves with the needed weapons, meet the defenders of Cymru upon their own ground, and refute them if they can; but no respect is due to those with whom a sneer is the principal argument, and the Roman historians the only possible court of appeal. It may, indeed, be well said, that if the motto of a too credulous Middle Age was, 'Omne ignotum pro magnifico est,' the motto for an age verging on the other extreme is rather 'Omne ignotum pro *falso* est;' a proposition at least equally unsafe.

It would lead me too far to speculate much on the causes which have created so bitter and intense a feeling of dislike for Welsh archæology and Welsh scholarship in the minds of some eminent English writers.

I do not now speak of political prejudices, or political necessities; of the national question, as between England and Wales; but of the absence of cordiality, or rather the openly hostile spirit which has marked, and which still marks, the Anglo-Saxon literary treatment of nearly all Cambrian themes. Doubtless something is due to the fact, that it *is* Anglo-Saxon, and that it *is* Cambrian; for a well known philosophic truth teaches how difficult it is to eliminate from the mind, that old indigenous sentiment of ethnical hostility, which is as surely transmissible as are national customs or family features; and, despite the influence of social intercourse and political fusion, there yet remains enough of this sentiment to colour deeply the opinions of writers on both sides.[1]

But such a cause of difference is disappearing with gradual acceleration, and, at the present day, other influences must be found if we would entirely account for the animosity which misguides the pens of English authors in their treatises on Wales—an animosity, indeed, wholly one-sided and peculiar to themselves. The chief causes I take to be these two: First, the imprudent conduct of some Welsh writers in treating of their national history and antiquities from the inspiration of affection rather than judgment; in accepting, without due discrimination, a heterogeneous mixture of facts and fancies, and in dogmatising on archaic difficulties, heedless of that calm and just critical spirit which, without rejecting earnestness and zeal, suffers no ingenuity to pervert reason, and no predilection to override evidence.

Unhappily, Wales has, among even her few distinguished writers, and undoubtedly great Celtic scholars, too many who misdevote their talents and their learning rather to the cause of Cymru *yn erbyn y byd*, than of Gwir *yn erbyn y byd*. Yet it is not so with all; and if we look with regret on the Druidic vagaries of a Davies, or the historical fictions of a Morgan, we can dwell with just pride on the varied and valuable researches of both a Thomas Stephens and an Ab Ithel.

The cause in question, however, is of course obnoxious to the scholarly instincts of our best English critics, who do not, in any similar degree, err in their treatment of Saxon and Norman periods; and if this were the only cause, they would be, to a great extent, justified in their antipathy.

But the other reason, equally cogent, lies in the very nature of Welsh archæology, poetry, and ecclesiology; in the remoteness of the theme in form and spirit from modern English sympathies; in the difficulty (far less, indeed, than it seems) of the Celtic dialects; in the assumption, quite a gratuitous and false one, that nothing relevant to existing English interests and to primeval ages in general, can be extracted from the Cymric Past; and it must also be added, in the more discreditable feeling of jealousy that there should be a system conterminous with the present law,

---

[1] There are two authors, Ritson and Pinkerton, whose hatred of the Celtic race amounts to monomania. The ludicrous aberrations of the first may be pardoned; but the scurrility of the 'Inquiry into the History of Scotland' is intolerable.

literature, and religion of the Anglo-Saxon race, claiming to have had a large share in the bases of all these: that there should be a tongue said to excel in structural capacity, copiousness, melody, and strength, which the highest resources of classical scholarship are unable to master; and lastly, that there should be claimed for Ancient Britain a moral and material civilisation unborrowed from Rome or Greece, which has left a distinct though unrecognised impress upon the best forms of the civilisation of to-day.

Why, it may earnestly be asked, do not our English men of letters co-operate with, and aid, instead of obstruct and ridicule, their literary brethren, whether Welsh, Irish, Gaelic, German, or French, who devote themselves to Celtic studies? Why do they not acquire the Celtic dialects, *and principally the Cymric*, now the chief representative of the family?[1] Why do they not help, by supporting the Welsh Manuscript Society, to remove the veil of obscurity, and to dissipate the cloud of error under which, as they assert, the subject lies? Why do they not investigate for themselves, and help to discover, the many memorials of our British forefathers, whether traditionary records or structural remains, which exist, or are suspected to exist; and thus develop and extend the knowledge of the early history of mankind in general?

Surely this is no unworthy aim for our most accomplished scholars! There have been few more accomplished scholars, or men of larger experience, than he who has told us, 'Nulli quidem mihi satis eruditi videntur quibus nostra ignota sunt.'[2]

When this happy end shall have been attained, we shall perhaps have no more extreme theories on either side, but be equally freed from Trojan dynasties and Druidical exaltations, and from the ethnology of a Pinkerton and the antiquarianism of a Wright; and then, perhaps, the woad-stained Briton may vanish from our schoolbooks, and the unlettered barbarian be no more heard of in our college halls.

---

[1] 'But even if the language of the Cymry were less ancient, or its stores less valuable, yet so long as it is the living language of half a million of our fellow-Christians and fellow-subjects, it must richly deserve, and abundantly repay, whatever labour or encouragement may be bestowed on its cultivation.'—*Bishop Heber.*

'The Welsh may now be justly termed the primary and most important Celtic dialect, and its cultivation is highly desirable.'—*Brate Poste.*

[2] Cicero, 'De Legibus.'

WELSH ANNALS AND ANTIQUITIES.

> . . . . . ' *Madam, thy Cymry seek*
> *Support in these that make their state unique—*
> *Tradition, custom, language;* ' . . . . . PAGE 42.

FEW persons, indeed, out of Wales, suspect that the Welsh have *any* peculiar annals or traditions; and of those that are at all acquainted with the subject, the majority know only sufficient to dispose their mind to ridicule and unbelief. Want of time, want of candour or of patience, and, above all, the secular spirit which, averse from introspection or retrospection, links itself only with the present, and with what is called the *practical*, stand generally in the way of such studies as those under consideration. In particular it is voted very idle and ridiculous to claim any regard for Ancient Britain. Critics petulantly evade a theme which they *cannot* handle with intelligence, and *will not* with kindness; scholars sneer at a language and a literature not comprised within their curriculum; compilers of historic manuals vacantly copy one another till the story of the idolatrous Druid and the rebellious Prince is recited in every dame-school, and improved in every Bible class. Journalists are never weary of declaiming on the supremacy of the mighty Anglo-Saxon Race; and innumerable consulters of those national oracles—oracles indeed in the faculty of dubious and double utterance—are never weary of listening to the flattering statement. The student who would call attention to forgotten facts, or unacknowledged conclusions, is pitied as an enthusiast, or disliked as a bore. The age of steam and telegrams is little disposed to pause at the beginnings of war chariots and vocal song. Borne on the broad river of time we have no leisure to look back on the fountain ever mistily receding from our gaze.

Archæology is a harmless weakness, ethnology a speculative toy.

Why should we line the nests of our minds with decayed sticks from the wood, or doubtful fossils from the quarry, when last year's hay is at hand, and when penny newspapers are to be had at every corner! It is true we may dive into fathomless geological depths, argue back for myriads of years the formation of the world, and theorise on the Natural Selection of Man. We may even descend to explore the mysterious cities of Mexico, the submerged log-huts of the Swiss Lakes, or the flint implements in the drift of Saint Acheul. But to examine records, traditions, and vestiges nearer to us in time, and closer to us in relation, is thought only in the smallest degree worthy of encouragement. Thus it is that the past of the Welsh people and the Welsh land is little cared for or comprehended by the nation which has borrowed much from it, and benefited much by it, but which now seeks only to absorb it, and strip it of its separate characteristics.

How more and more true become the words of Southey:—
'One maxim of this age is that the past is good for nothing. I wish it was not a corollary with those who hold it, that the future is worth as little, and that the present is all that it behoves us to care about.'

And indeed there is also an analogous prejudice or ignorance respecting the Wales of *to-day*. Despite the many points of contact with its people, the community of pursuits, the appreciation of its tongue by continental scholars, its tourist-trodden and much-painted valleys and hills, it seems to be regarded in the same spirit though modernised, as that in which North Wales was once regarded by the inhabitants of the South—as a region of mystery, eccentricity, and superstition.

Results like these are produced and perpetuated by political theories not less than by popular prejudices. Yet surely this ought *not* to be so! Surely the ties binding together England and Wales, as England and Scotland, under one Crown and one common name of Britain, are broad and general enough to admit of the differences peculiar to the Celtic nationality, just as variety in the scenery of mountain and plain produces the greatest natural charm of the island; or just as dissimilarity in the complexion and blood of its inhabitants promotes the superior strength and beauty of the united race. And if also the individual leaders of thought and action, and all intelligent and benevolent men,

instead of standing aloof with indifference, or drawing nigh only
with the weapons of sarcasm and ill-will, would qualify themselves
to understand the antecedent literature and history of the Cymry,
and would sympathise with, and encourage, that love of liberty
and fatherland, of music, poetry, and song, of unformal religion
and home affections, of free movement and free breathing, which
gives nobility to character and refinement to manners, and which
counteracts the degrading effects of trade; they would not only
advance a great divine principle, but promote their own intellectual and social enjoyments in no ordinary degree.[1]

---

[1] 'Un singulier mauvais vouloir anime certains hypercritiques contre
les peuples d'origine celtique: on a tout disputé à ces peuples, leur
langue, leur poésie, leurs lois ; voilà qu'on se met à leur disputer leurs
tombeaux ! Il est cependant assez probable qu'ils mouraient et qu'on
les enterrait.'—De la Villemarqué, *Mémoire sur les Pierres et les
Textes celtiques :* read at the Celtic Congress of St. Brieuc, 1867.

WELSH COLLEGES, OLD AND NEW.

' *To watch o'er choir and college, cell and shrine,*
Where burned through centuries dark, Song, Learning, Faith
divine.'—PAGE 49.

THE colleges of South Wales, such as Llandovery and Lampeter, claim our particular regard as being in some measure the representatives of those ancient institutions to which the names of David, Dubricius, Padarn, Illtyd, and Teilo have given imperishable renown. Perhaps if we were to mark the two divisions of the Principality by any broad characteristics, we must assign to the *Dehenbarth* the pre-eminence in secular learning, and the glory of first receiving and fostering the early Christian faith; while to the North belong the championship of the national liberty, and the preservation of the purer forms of the national tongue. But who shall venture to infer any meritorious distinction between the lamp that lights and the sword that guards—between the valour without which knowledge is feeble and the knowledge without which valour is blind! Wales has too much reason to be proud of the fair stream of her history ever to unmingle its waters, or analyse its springs: and she has too much need of the services of her united sons ever to inquire whose are of the head, and whose are of the heart: an inquiry indeed which, in the present day, with *all* the past for a basis, would be as impossible to answer, as it would be ungracious to propose.

That a Welsh professorship at Oxford should be instituted is more and more desirable every day; but, with the growing need, comes the growing difficulty of success. Oxford is one of the centres whence are launched the envenomed arrows of sarcasm and slander from behind the safe shield of anonymous criticism: and the whole range of Welsh subjects—tradition, history, archæo-

logy, scholarship, social and political interests—topics which few
Englishmen have time to examine, or inclination to defend—are
singled out as convenient objects of attack, by the Ishmaels of
literature with whom not to abuse is not to exist.   I by no
means believe that the general public mistake wit for reason, or
audacity for power.   I think that they merely seek what is
amusing and exciting, rather than what is philosophical or in-
structive. The present is an age which, while it sharpens thought,
deadens feeling, by the hard practicalities of life ; which in all
things finds it easier to laugh and to doubt than to believe and to
admire ; and which above all things consults the pleasure of the
hour and the profit of the individual. Thus it is that the same
craving for relief from daily cares, which, taking the debasing tone
of these cares, and vulgarising the word to express it, feeds upon
sensation in a thousand forms, from the spangled rope-dancer to the
mitred bishop ; maintains also leading journals and critical reviews,
adapted to present that side of a subject which is the most ludicrous,
or the most bitter, and to sneer down any assertion of exalted
principle, profound thought, or generous feeling. which may be
at variance with the selfish and superficial standard that has
been set up.

DURATION OF LANGUAGE AND NATIONALITY IN WALES.

' The Briton's tongue shall cease not,
Nor the Briton's lineage fail.'—PAGE 61.

THE celebrated prediction of Ionas Athraw (or Mynyw) in the tenth century, long attributed to Taliesin (who certainly wrote 'Tra mor, tra Brython '), must always be referred to when this is the theme :—

Eu Nêr a volant ;
Eu hiaith a gadwant ;
Eu tir a gollant ;
Ond gwyllt Walia!

Their God they shall worship:
Their language they shall preserve ;
Their land they shall lose,
Except wild Wales.

Hardly less striking is the reply made to Henry II. in 1163, reported by Giraldus Cambrensis, of an old Welsh nobleman, who had forsaken the cause of his country and joined the army of the king, and whose testimony, therefore, may be admitted to possess considerable weight : —' Unde et Anglorum rege Henrico secundo in Australem Walliam apud Pencadair quod *Caput cathedræ* sonat, nostris diebus in hanc gentem expeditionem agente, consultus ab eo senior quidam populi ejusdem qui contra alios tamen vitio gentis eidem adhæserat, super exercitu regio, populoque rebelli si resistere posset, quid ei videretur, bellicique eventus suam ut ei declararet opinionem, respondit : " Gravari quidem, plurimaque ex parte destrui et debilitari vestris, rex, aliorumque viribus, nunc ut olim et pluries, meritorum exigentiâ, gens ista valebit. Ad plenum autem, propter hominis iram, nisi et ira Dei concurrerit, non delebitur.   Nec alia, ut arbitror, gens quam hæc Cambrica, aliave lingua, in die districti examinis coram Judice Supremo, quicquid de ampliori contingat, pro hoc terrarum angulo respondebit." '— *Cambriæ Descriptio*, lib. II. cap. x.

The prediction of Ionas Mynyw has been distinctly verified as regards the worship and the language of the Britons; but if he indeed wrote the *Awdl Vraith*, I cannot see the force of the last part of the prediction. *A gollant, they will lose*, should be, *A gollasant, they have lost*, for the subjugation of the Loegrian Britons had been complete for at least two hundred years.   It seems difficult, however, to suppose that the writer could refer to accomplished facts, in the terms of the four preceding and the two succeeding stanzas. 'O Lord God! how grievous and miserable will be the fate of the Trojan race. A wily, proud, and cruel German Serpent with her armed train, will overrun all South Britain and the Lowlands of Scotland, from the German Ocean to the Severn. Then will Britons be held, like captives, in the power of aliens from Saxony. Their God will they worship, their language will they retain, and their land will they lose, except the wilderness of Wales; until such time, after long suffering, that the sins of both be had in equal balance. Then shall Britons recover their territories and crown, and the strangers shall dwindle away.'— *Myvyrian Archæology*, vol. i. Translation of Edward Jones, *Bardic Museum*, page 33.

· Let others rove from foreign spot to spot.'—PAGE 133.

THE more imposing dimensions of the Alps do not *on that account* afford finer views, or threaten greater difficulties, than may be met on our Scottish and Cambrian hills. It is not scale, but conformation, season, and accessory groupings, that make up the beauties and terrors of a mountain,[1] and our Europe-roving tourists would do well to remember that their native heights possess qualities in this respect quite as attractive as those for which they abandon them in their annual flight. I could present our wandering ladies in search of the *picturesque*, with Welsh extracts from the book of Nature, so varied and so fair, that the single disadvantage attending them of being readable at home without a foreign translation, may well be excused; and I could introduce our ardent youths of the Alpine Club who would consent, *pour la rareté de la chose*, to forego for one season the expense of Chamouni, and their desperate attempts upon the tremendous and unconquerable Matterhorn,[2] to the incidents of a descent into the crater of Cader Idris, under a thick autumn mist, or of twelve hours' exploration of Snowdon in a genuine freezing winter.

---

[1] Mr. J. O. Halliwell has some excellent remarks on this subject at the commencement of his 'Notes of Family Excursions in North Wales.'

[2] Written in 1862. The Matterhorn is now added to the conquests of the Alpine men who, emulous of Hannibal,

I eem nothing done while aught remains to do.

TWO WINTER DAYS ON SNOWDON.

'Come hither fearless in the time of snows.'—PAGE 141.

I HAVE long been of opinion, that the winter scenery of the North Cambrian Hills surpasses in real grandeur, and in beauty not only of form but of colour, any that is presented during the summer and autumn months. And I therefore believe that tourists would do well to diverge a little from the beaten track and fashionable custom, and to extend the Welsh 'season,' or rather add a new one, by exploring the country at a time when some of the most impressive Alpine effects may be realised with all the enjoyment they afford. It is true that for this purpose a real winter of snow, frost, and ice, with clear skies and an equable temperature, is essential—conditions which of late years have not been easy to obtain; but it is always possible to select at least a few days when the mountains wear the desired aspect, and do not threaten more than an ordinary degree of danger or difficulty to the traveller who would penetrate their recesses and conquer their heights.

Among seventeen distinct excursions in North Wales I look back with the greatest satisfaction upon those made in Caernarvonshire and Merioneth at a period when the hotels were empty and the coaches laid up, when a freezing north wind swept vainly over the great tarn of Cader Idris, and when Eryri wore his coronal of spotless snow. The last, however, of my excursions has been the most gratifying of all, owing to the decided characteristics of winter which will make the Christmas-tide of 1860 long memorable. And I propose to give an outline of this, hoping that many may be induced to tread the same ground, and obtain the same results.

In company with an esteemed friend, I left Caernarvon at five o'clock on a cold starlit morning, and took the road to Beddgelert. Passing the dark silent towers of the castle which stood harmless over the sleeping town, we amused ourselves with contrasting the present with many a Christmas of the fourteenth century, when strength and cruelty garrisoned these walls, and overcame the desperate but weak efforts of native patriotism. Further on we walked over the Roman city, of which hardly a trace survives, and came to the mediæval church Llanbeblig with its massive tower. Here, while we halted by the wayside to take some refreshment after our long railway night-journey, there came from the church a weird gleam of light over the snow, and sounds which I was disposed to think might be connected with some premature *Plygain*,[1] until we resolved them into the utterance of a pair of bellows with which the sexton was blowing up his early fires.

As we proceeded the snow deepened, and it was over our ankles when we ascended into the open country, and felt the keen mountain breath on our faces. At daybreak the hills growing out of the gloom, unveiled to us their familiar forms on either side of the valley and in front. The Roman Dinas Dinlle peered from the right, still wet with the sea-mist, and recalled to us the celebrated road to Heriri Mons, in the direction of which we were travelling. To the left, Eilio presented his great snow-slopes and broad bulk, behind which Snowdon was concealed; and Mynydd Mawr reared his savage head and showed his *cwm*-indented sides. Soon that fair mountain *triad*, older than all bardism, and eloquent with the undying language of Nature, Yr Eifl, lifted his peaks on the western horizon, and we could hear in fancy the hollow sea sounding in the depths of Nant Gwrtheyrn.

Next, the crags of Silyn rose before us, and the bleak expanse of Llyn Cwellyn, guarded by its rock-rampart of Castell Cidwm. It were vain to try to describe the varying effects of the clear winter dawn upon all the peaks, crags, and waters now in sight. Suffice it that we reached our breakfast place, the 'Snowdon Ranger,' keenly impressed with the beauties of our walk, yet not less keenly hungry; and we reached it just in time to avoid a smart snow shower that suddenly swept down darkening the sky.

---

[1] The early service on Christmas morning, in which carol-singing is a conspicuous element—an immemorial Welsh custom. (See page 239.)

At noon came a burst of sunlight and a wide reach of blue, and we were tempted to try the ascent of Snowdon from this point, although the day was so far advanced. We started upon the track well described of old by Pennant and by Bingley. The word *track*, however, is not very applicable to the rough hillside we traversed, covered with yielding snow, in which we sometimes sank thigh-deep. But the splendid panorama that revealed itself as we rose, comprising the dark grey sea, the gleaming Menai, the wild white mountains of Lleyn, the near rocks of our valley, the slopes of Moel Eilio, and, above all, the sterner side of Snowdon, Cwm Clogwyn, with three lakelets lying frozen in its folds, more than recompensed us for the difficulties of the ground. Skirting Maes Cwm with Moel Cynghorion (Hill of Councils), now vacant of all living sound, to our left, and Bwlch Cwm Brwynog before us, we made for the dark precipitous ridge of ClogwynDu'r Arddu, which should lead us up to Y Wyddfa, over the great hollow mentioned. But in the words of the old ' pennill,'

> Hawdd yw d'wedyd dacew'r Wyddfa,
> Nid eir drosti ond yn ara';

and on reaching with some labour the bosom of this *cwm*, and the margin of the Llyn Ffynnon Gwas at the foot of Arddu, we were overtaken from the north-west by one of those sharp sudden storms which are so characteristic of mountain countries, and which, when they occur in winter, can by no ingenuity be called agreeable. The snow encrusted our clothing, the hail lashed our faces, the wind howled sullenly around us, and, worst of all, a dense mist enveloped us spreading up from the valley. To stand still in two feet of snow was beyond endurance. To go back, beside being inglorious, was more uncomfortable than to go on. But it was the best thing to do as the mist was deepening. After gazing, then, once more on Llyn Gwas, and thinking of the poor farm servant who was drowned in it on perhaps such a day as this, thus giving its name to the tarn, we commenced our retreat.

At first we lost our bearings in the indistinguishable mass of snow and sky, but soon recovering them by help of the compass, we set out in a bee-line for Pont Rhyd du Gate on the Beddgelert Road. The situation suggested to my companion one of his old adventures on the Alpine cols or plateaux, while to my mind it vividly recalled a four hours' imprisonment on Cader Idris,[1] and a memorable Christmas night's wandering on the Glyder Vawr.[2] For about an hour and a half we forced our way down, now struggling over a stone dyke, now pausing behind some enormous fragment of rock, through wood, and marsh, and brook, through mist, and hail, and snow, until at the desired point we struck the road which was become almost invisible in the advancing night and the blinding drift. Thence to the mistress of three vales, the romantic village of Beddgelert, was an easy descent; and there, under the shadow of Moel Hebog and Craigyllan, we enjoyed ten hours of uninterrupted sleep earned by hearty fatigue and free exposure to the elements, in which, however, there was a rare mixture of pleasure in the endurance, as there will always be in the recollection.

We awoke to find the sky stainless blue, and the earth locked in frost, after the coldest night that the villagers had known for twenty years. The little river Colwyn, which we had left sparkling and dancing to its own music in moonlight, now lay dumb and still; and the trees which we last saw swaying naked in the storm, were now crisp and motionless with every bough beaded by glistening rime. A pale rose-tint suffused the upper slopes of the Hill of the Falcon, which gradually deepened into ruby as the sun ascended over Aberglaslyn. All looked so promising that, with a joyful impulse, we determined to attack Snowdon once more, seizing at least the beginning of the day whatever might be its end.

After two preliminary miles on the Caernarvon road, occupied with encouraging views of Hebog, Silyn, and the crags of Mynydd Mawr towering over the Nantlle valley, we came in sight of Aran, the southern outpost of Snowdon, and next, of the grander front of Eryri itself stretching, in an unbroken curve, from base to summit an intense snow-line against the intense azure of the sky. Never

---

[1] In July, 1856, I found myself among the splintered basaltic crags of Cader, unable to see three yards around me, and I had no easy task to extricate myself and the young friend accompanying me. But the view of the mist, boiling and surging up as from a cauldron, in that fantastic amphitheatre of black jagged rocks, as the eye peered over some dripping precipice, while the foot, arrested in its progress, held fast for life, would have been a rich recompense for even a longer imprisonment.

[2] See the poem 'Nant Ffrancon,' p. 71.

did we see the mountain more beautiful in form or hue, although in mere height it is considerably dwarfed on this side by the elevation of the road skirting its base.

Leaving the road at the Pitt's Head Rock, we passed through the farm of Ffridd Uchaf, where the good people seemed astonished to hear of our intention. Drawing a bee-line from this farm to the lowest part of the Llechog, we pressed on through the snow, which presented an unbroken even surface with a depth of about two feet. An hour's rather toilsome march brought us to the Llechog's side, and here was, perhaps, the hardest climbing of all. We were obliged to grasp the rock and force a way over the rough fragments that strewed the slope, and whose interstices were filled with deep snow, in which the leg had to be plunged and withdrawn in a very fatiguing succession. Often did we find the supports treacherous and the foothold uncertain, and slip back, or tumble headlong, burying face and hands in the snow. But we always came up like Antæus, fresher from the contact as from a bath, and we had even here many sights and sounds of interest in the fantastic wreaths overlapping the crags, in the miniature defiles through which we waded, in the breeze singing among the upper rocks, and skimming off into vapour the fine powder of crystalline snow, and in the faint bubbling run of the buried and unfrozen rill heard beneath the feet, suggesting the fairy tales connected with this part of the mountain. Icicles too, in every variety of form and colour, adorned with their sparkling spear-fringes each exposed little ridge. But our great icicle-picture was on the following day, in the Pass of Llanberis, where they hung in most grand and romantic shapes—organ pipes—tilting lances—cataracts.

It was a relief, however, to gain the crest of this troublesome brae, and to step out upon the brink of Cwm Clogwyn, that fine amphitheatre, whose walls form nearly one-half of the mountain's vertical section, and above which, bending to the northward, is piled the rocky framework constituting the mural barrier of the still greater Cwm Llan, and culminating in Y Wyddfa, the conspicuous type of dignity and repose.

This we seized at a glance, and the eye then dwelt on the rounded snow-slopes of the Llechog, seeming to stretch over Cwm Craigog to the foot of Aran below, and on the domelike eminence directly above us, melting into the calm blue heaven. The snow

had been here much blown about, drifted and sifted by the prevailing winds, hanging sometimes on the very edge of the precipice, then receding from it, leaving spaces of herbage where we
gathered mosses. The dark basaltic sides of the cwm were beau-
tifully flecked with snow and glazed with ice. The white covering
lay on the brow generally to the depth of from two to three feet,
and it had been formed into *spiculæ* and crystals of singular sharp-
ness and delicacy. There were snow-cornices too of indescribable
beauty, now resembling the fretted lines of the choicest stone
tracery, and now a frozen image of some deep-curving wave.

We doubted not that, after a few more days of frost, the snow
would be hard enough to bear our tread, which would make the
passage of the mountain far more easy, but much less safe, as the
snow is of positive service in detaining the foot and steadying the
body. We looked for a few minutes on the scene below, and
chiefly on the ' Rivals' rising far in the distance, on the cwm of
Craig Silyn, down the rich mineral valley of Nantlle, at the head
of which, upon Llyn Dywarchen, we saw the farmhouse where we
were hospitably treated in 1857, and at the notable mountain-
barrier Moelwyn, beyond Beddgelert. All these were touched
with the last rays of the sun, and we hasted on eastward up the
steep side, bringing the sun up with us, to the sharp wedge-like
peak of Bwlch y Maen, and thence northward to the *aiguilles*—for
such they almost are—of the Clawdd Coch. Here we overlooked
the great cwm of Snowdon, and here the moon came out to meet
us above the peak of Lliwedd.

From this ridge were visible Cader Idris, the Berwyns, and a
vast wilderness of hills to the eastward, the hills of Lleyn, Bardsey
Island, the Bay of Cardigan, with the tremulous fires of sunset
playing on it over Port Madoc, the entire plain of Anglesey,
Holyhead, the dark sea to the north, and the shining Menai on
the southern border. A bank of compact clouds was settling over
Caernarvon Bay, veiling distance in that direction. Of the near
view of lakes and mountains, I will now only mention the magni-
ficent Lliwedd rising sheer from Cwm Dyli and Cwm Llan, and
forming the bold eastern outwork of Snowdon.

But the fast sinking sun and the hazardous character of the
' Red Ridge ' made us push on for the summit. The real difficulty
was now, indeed, to begin in the passage of the Clawdd, which is
hardly anywhere more than three yards wide, and which presented
a tableau of snow and crag mingled in the wildest manner, and of

wreaths and icicles fantastically suspended over the abyss on each side. Breaking through the breast-high cornices, sounding cautiously every step with our sticks, holding on by the hands in places where a slip would have sent us rolling hundreds of yards to the right or left, one of us taking care to tread in the steps formed by the other, we clambered slowly across the neck, and reached the shoulder crowned by the chief summit. During the hour occupied by this part of our journey, we had the same splendid weather that favoured the beginning and the end of it. Standing in the centre between the two *cwms*, where we could plant our feet against rock, with the faintest breeze from the north-west, in the full glitter of the risen moon, with the keen frost deepening the azure air and crisping the virgin snow, we were at liberty to enjoy in tranquillity the wonderful beauty of the scene. But if the snow had been wholly converted to ice, if a strong wind had blown from any quarter, or if a close mist had enwrapped us, our position would have been perilous, for tourists unacquainted with the hills, or unsteady of foot and eye. If we had fallen from this saddle in opposite directions we should probably, in a few seconds, have been half a mile asunder. But we were both fair cragsmen, accustomed to depend on our own resources, and able to take the proper steps under most circumstances of mountain danger. We had made a previous ascent on a winter night (in 1857), but the essential element of snow was then absent, and we missed some other of the grander aspects of Eryri, although upon that occasion, as upon this, we were deeply impressed with Clawdd Coch and Bwlch y Maen (which we then approached by an extemporised route from the foot of Aran), particularly as seen from the end next the Wyddfa, for the skeleton of Snowdon is here narrowed to a bone, and the rock-bridge of some four hundred yards long seems absolutely aerial.

Passing to the summit we found no greater depth of snow. The air was perfectly calm. The cold was intense. Our observations however, on this point, are valueless, as we had no instruments with us, but the temperature must have been many degrees below zero.[1] Its effect on our limbs was such that we could only

---

[1] At Downham Market in Norfolk, on this Christmas Eve, the registered average temperature was 11° below zero; and on the Yorkshire Wolds it was 7° below zero.

retain life in them by violent motion, while the well-known sensation of sleepiness stealing through our veins made movement difficult and wearisome. After a hasty refreshment, we paced round the rocky knoll, surveying all the peaks and cwms grouped about our central station. No picture could be more grand or solemn. It can be but faintly indicated. Cwm Llan and the Vale of Gwynant lay in broad masses of light and shadow, the upper part being snow-slopes of dazzling white, the lower part flecked and intermixed with the signs of road, wood, and stream. Cwm Dyli yawned still more precipitous, enclosing Llyn Llydaw, whose deep pure waters of seeming inky blackness were streaked with one vivid shaft of moonlight. The great peaks Crib Goch and Crib Ddysgyll stood out as the northern body-guard of the monarch, while the savage head of Glyder Vawr and the picturesque lines of Moel Siabod, seen across the respective valleys of Llanberis and Mymbyr, formed on other sides the advanced posts of Snowdonia. At our feet, seeming to defy access, lay the Lliwedd, perhaps the finest single peak in Wales, Tryvaen excepted, and which, seen from Cwm Dyli or Gwynant, looks only less imposing than the Wyddfa itself. The moon, nearly at her full, flung over all these her whitest wintriest lustre, and the long tracts of unspotted snow gleamed colder under that lifeless light. Two or three of the greater stars burned sharply in a sky dark with azure, and bared from horizon to zenith. One wide circle of the world of Nature and Man was gathered into our vision, but not the faintest human or elemental sound flitted across that intense silence.

> . . . . The very Winds,
> Danger's grim playmates, on that precipice
> Slept clasped in his embrace.

Imagination needed very little stimulus to realise the aspect of Snowdon at the far-remote period when humanity was not, when Cwm Dyli presented a vast basin of ice, and glaciers rolled down from every side, encumbering the narrow gorges, and overflowing into the deep valleys.

I have seen the best mountain beauty of North Wales—Aran Vowddwy from Bwlch y Groes; Cader Idris from Llanelltyd Bridge, or from its own great tarn; Carnedd Llywelyn from Bethesda; the Rhynnog hills from Trawsfynydd; and the Eifl

group from Caernarvon Bay; and I have stood on all those peaks,
and explored the recesses of Snowdon itself in all seasons; but I
never looked on so impressive a scene as that spread before me on
this memorable Christmas Eve.

The descent to Llanberis offered few additional features beside
the increased depth of the snow over the Llechwedd, and in
Cwm Brwynog where it had obliterated the horsepath. The
Glyders showed their rugged peaks for the last time; Clogwyn Du'r
Arddu, the most savage, dark, and precipitous of the Snowdonian
crags, and a most striking object seen in approaching Llanberis
from Caernarvon, looked still blacker and ruder now; and the
beautiful Llyn Padarn, almost constantly in sight during the
downward walk, lay fair in moonlight awaiting our coming.

The rest was desolation unrelieved by grandeur, yet not without
interest or meaning; and passing through the little firwood, we
reached the Victoria Hotel, invigorated rather than fatigued by
the eight hours on Eryri, and with sincere emotions of love for the
country which had so often yielded us these pure pleasures, and
of veneration for Him Whose Almighty hand prepared the mountain glory and the mountain gloom.'

January, 1861.

---

¹ We were preceded in this excursion by Professor Tyndall, who with
two companions and a guide ascended, a day or two earlier, from the
head of Llanberis Pass.

Dr. Tyndall, who is a practised Alpine traveller, and an excellent
authority in mountain matters, scenic as well as geologic, said that
hardly on Monte Rosa, the Görnergrat, or Mont Blanc itself, had he
enjoyed such glorious moments as upon the top of Snowdon that day.
See his narrative of the ascent in the *Saturday Review* of January 5,
1861.

THE VALE OF MOWDDWY.

' Valley, which green hills invest,
  Crags and summits tempest-torn,
  River, from their twilight breast
  Falling southward to the morn!'—PAGE 193.

FEW even of our hardiest pedestrian travellers are sufficiently acquainted with this corner of Merioneth. The genius of guide-books has flattered over Gwynedd on very weak pinions indeed, feeling most at ease when near the line of the Chester and Holy-head railway, or the great Holyhead road, where he could get a timely lift, and without fatigue describe glibly the beauties of Bangor, or the amenities of Llangollen. The egregious swarm of ' tourists' whom ' cheap excursions' and summer skies draw annu-ally to wild Wales, and who *do* the country, to its detriment with closed eyes, yet to its advantage with open purses, are not exactly authorities as to the Mowddwy district, though many of them have been hospitably entertained at the table of its rector, while on the way wearily sighing for the hotel at Mallwyd, Dolgelly, or Bala. And the flippant book-makers of the Miss Louisa Stuart Costello class,[1] the *feeders* of the guide-books, who lisp out a calumny against the music, or a protest against the language, and without the head to perceive, or the heart to appreciate, any-thing a little beneath the surface, complacently roll through the turnpikes, thinking they do enough in collecting materials for a few pretty pictures and anecdotes, need not be consulted for any details of the Valley of *spreading waters*. But Pennant among the old writers, and Cliffe among the new, are well worthy of credit, especially Cliffe, whose *Book of North Wales* had the advantage

---

[1] Falls, Lakes, and Mountains of North Wales. Longmans, 1845.

of being revised by Ab Ithel. The reader, however, would do best
to judge for himself of this most remarkable little glen; and he
will not then accuse me of any attempt at 'fine writing' if I seek
now to give him a verbal impression of its wildness and its beauty.

From the high ground eastward of Bala, on the Corwen Road,
the traveller to Dolgelly sees straight before him, rising afar in
picturesque grandeur, the two Arans, Benllyn and Mowddwy, and,
beyond them, he may even catch glimpses of the tall peaks of
Cader Idris, where the mountain gloom and the mountain
glory, to which Mr. Ruskin has devoted some of his most eloquent
chapters, find one of their fittest Cambrian illustrations. If that
gentle wind, from the

> · · · · south-west, that blowing Bala Lake
> Fills all the sacred Dee;

be then prevailing, it will refresh his cheek with the pure coolness
of those hills, and woo his footsteps to seek their romantic recesses.
As he passes along the margin of the Llyn—it matters little whether
on the Llanycil or the Llangower side—the region he is approaching
assumes an aspect of most attractive mystery. Aran Benllyn, at
the head of the lake, which its name implies, grows more and
more imposing as a barrier or a guard. At Llanuwchllyn the
Dolgelly Road turns the west flank of the mountain, and soon
becomes uninteresting. Yet *that* of course is the popular road, for
does not a coach traverse it daily, and is not the *Golden Lion* at
the end? I invite our traveller to another road, leading to
Bwlch y Groes, the celebrated Pass of the Cross, to the eastward
of the Arans. Like most celebrated things, this fine scenery has
suffered from over-statement. Too much has been said, even by
Pennant, of its difficulties and terrors; too little by all writers of
its peculiar excellences. There are not many places in Wales
capable of presenting at all seasons a succession of pictures equally
vivid. The road, gradually growing narrower and steeper, ascends
the long valley of Cwm Cynllwyd,[1] where, far down, the brawling Twrch[2] flows from its rocky fountain under Llechwedd Du,

---

[1] Meaning, the hoary-headed hollow, or the primeval grey gorge.

[2] Burrower, mole. 'Or sullen Mole that runneth underneath.'
Milton.

leaping, *burrowing*, and dashing on its way to Llyn Tegid. To the right hand, opening into this valley, is Cwm Groes, one of the desolate vestibules of the mountain shrine. Bisecting it is a silver threaded torrent which struggles into the Twrch. Above it, the twin heads of Aran, massive and majestic, pierce the clouds. If, as I would fain believe, the Twrch is the Dee, in, as it were, a state of pre-existence, then the springs of the holy river are at our feet, and the glorious verse of Spenser and of Drayton, mixed with the Arthurian legends, fires our imagination.[1]

We turn awhile, and Arenig is before us, grandly filling the sky-line to the north-west. Descending the Bwlch on a clear autumn morning, I have seen, across the white glitter of the lake, this lofty hill struck by the early sun with such a roseate blaze, that it resembled a floating golden cloud ever and anon streaked with opaline bars, and wearing an aspect so unearthly in its beauty, yet so vividly defined, as to suggest one of the fabled Islands of the Blest.

Soon the track grows rude and tortuous and winds along the shoulder of the hill beneath impending crags, into the Pass of the Cross. The valley seems to retreat and deepen as we go, till at

---

[1] However, the *antelacustrine* Dee has been alleged to be the stream called indeed Dyvrdwy in the Ordnance map, rising under Penmaen (where is a carn), near the eighth milestone from Bala, on the Dolgelly Road. This stream is the Avon y Llan mentioned by Pennant, and receives, not far from Llanuwchllyn, the Avon Lliw, which has its sources in the hill-waste between Arenig and Cwm Prysor. These two streams have been said to form the Dee. But it must be remembered that, at a point near old Caer Gai, the waters of the Twrch receive, or are received by, those of the Lliw and Llan, and the united three pass into Bala Lake. Which is the parent stream it is difficult to say. Pennant somewhat confuses the question, and Black places the head-waters of the Dee at the foot of the Berwyns, thinking perhaps of the stream that falls into the lake at Llangower, but which can have no better claim than the Llavar on the opposite side. Science may smile at the tale of a Welsh Arethusa (what could be better fitted than the Twrch for such an exploit?), but it may be substantially true, if we consider Llyn Tegid as an expansion of the triad of streams we have been describing. I do not know what Catherall says on the subject. He is reputed to be 'very learned on the sources of rivers.' I write from personal observations.

last it terminates in a true amphitheatre of the wilds. There one solitary farmhouse called Blaen y Cwm from its position gives a human interest to the spot, and, maybe, the faint cry of a sheep, or the quick bark of a dog, breaks the ghostly silence with a peculiar charm. I have passed over these hills in mid winter, when the cwm was locked in frost and flecked with snow, and when the moon, labouring under great cloud-masses, broke out fitfully upon the ancient region, flinging alternately broad shadows and piercing shafts of light. Arrived at the summit of the Bwlch, we find, instead of the old cross which gave a name to the pass, a cam placed by the Ordnance surveyors on the exact confines of Montgomery and Merioneth. Without entering the former county, we proceed along the swampy level, whence the peaty substitute for coal, called *mawn*, is procured; and, turning suddenly, descend into a completely different district, that of Mowddwy. Now the mountain side is on our right hand, and on our left a deep ravine, which encloses the tiny river Rhiwlach, with the mural ramparts of Moel y Gordd towering over it.

As the rough track leads us down between these and the green ridges of Yr Eryr, into recesses more and more secluded and overshadowed, a feeling of oppression and sadness steals over the mind, and we doubt for a moment whether the district we are approaching be like the happy valley of Rasselas, or rather like that brooded over by the dread lethiferous wings.

At the bottom, however, gloomy thoughts take flight. The rejoicing little Rhiwlach is content to blend its existence with that of its infant playfellow Dyvi, who, as if conscious of the more brilliant destiny in store for it, of traversing pastoral plains and bearing ocean-spanning ships, comes dancing from the lonely tarn hid in the heart of Aran Vowddwy, down Llaithnant,[1] the broad cwm opening on the right hand at the foot of Bwlch y Groes. Turning also to the left, we follow Dyvi into the valley of Llanymowddwy,[2] at this spot fitly called Vale-head (*Pen-nant*), and become acquainted with an almost unique combination of scenic

---

[1] The *moist ravine*, if the Ordnance map is correct; but if *Llaethnent* be the right orthography, as local legends indicate, the meaning would be the *milky brook*. The Dyvi, however, was once called *Llaith*.

[2] Accurately Llanymawddwy—the sacred inclosure (or church) of diffused waters.

sublimities. Fronting us, or a little to the right, is Moel Ffridd, a hill now utterly *unwooded*, of the boldest outline, presenting on this side a wedge-like or pyramidal section quite as picturesque, though hardly so grand, as Trivaen in Nant Ffrancon. To the left the still descending road develops a lofty barrier of hills rising with every variety of slope and contour, and broken in the near distance by two *cwms* penetrating them at an angle, as savage and romantic as any I have seen. These are respectively Cwm Cerddyn and Cwm Llygaed. Each is traversed by a torrent, and inclosed by dark discoloured precipices. Between them is Moel Vryu, a round picturesque hill, outjutting like a promontory, easy of access, and affording a curious view of the valley and of the distant mountains to the north and west.

The valley is here, and at Llanymowddwy itself, contracted to very narrow limits, being almost a mere gorge, marking the descent of the Dovey. It expands very gradually with the river, and may be said to be terminated by the fine bluff hill Moel Dinas, beneath which the ancient capital city Dinas Mawddwy cherishes in its street of hovels, its mayor, corporation, and all privileges appertaining; and the Dovey, which has flowed past all the grandeur and all the decay, flows on as ever, widening and deepening, in the open valley to Machynlleth.

Llanymowddwy Church, a very small and utterly plain building, and the rectory adjacent, a low rustic cottage, stand at about a mile from the foot of Bwlch y Groes.

The living, when Ab Ithel was preferred to it, was in the diocese of St. Asaph, but it had been, before he left it, transferred to that of Bangor. Its yearly value is little more than 200*l*. The parish embraces a wide circle of hill country, which Ab Ithel's high reputation and character practically much extended, for the people flocked to him from Dinas, Mallwyd, and Montgomery parishes, as to a loved pastor, who sympathised at once with their personal interests and their national predilections.

The patron saint of Llanymowddwy is the great Tydecho,[1] of

---

[1] See the *Cywydd Tydecho Sant yn Amser Maelgwn Gwynedd*, by Davydd Llwyd. 'This illustrious bard informs us that Tydecho had been an abbot in Armorica, and came over in the time of King Arthur; but, after the death of that hero, when the Saxons overran most of the kingdom,

whose residence and actions here some curious legends survive. In the churchyard stand two yew-trees, reputed to be older than the more celebrated ones at Mallwyd. They give to the enclosure an air of weird antiquity somewhat inconsistent with the modern little church, but quite in harmony with the surrounding scene. The little rectory, like the church, nestles under the bold masses of Moel y Ffridd, where it is well protected from north-west winds. In front of it, stretching to the Dyvi, are the few glebe fields, and opposite, beyond the river, yawns another fine *cwm*, that of Pen y Gelli.[1]

The great precipice of Cwm Pen y Gelli forms a deep indentation of the mountain wall, closing the valley of Llanymawddwy on the eastern side.

Well worth regard is the aspect of this *cwm* from the Rectory, or from the Manor-house of Bryn. Deeply recessed in the hill, and seldom penetrated by the sun, it has more to do with shadow than with light, and whether half-veiled by the thin mists of morning, or sunk in the glooms of eve, or tinted by the fleecy clouds of noontide, there seems a curious constant horror upon it—something which moves the mind to images of pain, cruelty, and despair. But it is when winter settles within it, sharply defining the dark steep crags against the freezing sky; spreading sheets of snow

---

the saint retired, and led here a most austere life, lying on the bare stones, and wearing a shirt of hair; yet he employed his time usefully, was a tiller of the ground, and kept hospitality. Prince Maelgwn Gwynedd, then a youth, took offence at the saint, and seized his oxen; but wild stags were seen the next day performing their office, and a grey wolf harrowing after them. Maelgwn enraged at this brought his milk-white dogs to chase the deer while he sat on the blue stone to enjoy the diversion, but when he attempted to rise, he found himself immovably fixed to the rock, so that he was obliged to beg pardon of the saint, who on proper reparation was so kind as to free him from his awkward pain.'—Pennant's *Tour in Wales*, vol. ii. p. 227.

Tydecho's chair (the blue stone) is still visible at the top of the wooded ravine of the Pymrhyd, close to the rectory. There is also Tydecho's bed on the cold flank of Aran, approached from the same direction.

[1] *The head of the hazel grove.*—As little wood remains as upon Moel Ffridd. This inconsistency, so frequent in Welsh names, proves their antiquity.

along the stony slopes, like cerements on the face of death; hanging giant icicles adown the mural front, and bright bands of drift in every crevice; trampling into muddy ruin the hardy mosses and lichens; binding the torrent between the shapeless stones of its bed, save only in its impetuous sweep over the crag, which not even winter can arrest; and in fine, transfusing all with a spirit of dumb and utter desolation: it is then that Cwm Pen y Gelli puts on its most awful aspect, and most resembles a vast lair where couches some gigantic wild beast, fierce habitant of a world from which human life has died out.

Above this romantic hollow, upon Carreg y Vrân, runs the dividing line of the two counties. To the left hand, the valley seems closed by Moel Vryn, where, in autumn, a good example may be seen of those beautiful tints in which the hills of Meirion in general excel the hills of Arvon, as the latter excel the former in crag. To the right hand, the group of humble tenements along the road, forming the village of Llanymowddwy, redeems the prospect from utter loneliness. The population is small, poor, and widely scattered: speaking only Welsh, and living only by agriculture and sheep-farming. They are of simple life and manners, fond of music and song, warm-hearted, hospitable, superstitious, and devout; and in short, exhibit the typical Welsh mountain character as it has been from the days of Giraldus to the days of Pennant, and thence to our own time.

In all respects is the Mowddwy district worthy of more attention than it has received. To every class it offers attractions hardly to be met elsewhere, grouped within similar bounds. The student may find a harmonious sphere for quiet thought. The man tired of the pleasure or business of cities may enjoy pure relaxation and undisturbed repose. The pedestrian may discover splendid employment for his legs and lungs. The lover of field sports may harass to his heart's content the trout on the river, and the game on the hills: and if he have strong limbs and steady eyes he may follow the fox in places which would try the mettle of a Leicestershire squire, and shatter the nerves of a pigeon-shooter of London.

Nor is the valley less eligible for intellectual tastes and uses. Art may delight in several picturesque water-falls and river-reaches, as well as in grand mountain groupings. Geology and Botany may find in the noble sections of Cowarch and Aran, and on the wild summits around Carreg y Big, much to enrich the cabinet, of moss and of rock. Romance may have ample materials in the fairies and *ellyllon* born of the winds, woods, and waters, who haunt this region: in the tales, legends, and even relics, of saints, princes, banditti, and wizards, and, above all, in the wild and wayward ghosts whom no power ecclesiastical or mechanical can *lay*.[1] Archæology may find suggestions in abundance, of Roman roads, and Celtic carns and circles; with some curious mediæval traces. And Poetry may dream at midnight in those secluded dells, when nothing is visible but the keen stars burning above the black mountain-crests, and nothing audible save the faint song of the river flowing over the polished stones. Or she may take her stand upon Moel Ffridd on an autumnal morning of sunny promise, and watch the surging columns and wreaths of mist in the valleys, and the multitudinous hills tumbled about in all shapes of grandeur and grace over the horizon, with their tops islanded in a milky sea, or their dusky backs upheaving like uncouth monsters of the Pleiocene. Or she may listen to the rolling thunder, and the fierce north wind sweeping down from the caves of Aran through the shivering firs; scattering the lingering berries of the ash, loosing the secret springs, maddening the torrents, wreathing the cwms with feathery snow, or hurling a deluge of rain upon the fields.

Of atmospheric vicissitudes, indeed, vulgarly called 'changes of weather,' Mowddwy has had always more than its share, even for a hilly country. However sublime it may be to the mind, it is by no means comfortable to the body to be caught in a sudden storm on the Welsh hills. It is a fine thing to be 'a portion of the tempest,' but it is peculiarly pleasant to be so from a snug

---

[1] The presiding ghost of Mowddwy keeps his court at the old manor-house of Bryn. The writer, who has a considerable sympathy for ghosts, once passed a winter's night in *the* room; but he is not at liberty to say more. As to fairies, he does not *insist* that the Tylwyth Têg still occupy their ancient ball-room in the great *cwm* of Aran, though he knows some persons who *do*. He is, however, quite willing to believe that an old patriotic grey wolf, the same that did the harrowing for Tydecho, lurks still in Cwm Llygaed, and often casts a wistful eye to the sleek Saxons who admire the *cwm* from the road in the autumn twilight.

study-window, or a balcony well sheltered and lightning-proof. *Experto crede.* One of my keenest enjoyments of a storm night was at trite over-thronged Llangollen, where I watched the glorious play of the elements from a window of the hotel. And one of the most wretched nights I ever passed, was amid the solemn wildness of the Carnedd Llywelyn range, where the day had closed magnificently, and the highest poetical stimulants abounded. *But it began to rain.* A little while before, I had found a delicious spring, and had quaffed, and quoted with fervour,

> . . . . solicito bibant
> Auro superbi: quam juvat nudâ manu
> Captásse fontem!

But *now* I had to turn for safety to a stimulant the reverse of poetical—which, however, our Armorican cousins call, with a fine accumulative significance, *gwinardan*,[1] and their Gallic neighbours as emphatically *eau de vie.*

That Mowddwy has been afflicted with an excess of rain from an early date, appears from the adage of the three things which she wishes to send out of the country, namely, detested people, blue-marking earth, and *rain*.[2]

This great humidity, and the extreme contractedness of the valley, which hardly permits the sun's direct rays in winter to penetrate the houses before noon, are the chief disadvantages of Llanymowddwy as a place of residence. For temporary seclusion or holiday resort, there are few more eligible spots on Welsh soil.

---

[1] *Gwin-ar-tân,* wine on fire.

[2] O Vowddwy ddu ni ddaw, dim allan
A ellir 'i rwystraw.
Ond tri pheth helaeth hylaw,
Dyn atgas, nod glas, a Gwlaw.
  Quoted by Pennant, Tours in Wales ii. p. 234.

THE WELSH LANGUAGE.

' And oh the dear speech of the Awen and Altar !'—PAGE 33.

SIR,—In your paper of November 20 there appeared a letter from Ab Ithel justly reprehending the remarks of a Mr. Miller, of Aberystwyth, in disparagement of the Welsh language, and proposing a prize of 10*l.* to be given for the best essay upon the most effectual means of maintaining and extending the Cymraeg. In your paper of the following week, 'Mervinian' suggested that the prize should be 100*l.*, and offered some practical suggestions as to the manner of raising the money.

As a sincere lover of Wales, I beg heartily to respond to Ab Ithel's call for assistance and co-operation in this matter: and if the humble comments I am about to make from my own point of view—that of an Englishman and a student—serve to awaken or increase attention to the subject, either in England or Wales, I shall welcome the result with the warmest satisfaction.

It is not to be denied that the Welsh language is declining in respect to the area over which it is spoken. But while admitting what is a plain fact, let us not be supposed to admit what critics and reporters, more or less prejudiced or ignorant, are in the habit of affirming to the world. Welsh is not declining so fast as they suppose, or choose to assume. Welsh is not dying from inherent weakness, or from inability to breathe nineteenth-century air and to crawl out of the way of the wheels of Civilisation's car. It is weak and languishing truly, but its sickness need not be unto death if only the proper remedies be administered: and it is in the power, as it is the plain duty, of Welshmen. of those who speak it, have spoken it, or ought to speak it, to support and strengthen their mother-tongue against both external animosity and internal indifference.

'The Cambrian idiom,' says the historian of the Norman Conquest, 'is still spoken by a sufficiently extensive population to render its future extinction very difficult to foresee.' And if that population do their duty with their idiom, it may be that the possible future historian of another conquest of Great Britain will have to repeat the same words, and, let us hope, in the same spirit. But admitting that the Welsh language is now geographically declining, I would glance at the causes and the cure.

The most obvious causes are the overt interference of the State: the influence of manufacture and commerce; and the too habitual indifference of large classes of the Cymry themselves—the last the most lamentable of all. It behoves every Cymro to keep steadily in view these main facts.

It is well known that under the Hanoverian dynasty, a policy not less shortsighted than oppressive, has for the most part been pursued towards the Welsh language, literature, and institutions: and though of late years, open coercion has been in some degree replaced by more insidious measures, the *animus* of the Executive has continued to bear most hurtfully upon the nationality of Wales. In the present Ministry, however, we may discern better tendencies, and we have ground for believing that the time will soon arrive when just views will prevail in the seats of power, or when the enemies of Cambria will at least refrain from accelerating the extinction of her language, which, they profess to think, can be effected by the lapse of time.

I have called the repressive policy, however it be exercised, *short-sighted*, and it is so, because it is based on erroneous assumptions and ridiculous apprehensions; because it seeks to obtain a small good at the price of a great evil; and because it works unaided by the light of experience or the sanction of truth. What is really comprised in the phrase 'Welsh nationality?' I am sure the majority of intelligent Welshmen are agreed on the question. Is it a reverting to things past—an archaic curiosity— an antique fossil to be unearthed and unmuseumed for the learned delectation of the few, or the vulgar gaze of the many? Is it an ode or an epic—something to be shouted from the platform, or sentimentally wept over in the drawing-room? Is it, in its separation and difference, anything antagonistic or inimical to the country at large? Is it, in short, something half-barbarous, half-romantic, a sort of dangerous impossibility? Not so indeed! It is a right, a truth, and a privilege. It is what no Government can justly take away, because no Government has given it. It seeks no disunion from the State of which it can be an independent yet harmonious element. Far from cherishing hostility to the British Constitution or Crown, it would always be, as it often has been, its defence and ornament. It looks with an eye of respect and affection upon its own history, and would conserve all that comes from the past, stamped by the impress of true nobleness and freedom. It remembers the long struggle for liberty during 1500 years, against invading nation after nation, and while venerating the devotion, bravery, and genius of those who fought for it, wrote for it, and died for it, it cannot refuse to regard with reprobation the names of those, whether Roman, Saxon, or Norman, who oppressed, injured, and insulted it. But it nurses no resentment against the great Empire of which it is now an integral part, with which it is bound by community often of blood, always of interest, and which it is proud to acknowledge to the world under the common name of British. It asks only to be respected and recognised in those circumstances wherein it is different from England, and by means of which it has preserved its characteristics, while other Celtic nations have lost them. It asks only to be left to enjoy its comparative simplicity of manners, its attachment to the soil, its genealogical honours, and its own form of worship. Above all it claims to keep its language—the great cabinet which alone holds what it possesses of most valuable and most dear—the voice that can alone interpret its aspirations—the power that alone can perpetuate its existence. Is there in all this anything inimical to England—anything inconsistent with public virtue, order, or security? But it is said that the existence of two languages under one Crown is an unmixed evil—I deny it. In respect of whom is it an evil? Is it against the State? The Cambrians have spoken their language for centuries under the British Constitution as they now speak it. Have they been, or are they now distinguished by disloyalty and discontent? Have they used their language for seditious purposes, or indulged other habits and pursuits than those of peaceable and obedient subjects? No! Is it then against Society? Consult the records of crime and vice, and you will find no undue proportion of Welsh offenders. But the Welsh (I quote from Government authority) is a language of old-fashioned agriculture, of theology, and of poetry. Indeed! Why the inspector who made the remark thought it peculiarly so, I am at a loss to tell, since he probably understood not a word of it. Yet if it were so? Get rid of the old-fashioned farming by all means, if it is unproductive and exhausts the land, and you can find bran new English names for the new tools and processes. But keep the rest with heart and soul. Long may religion be associated in this honourable manner with the Cymraeg! God grant that the language which first in these islands was vocal with the one true faith, may long deepen and preserve among the worshippers in Wales that faith which it is so eloquent to interpret! We know that religion has reacted on the language and given to it depth and vigour. Ought we not to regard this as a Divine blessing? If Dissent have effected such a result rather than the Established Church, it is owing to reasons not perhaps wholly creditable to the latter, and as a critic I am bound to acknowledge what as a churchman I must deplore.

Then the Cymraeg is accused of poetry. Poetical and nothing else! As if that were not the Alpha and Omega of a language— as if that which expresses eternal truth and eternal beauty, which is laden with the deepest emotions of the heart, and is prolific of all that is most manly in man, should not endure the longest as it is uttered the first! In a poetical language there must be vigour, nervousness, strength; qualities that will keep it living, if only its people be true to it, when the superimposed refinements and technicalities, which time drafts in, shall be blown out by the breath of change to make way for new modifications. But it is true that this is not a poetic age; and the inspector telling us in his categorical way that the Cymraeg is a language of poetry, is only a product of the age. We blow away the envelope of the sneer, and seize the jewel of the truth. The Cymry will keep their agricultural, theological, and poetical language, and yet be as good 'men of business' as the inspector. *Nullum numen abest si sit prudentia.*

And this leads me to consider whether the 'unmixed evil' discovered by another 'authority,' and before spoken of, be against the Welsh themselves as regards their material interests; and how far, and why, the undoubted influence of trade and commerce has caused the language to decline. I shall only allude in general terms to the over-trading tendencies of the day, and to the spirit which practically teaches that to be rich, is to be happy and good. I could wish that Trade were less dominant in Britain, because I am quite sure it is, in one form or other, using up the intellect, the manliness, and the virtue of the land. It monopolises the choicest hours of life; it imprisons the affections, and distorts the judgment; it grasps both brain and muscle, strikes at thought, health, and repose, and looses some of the most mischievous passions from the guard of reason and temperance. It buys up science and art, and makes marketable commodities of virtue and genius. It converts man into a machine to drive or to be driven; woman it prostitutes; childhood it destroys. It draws a smoky veil between our eyes and the dome of heaven, as between our minds and the light of truth. It pulls down the standard of simplicity, humility, and contentment, and sets up a luxurious and inflated idol to be worshipped at the sacrifice of first principles and home affections; of our duties as Christians, and our privileges as men. And it does all this, not because it is bad in itself, but because it is abused, and made the end, instead of the means, of existence. It is not for a moment to be supposed that trade is not necessary and honourable, and may not, when conscientiously and temperately used, be fruitful of blessings. And in pursuing trade as a means of satisfying the physical needsof an increasing population, the Welsh people are of course only acting agreeably to the dispensation of Providence. It would no doubt be better that agriculture were more largely developed, and that the thousands of barren acres in the Principality, capable of cultivation, were made productive. But looking at things as they are, what is there in the mine, in the warehouse, in the forge, or in the workshop, that should hinder a Welshman from cherishing his native language? That there *is* something is evident, and I doubt not that this exists because the sordid, and not the humanising, spirit of commerce has been too much invoked.

The English tongue is certainly well adapted to business, as it has grown up with business, and the English people must, of course, be gradually brought by time into closer connection with the Welsh people. But, at best, this is an argument for learning English, not for neglecting Welsh. I do not even admit that Welsh is not adaptable to modern business, and I think it ought to be universally spoken in Wales among Welsh people. As to new terms and technical phrases, for which the Cymraeg has no equivalent, it seems easy to adopt the needful English words, just

as the English language adopts classical words for purposes of art
and science, or the words of some continental idiom, to render
certain expressions with more clearness or force. But even suppose that English were to be made the general language of commercial dealing in the Principality, will that include necessarily
the laying aside of Welsh? What is there to hinder us from
retaining one as the idiom of the shop and factory, the other of
the home and heart? Nothing, I apprehend, unless it be that
we too often place our home and our heart in the factory and the
shop. Is it not practicable to use two languages, one as acquired,
the other as native? The example of continental nations, where
two idioms prevail—as Belgium, Holland, Russia, Poland—is
before us, and countless domestic instances of the advantages of
a double utterance must occur to us. Let every child in Wales
be taught Welsh first—this is essential—as the mother tongue.
Let him be instructed in English and everything beside, through
the medium of Welsh, and let him be accustomed to Welsh only
in his intercourse with home and his prayers to Heaven. No person in Wales ought to be ignorant of the English, since, quite
apart from the purposes I have been considering, there is the
sterling value of the language itself, and the treasury of literature,
art, and science to which it is the key. Let the two languages
flourish together on a common British soil, and minister to the
true happiness and prosperity of the united subjects of one Sovereign.

I am aware that this course is to some extent now adopted as
circumstances compel, but owing to political repression, to native
inertness, and to a want of agreement on the subject, and of system
in working out a plan of counteraction, the English element is
preponderating, and the Cymraeg is only tolerated, not encouraged.
The danger, of course, is the most pressing along the coastline,
and in the border counties, some of which, as Radnorshire, have
almost lost their national speech. The continued introduction of
railways will operate largely in the degradation of the language,
and be a potent agent of denationalisation. Bringing some un-
questionable benefits, will not this also bring grave evils? I call
upon the young men of Wales to rise energetically to meet the
present emergency. Do not believe that the existence of two
languages in our country is an unmixed evil, any more than that
the existence of two climates or two kinds of scenery is one.

You who are born and also live on Cambrian soil, be the earnest and consistent advocates of your nation's rights, the vindicators of its fame, the representatives of its genius and worth.

Be assured that it is possible to fulfil an honest calling, and to perform all the duties of social life, without ceasing to be patriotic Welshmen, or losing a syllable of the noble language which ought to be endeared to you by so many national and personal associations. Be zealous in promoting Eisteddfodau, and every other means of strengthening the Cymraeg, and guarding all that it enshrines of music and of song. Support any Society that will multiply Welsh books, deliver Welsh lectures, promote the free colloquial use of Welsh, and obtain the mitigation of the disabilities which exclude it from too many churches and schools, and from all courts of justice. Use well the English language too, not only for the purposes of life and knowledge, but to vindicate and popularise your cause among your English neighbours. Multiply and support Sunday Schools, those instruments at once of piety and patriotism, which aid and extend the language, while training it to the glory of God. Do all things according to your ability and opportunity for your country and your countrymen, and do it unitedly and unanimously, remembering that *Nid cadarn ond brodyrdde*. Wales can only save her language through the efforts of her people. Be it your glory to make that effort—your happiness to secure that triumph!

I would beseech the great families of the land to help this movement; not to throw the weight of their influence into the wrong scale; not to live isolated from national interests, and cold to national inspirations; but to use their responsible power in the service of Wales, never forgetting that they are Welsh by descent as by possessions, and that it is the Welsh whom they are called on by the highest motives that may animate the breast, to respect, to support, and to benefit. Nothing in all Wales strikes a thinking Englishman more forcibly than the apathy and isolation of too many of the noble houses, in regard to questions which even Englishmen can admit to be vital to the national welfare.

In conclusion, I would say a few words to my own countrymen in and out of Wales. Abandon the ignorance, correct the prejudice that has so generally obscured your perception of Wales and the Welsh. In the face of contrary evidence and probability, do not believe that the early Britons were painted savages, or the Druids heathen monsters, as your nursery histories teach. Rely

upon classical authority if you will, but accept it in its fullest
extent, not from the point of view of a particular author; and
bear in mind too, that much of classical history was written from
hearsay, much with the conqueror's animus, much with the rhe-
torician's passion for effect. Do not despise oral tradition, or
accuse the Welsh annalists of mendacity and corruption. Why
cannot you accept at once the spirit of the Triads and of the Saxon
chronicle? How can you believe in Homer if you doubt Taliesin?
Study Cambrian history, not only in the pages of 'standard' English writers, where it is either distorted or suppressed, but also
from the sources supplied by the great body of bardic, theological,
and historic literature existing on the subject, but most of which
is unknown or misunderstood by English critics and readers. Do
this in no captious spirit, but philosophically and candidly. And
in order to do it well, study the Welsh language. Do not look
upon Wales as a pleasure ground for excursions only, or as a field
to make money in, or as a place for enjoying the beauties of nature
and the amenities of life. Mingle with the people—interest yourself in their welfare, support their institutions. And in order to
effectually do this, I again say learn the language. In every respect it will amply repay you, and you will be glad to aid the
endeavour now about to be made for its preservation.

To the scholar, I would especially say, How can you look with
complacency upon the decay of this, which, with its congeners the
Irish and the Erse, is the only remaining healthy branch of the
great Celtic idiom? For the Breton dialect is rapidly losing
purity and territory, and few traces remain in any other part of
Europe. And even more than the Erse or the Irish, interesting
as the remains of these are, is the Cymraeg worthy of preservation, by reason of its more perfect structure, its superior strength,
flexibility, and melody (let who will, deny), as well as the service
it has rendered to the literature and history of mankind.

I do not presume to offer to the Welsh people any scheme of
my own for giving effect to Ab Ithel's appeal. I merely second
that appeal as an Englishman. Whatever course be chosen, it
should be adopted speedily, for every day the necessity for action
becomes more urgent; and earnestly, for coldness and hesitation
would destroy our chances of success. Let us by union and
energy do all that can be done, remembering always that 'the
disgrace of defeat is not so great as the glory of endeavour.'
Non tam turpe vinci quam contendisse decorum!

WELSH LITERARY SOCIETIES.

Sir,—I have attentively read the letter of Ab Ithel in your impression of the 15th ult., and the replies of 'Clynnogian' and 'Gwyneddon' in that of the week before last, and I beg leave to offer some remarks on the subject, with the endeavour to show that the general view taken by Ab Ithel of Welsh Literary Societies is perfectly just and reasonable, and also that there need be no real impediment to the cultivation of the English language and literature, in strict harmony with that view, and with the fundamental principles of nationality which ought always to be remembered and respected.

Ab Ithel, I conceive, was very praiseworthy in resenting what he supposed to be an attempt to alter the exclusive national character of the Bangor Society. It is the spirit of this attempt, rather than the particular direction it assumed, that lies open to reprehension. The principle of nationality affirmed by Ab Ithel to be the guiding principle of a Welsh literary society, has my cordial concurrence as an Englishman viewing the whole subject dispassionately and at a distance, but animated by a warm feeling of regard for the interests of the country in the highest and best sense. If there is anything in Wales—language, institutions, traditions, privileges, usages—worthy of respect and conservation; if there exists a known tendency to decay or change, which negligence and dissension may increase, but vigilance and united action arrest; if influences are openly at work on the degradation of what all profess to admire, and hope to retain; surely it is time to organise efficient means of grappling with such evils, and surely it becomes all persons who are not timeservers or egotists, but patriots, however despised be the word, to support in the most unreserved manner, and with the most hearty unanimity, those institutions that were established, and continue to exist, for the plain purpose of strengthening the hands of Welshmen for the service of Wales.

The most important and valuable of all things connected with Wales is her language. I have heard of no native so base or foolish as to deny the merits of his language *per se*. Scholar and peasant are agreed on this point, though unhappily there is a variety of opinions about its comparative value and the policy of retaining it.

Now, what is the state of the language in the Principality? The question has been asked and answered many times. Yet there are some whom no evidence seems to satisfy, and no danger to warn. The language is, indeed, losing ground—passing gradually out of the minds and hearts of the people—declining not from internal weakness, but from external neglect. And what are the comments of a large section of Welshmen who stand by and watch this state of things? Hear Clynnogian, 'It has braved the battle and the breeze for centuries, and it is as likely now as ever to continue. If it be a language to die, any attempts to preserve it will be in vain; but if it be to continue, the offering of prizes at literary societies will do it no harm,' &c. &c. Would anyone but a helpless fatalist entertain such a sentiment? Does Clynnogian apply this axiom of his to every day affairs? His trade is depressed: his health is declining. Never mind. If it is to sink his attention cannot save it: if it is to revive, his neglect cannot injure it! So he will not call in the physician, or examine his account books. And he will calmly let the Cymraeg take its chance, no matter how different its present may be from its past —no matter how evident it becomes, day by day, that it is as necessary to use the proper means to retain, as to acquire, a language.

Now I thoroughly agree with Ab Ithel, that the Welsh Literary Societies are the natural and only powerful guardians of the native tongue, and it is there that the Cymraeg should sit as upon an hereditary throne. Whatever mutations prevail out of doors, whatever Fashion insinuates, or Trade demands, the Societies ought boldly and persistently to pursue their course, and radiate throughout the country as from so many centres, the influences able to support, revive, and extend the language of the Bible and the heart.

The highest in rank and mind in the Principality should gladly unite as their leaders and defenders. The lowest in station should be invited to share in the benefits open to all. Above all things, there should be union and co-operation.

What should be the plan and basis of action for such Societies? They are by no means designed to fill the office of schools, though education is a main feature. Lectures, essays, papers, the editing and printing of MSS., an ample library, classes of a high character, are among the most obvious of their resources. All the proceedings should be conducted in the Welsh language, and the Welsh language should be the groundwork and medium for every kind of study and business. Not an iota should be abated in this respect from their nationality. Now, surely, Ab Ithel and Eben Fardd can agree in this view. Let the latter eminent man insist on retaining the purely Welsh character of the Society, as to language, and I doubt not that Ab Ithel will gladly consent to the teaching of English composition to all who need it, by means of prize essays or otherwise. For it is not I who would question the excellency of my native language, or its value to the young men of Wales.

Much has been said, and said justly, on this topic. There can be no doubt that, both socially and intellectually, an ample knowledge of English is of advantage to Welshmen. It is merely to assert truisms to say that Wales is so connected with England, that many interests are common to both, and that so long as the natives of one country mingle with those of the other, a knowledge of both languages is essential to both parties, though in a greater degree to the Welshman. I have ever been, since I first knew Wales, an advocate of the duality of language for purposes of business and literature.

Fully admitting the value of English to the youth of Wales, I am bound to express my conviction that the value has been by writers and orators in the Principality much overstated, and that the advantages held out as accruing from a knowledge of our language are neither in quantity or in number entitled to the advocacy they have received. Gwyneddon wisely remarks that Welshmen are not generally great and successful, because they are acquainted with English, but that they are not recognised as such without at least some knowledge of it. And I will further beg him to remember that the knowledge of English which, under ordinary circumstances, a young Welshman may hope to attain, is by no means calculated to advance an Englishman himself far in the world.

Thousands of our young men in shops, factories, and counting-houses; thousands more working at handicraft trades; who have been educated in national and commercial schools, and have, perhaps, in addition, attended Institute-classes and evening schools, are barely competent to perform their duties as far as knowledge is concerned. Very few are able to do more. Knowledge is undoubtedly extensively and generally spread over the community, but it is superficial in the same ratio. There is little time to instruct—less still to educate. The study which is not long cannot be deep. Trade interrupts and engrosses all.

Yet I quite admit there is no reason why the youth of Wales should not acquire the knowledge of their English brethren, whatever that may be. Only do not let them be misled by high-coloured representations of gaining distinction in England, or by statements that the literary Societies of their country would be acting against their moral and material interests by declining to teach English on any predominant scale. It is not the proper office of a literary Society so to teach it. Clynnogian has many remarks on the necessity of retaining and extending the young man's knowledge of English after he leaves school. But are there not, or ought there not to be, evening schools in Wales and special classes open, as in England, for this purpose? Cannot the literary Societies, without excluding the study of languages, be of a higher character and for a higher purpose, as they are in Germany, Poland, Sardinia, and some parts of England? I lament most of all that such unworthy stimulants are offered to the Welsh youth by so many of their countrymen. Gain, worldly interest, distinction, are given as far greater incitements to learn English than the merits of the language itself, and are put forward and dwelt upon as the chief ends of life. Vulgar epithets are showered on those who dare to question the alleged desideratum, and who strive to moderate the fever, or, as it has been called, the mania. I, as an Englishman living in a great trading district, knowing what my young countrymen in the mass are, what knowledge and opportunity they possess, and what are their position and prospects, cannot join in this too popular cry. I love nationalities of all kinds if they be consistent and virtuous, and I desire to see Wales distinct from England in all that in which she has received a distinct impress from Heaven, and yet united to England in all that concerns the real interests of both countries. And I would far rather see developed the native resources of Wales, especially her agricultural resources, to meet her increasing population, and her young men kept upon the soil, than I would witness the extension of trade, the ramifications of railways, the introduction of English usages and manners, and the dispersion of the Cymry over the kingdom and abroad. I believe that the one policy leads, perhaps, to riches, though that is doubtful, but certainly to national disorganisation and decadence, and to individual deterioration of mind and heart; while the other policy strengthens and consolidates the national cause, and denying no mental or social blessing, gives to the individual that contented mind which enables him to live happily in an unquiet and feverish world.

Much cant is uttered and circulated about the English language and the English race. The current phrases of the day tell of 'Anglo-Saxon predominance' and of the 'Anglo-Saxon language, the language of civilisation;' and I lament to see that not only Englishmen, but also Welshmen in and out of Wales, are taking up the cry.

The 'language of civilisation' means the language of commerce and money-power. We carry those principles into all the world, China and Japan being the latest instances. We make the term 'civilisation' cover a multitude of sins. The English language is not in itself, I believe, superior to the Welsh for any purpose save that of business. Nor is it improving in quality. How much better is the language of Milton and Addison than that of the House of Commons and the 'Times'! English is said to be the gate to the art, science, and literature of the world. It is a gate truly, but why say the only one? Doubtless the greatest works have been produced in English, as I rejoice to affirm, but cultivate the Cymraeg, and you will produce great works in it also.

The English has borrowed largely from all languages to interpret art and science—so let the Welsh. As to the acquisition of other languages, Welsh is at least as eligible as English. It is indeed not so available, but make it so by cultivation. Support your bards and scholars, promote cordiality and union among them, establish and extend literary Societies. They are the instruments of power and good. Give to them a distinct national character.

I appeal to the literati of Wales to enter into this great question of literary Societies with one mind and one heart. Why is it, asks the Englishman, that North and South Wales are opposed so much? Why are accidents of religious persuasion, of profession, birth, habit, locality, suffered to mar the success which united action is certain to eventuate? Why do you not erect among you one great parent Institute to which Cymmrodorion, Welsh MSS., and archæological societies, the Cambrian Institute, and other existing associations, may give support and look for support? As it is, an Englishman wishing to cast in his lot with Welsh interest, is distracted and disheartened by the dissension everywhere prevalent.

In England our literary Institutes are on the whole decaying, but it is for want of a high scope and purpose, and of one common bond of nationality. In Wales you have that bond and that purpose—why will you not avail yourself of it?

These letters of ten years ago are still entirely relevant to the present day.

What I have written of the necessity of arresting the decay of the language may, *à fortiori*, be re-written now. That this language will, or *can* perish, I do not believe. But that it may be injured by the neglect, or strengthened by the support, of the Welsh people, needs no demonstration. Let the Youth of Wales remember this. The splendid example of the Bretons is before them. The International Congress held last year at Saint Brieuc has revived the enthusiasm that slept, and encouraged the hope that languished, in our Celtic Arvor. Poets, historians, and antiquaries, have led: an earnest-hearted people has followed. The Congress will again meet. May it become more and more international! Let the Welsh depute good and true men to attend it, and let it in return be held on their own soil.

They have especially three things to promote: Devotion to country and language; Unanimity of purpose and action; Sympathy with the Celtic brotherhood of other lands. Let this be stedfastly done, and the words of Taliesin will be verified—Cymry vu, Cymry vydd! (1868.)

THE PLYGAIN.

' And when came the appointed close
Every voice in carol burst.'—PAGE 195.

AMONG the popular customs which Ab Ithel encouraged as favour-
able alike to piety and to patriotism, the *Plygain* well deserves
mention. The word, little euphonious, doubtless, to Saxon ears,
for no gentle onomatopœia is in it, means *early dawn*,[1] and is
applied to the special service of Christmas-eve or Christmas-
morning, held in many churches and chapels in Wales, and which
is peculiarly grateful to the Celtic character. A religious service
on this vigil is indeed common to nearly all Christian countries,
and carol-singing, which always forms the essential portion of the
Welsh observance, is universal in some form throughout the
Christian world. But it is only in the Principality, where religious feeling acquires an intense development, and where the love
of vocal song is ineradicable, that the celebration of the Nativity
exhibits the characteristics of the Plygain. I have been present
at these meetings in different towns and villages, but nowhere
have I seen the typical Plygain so fully marked as at Llanymowddwy.

Let me snatch from the receding years some memories of Christmas-tide in that quiet valley, while as yet the Genius of the place
was present in Ab Ithel, and no railway works abraded the meads
of the lower Dovey, or polluted the borders of the free lake of
Bala.

Night has long gathered over the Pass of the Cross. The
church bell of Llanuwchllyn, feebly ringing welcome for the great
Advent, has died away below. The last light has faded from the

---

[1] *Ply-cain.* Owen Pughe. (The *y* has the sound of the English *u*.)

lonely farmhouse of Blaen Cwm. We rise into the spiritual darkness of the hills. Broad tracts of table-land broken by shelving ridges and abrupt peaks, stretch around us in distances not measured by the eye, but felt by the mountain instinct. The pure frost-wind flows steadily without pause or gust from over the double crest of Arenig, and the remote crags of Snowdon, on across the Berwyns and many a Montgomeryshire *moel*, down to the pasture levels of Tanat, Vyrnwy, and Severn. Great belts of cloud swathe the moonless sky, and oppress the stars, save when a chasm of intensest azure cuts their black edges, and some separate star hangs tremblingly in it. As we climb the difficult path under the dripping rock-wall on the left hand, and above the deep *cwm* to the right; or stride freely across the open ground on the shoulder; or wind down the dark recesses of the Bwlch into the Mowddwy Vale; there rises in the bosom that rare and joyous sense, physical in part, intellectual in greater part, revealed not amid the haunts and employments of men; the sense of unfettered movement and self-reliance, all vacant of fear, unconscious of fatigue, keenly alive to the subtle manifestations of nature, and eager to meet the shadowy fancies and far-reaching meditations that then come forth, cleared of the dull passages of frivolity and care which too thickly overlie them in daily existence.

And when the site of the vanished Cross gleams on the summit of the Pass, a frozen area of peat ground, the heart swells with holier emotion, and the religion of Him Who was tempted in the wilderness, and transfigured on the mountain, sheds a better blessing on the hour and on the scene.

For surely no fitter time than the eve of His Nativity, and no fitter spot than one into such as which He was wont to go up to pray, could be chosen wherein to express our thankfulness for the Divine Incarnation that has taught the dust of Adam to contemplate its immortality, or wherein to utter our trustful prayer for the coming and crowning perfection of the human race! And under the shadow of the Arans, and around the desert springs of Dyfi, may not the Omnipresent receive that true praise and prayer equally as within gorgeous cathedrals and amid choral crowds, for, in the beautiful words of Gray,

> Praesentiorem et conspicimus Deum
> Per invias rupes, fera per juga,
> Clivosque praeruptos, sonantes

Inter aquas, nemorumque noctem ;
Quàm si repòstus sub trabe citreá
Fulgeret auro, et Phidiacá manu. [1]

Here, however, is no churchless wild, and the mountaineers are
not left to the teachings of natural religion, influential though
these be upon their simple lives; and now as we skirt the grounds
of the silent Bryn-mansion of ghostly reputation—and cross the
Pymrhyd, where, gliding down under thick foliage from Tydecho's
Chair, it cuts the road in the bottom ; the little bell of the unseen
church fills the clear air, and we overtake a mixed company of
peasants hastening to the holy tryst.

Some have crossed the Bwlch from Llanuwchllyn, some the
Dovey from the hill-farms on the east side. All are gay and
hilarious but without any boisterous merriment, nor is there the
slightest sign of intemperance. We follow them into the Rectory,
where before Ab Ithel's hospitable fires they shake off the midnight cold and mingle with the large company gathered there. To
many, Ab Ithel is pastor and friend, and to all, the good Welsh
patriot and preacher, whom it is well worth a long and difficult
journey to see and to hear.

And now all are bidden into the Church which is hardly distinguished by its dim lights through the black arms of the great
secular yews. It is a small undecorated place, yet large in the
ungrudging devotion of its people, and rich in the virtues and
talents of its minister.

Candles glimmer in the windows and along the seats : wreaths
of evergreen mark the season, and the taste of the ladies of the
Rectory. As much warmth as could be attained in such a place, at
such a time, has been given to the interior. But light and warmth
and ornament are in the audience, not the edifice. The people
supply all that is deficient and ennoble all that is mean. The Church
is filled, for nearly all the parishioners are there, and many belonging to other districts have wended their various way from mountain
villages and scattered farms, to hear the Bishop of Mowddwy,[2] and
to sing their Christmas song. There are old, very old men and
women present, for as Churchyard long ago sang, and as the Regis-
trar-General certifies, the peasantry of Merioneth enjoy great lon-

---

[1] Ode written in the album of the Monastery of the Grande Chartreuse.
[2] As Ab Ithel was familiarly styled.

gevity, the obvious result of very pure air and temperate habits. The
dames, who perhaps excel in this respect, wear the linsey woolsey,
the hose, and the coarse flannels of their country, together with the
ample frilled cap carefully whitened for the occasion, and crowned
by the imposing beaver, (the *bête noire* of modern masculine costume,
and certainly not less unbecoming to the gentler sex,) or by the
simpler round felt hat which is more generally used in North Wales.
The old men—and indeed all the men—are clad in a garb without
any character save roughness and plainness for the hard uses of life.
The young Cymry are tall and well moulded, though having the
air of reserve or diffidence which is associated with mountain
training, and which often covers high mental capacity, while the
obtrusive assurance of the townsman as often displays the want
of it. Of young girls there is an ample attendance, and the
beauty of the ' Morwynion glan Meirionydd ' is well indicated by
the rounded form, dark Silurian eye, clear-cut features, and glowing
cheek. Nor should the crowding, joyous, carol-burdened, wea-
ther-careless children be disregarded, the *plant* and *plantach* of the
parish, whether *llodesi* or *bechgyn*, to whom Christmas is a delight,
and church-going not a weariness ; who grow up under the shadow
of their hills, and in the practice of the religious customs of their
country, credulous, it may be, simple-minded, and unskilled in the
ephemeral babble of the ' certified ' schools, but with unloosened
hold on a true faith from which modern youth is drifting, and
with a clear conviction of first principles, which sordid habits shall
not debase, nor shallow sophistries darken.

But Ab Ithel takes his surplice from beside the reading-desk—
the church has no vestry—and the service begins. He reads in a
low earnest tone, and the Liturgy loses nothing in its Welsh setting.
The congregation join with fervour in the responses, lead by an
ancient grey-haired clerk, who most carefully and emphatically
marks the time and the sense. There is a plaintive character, almost
a sadness, in the Welsh responses, especially in the Litany, that
seems very appropriate to the confessions of sinners, and, in general,
there is no better language for rendering the utterances of religion
with clearness, solemnity, and strength. Religion, indeed, has
done much for the Welsh language, and the Welsh language has
done much for religion. In this poor primitive Church of course
no organ is found, but the musical service is well conducted by
Miss Williams, on a small harmonium belonging to the family.

The grand old Gregorian chants and the immemorial hymns of Cambria, rise eloquently from this humble instrument, bearing with them all voices and all hearts in that unsophisticated assembly.

After prayer and praise follows the sermon, a plain setting forth of the blessings of Redemption, a loving exhortation to seize the great opportunity of life which grows more fleeting with each revolving year. And now the benediction is pronounced, and there is a stir among the people, not of departure, but of preparation and expectancy. The carol-singing is to begin. And first Ab Ithel, divested of his gown, standing before the congregation, and his two daughters with him, lead off with a carol, doubly their own in music and in words. This short and simple song over, the old clerk advances, and with him two other singers, a ruddy stripling of twenty, and a weather-bronzed farmer of middle age. They group themselves before the altar-steps. The old man, the central figure, bears in one hand a candle and in the other the manuscript carol. The three bend over the paper. Though the voices are unequal and the tune monotonous, a reality and intensity of purpose stamps the performance with no common interest. Their carol is a long one of old verses connected and completed by original additions. It tells of the Divine dispensation on earth, from the fall of Adam to the Resurrection of the Messiah. It dwells on the persons, places, and events of Gospel history. It is briefly the universal carol recast into a Cymric mould. As it proceeds, the singers do not modulate their tone or alter their emphasis. The strain rises and closes throughout stanza after stanza in what seems an interminable equal flow. There is no attempt at effect or self-exhibition. It is a duty and a delight, not a task or entertainment. The three stand quiet and patient, the flickering light playing across their faces, and chant to the end the high burden of their song. At length it ceases with a long-drawn *Amen*. They glide into their places; but immediately another singer starts up and bursts into vigorous carol, taking a more joyous note than that of his predecessors, but with as little variety of expression or air. While he sings there is an anxious unfolding of papers and shifting of positions among the audience, and when he subsides satisfied, there is a springing forward of two groups simultaneously, of which one is selected, that of a boy and a girl, and their timid and sweet voices clothe the recurring carol with an interest that checks the longing for the end, inspired sometimes by the male performances. And now there is again a pause, and again a vocalist rises with a book or manuscript, or with only an exuberant memory; and again, and again, until at last the carol culminates in the votive offering of two stalwart mountaineers, who pursue it in mutual excitement through a maze of amplifications, heedless of passing hours and sleepless eyes. The winds rising in their strength sweep moaning round the church, laden with the funeral breath of the yews. Cold December darkness is outside, the feeble gleam of a few candles within. Heavy shadows flit along the walls, and over the faces of the people. The chill of the early morning creeps through your frame, and a weird restless feeling weighs upon your soul. But finally the tones fall away from your dreamy ear. The programme is ended. Ab Ithel dismisses the assembly. Then follow greetings and gratulations. All press around their pastor, and with many a *Nos dda!* and hearty grasp of the hand, the people separate. The rector and his family go to rest, as do most of his parishioners, but a strong band of all ages, with bosoms yet glowing with Christmas fervour, and with feet that spurn fatigue, march towards Mallwyd Church, five miles distant, where *another* Plygain awaits them—a service, a sermon, and a carol-singing, as earnest, as consentaneous, and as long.

All this is doubtless very simple, and may be deemed very uninteresting to witness, or very unnecessary to describe. But if the philosophic mind do not find in it some gratifying transcript of national character, something that indicates qualities honourable to humanity, and tastes which no wise social economy could advantageously discourage, then it would be vain to seek better examples among the Cambrian hills and valleys. And whatever may be the state of this Country when the wave of Anglo-Saxon assimilation shall have rolled over its boundaries, it is at least doubtful whether any of the new customs can compensate the blotting out of the old; and whether the new 'progress' of the people can bring them nearer to that substantial happiness which is neither a slave prostrate at the feet of Fashion, nor an infant pursuing the chariot-wheels of Time.

Spottiswoode & Co., Printers, New-street Square and 30 Parliament Street.